Praise for the

And Then There Was Her

This book really was a joy to read. As soon as I started reading this book I was hooked. I loved the premise. I loved the setting of a winery. There is something so romantic about it, and Shepard writes beautifully so you feel like you can taste the grapes and even feel the soil. I thought all the characters were well done. This was the right book at the right time and it's going on my 2020 favorite list.

-Lex Kent's Reviews, *goodreads*

The romance is very delicately written, a well-balanced slow burn with some spectacularly hot moments too! I could have written thousands of words on how much I love this book, the intricacy of the imagery, how much I want to punch Kacey, and how I can relate to the pain and doubt etched in Madison's soul. Anyone who has ever been made to feel "less than" will be touched by this narrative.

-Orlando J., *NetGalley*

I adore an age-gap romance, and this slow-burn story is incredibly romantic. There's something about the writing that is lush and elegant and beautiful, and it really suits the story that is set in a gorgeous vineyard. I highly recommend this gorgeous book for anyone looking for an escape.

-Karen C., *NetGalley*

This book plucked the strings of my romantic side on multiple occasions. I highly recommend this book to the romantics out there and even the aspiring romantics who just need a little encouragement.

-*The Lesbian Review*

Across the Dark Horizon

This is a well written and very fast-paced book. It is not overly long and there is quite a bit of action crammed into the pages. Shepard builds great tension throughout the book through both the plot and the bourgeoning relationship between Charlie and Gail. ...the result is heart-pounding excitement throughout!

-*The Lesbian Review*

Bird on a Wire

This is the second novel by Tagan Shepard. I said for her successful debut that it is a sign that many more fine books are yet to come. I am glad that I was right...With all main elements done well, this makes for another very good book by this author. Keep them coming!

-Pin's Review, *goodreads*

...She has become an author that I will automatically read now. If you are looking for a good drama book with a little romance, give this a read.

-*Lex Kent's Reviews, goodreads*

Visiting Hours

...*Visiting Hours* is an emotional tale filled with denial, pain, struggle, commitment, and finally, more than one kind of deep, abiding love.

-*Lambda Literary Review*

Queen of Humboldt

The story is told from both Sabrina and Marisol's perspectives and is nonlinear in that some of the chapters are flashbacks. I found these glimpses into the past to be a great way to introduce some much needed character history as well as helping to understand and sympathize with Marisol. This structure can sometimes be confusing, but Shepard does a great job using this device and I never felt disoriented or lost. It is a pulse pumper with a ton of action that will keep you excitedly flipping the page to see what is coming next.

-The Lesbian Review

Queen of Humboldt does not disappoint. This is a second-chance romance with a dose of opposites attract and almost a taboo feel thrown in for good measure. Be sure to pay attention to the chapter headings where a year is involved, because there are flashbacks interspersed and the timing definitely matters. I don't want to give any of the story away because this one is a doozy. A true roller coaster ride that ends with a bang.

-Karen R., NetGalley

Talk about an action book! I think I'm still trying to catch my breath over here. While Shepard writes mostly contemporary romances (and one futuristic book) I was excited to see her mix it up again with an action-romance. And when I say action I mean ACTION! I was completely glued to my seat. For me a read like this is just really fun and super entertaining. ...It's a "buckle your seat belt and hang on for the ride" kind of read.

-Lex Kent's Reviews, goodreads

Well, this came out of left field. I honestly wasn't sure about this one, because of the darker themes it promised, and it is hard to really balance that grit out with some hope. But dang, this is done so well. Marisol's character and life is well plotted, utilizing flashbacks to help slow down the breakneck pace a bit. I love that there are hints for what Marisol is doing in the shadows of her criminal enterprise, but when it's revealed, it's done so well that it doesn't lose any of its punch. Shepard avoided switching between Marisol's and Sloane's perspectives too much, giving most of the storytelling duties to Marisol, and it works well. Marisol is a compelling narrator and having events playing out through her eyes was great.

This is dark, pretty violent, but is also full of hope and goodness. Sloane and Marisol are well balanced characters, and one of the few examples where they don't have to grow that much to make them compelling. It is well paced, with some really great action sequences, some slower moments, and some truly emotionally impactful ones. This was a lovely surprise, and is quite possibly my favorite book this month.

-Colleen C., *NetGalley*

Swipe Right

There is a lot going on for both characters in their lives and some unresolved issues for both. Some of them are pretty heavy but Ms. Shepard adds a bit of levity and humor to balance it out, Ms. Shepard writes humor very well, and sometimes it made me laugh out loud. I appreciated that the levity wasn't so much in the online dating experience but in the relationship between Kieran and Pen. Those two have very good friendship chemistry, so much so that I'm glad that the author took her time to develop a romantic relationship between them. I loved the diversity in sexual orientation and gender identity in different characters and seeing Kieran's struggle to be accepted as pansexual gave me food for thought.

- *LezReview Book*s

Tagan Shepard's writing style is so lyrical and lovely and lush that it just draws me in immediately. I love first person and it really works here as we get to experience all the disappointment Kieran feels every time one of her dates is a disaster. This could have been a listing of faux humorous situations, and I'm so glad it wasn't. Her dialogue is witty without being like a sitcom script. Within the lovely writing, Shepard parcels out Pen's back story in increments that resulted in this being unputdownable for me.

-Karen C., *NetGalley*

TWO KNIGHTS TANGO

About the Author

Tagan Shepard (she/her) is the author of seven novels of sapphic fiction, including the 2019 Goldie winner *Bird on a Wire*. When not writing about extraordinary women loving other extraordinary women, she can be found playing video games, reading, or sitting in DC Metro Traffic.

She lives in Virginia with her wife and two cats.

TWO KNIGHTS
TANGO

TAGAN SHEPARD

BELLA
BOOKS
2022

Dedication

For my Knight in shining armor

CHAPTER ONE

The cattle prod's twin probes slammed into Marisol's side, sending waves of electricity through her muscles. Her fingers locked into claws and her wrists shook under the tightly knotted ropes. She jerked in spasms. Just when she thought she'd lose control of her bladder, the stick was yanked away and a last, sputtering lightning bolt arced between the probes.

A fist slammed into her right side, pounding into already bruised flesh. The pain eclipsed sound for a long moment and she thought she'd gone deaf. Just as her hearing returned, a fist smashed into her other side, glancing off her rib so the blow to her kidney was partially deflected. This time her hearing sharpened, the blood roaring in her ear, muting the rest of the world. Marisol thought she heard muffled laughter from above, but it evaporated as the first fist buried itself in her abdomen.

Brin screamed, begging for help, but Marisol couldn't move. Her legs were like lead and she couldn't feel her arms at all. She tried to shout, tried to scream as loudly as Brin, but not even a whisper escaped her lips. Her ears rang with evil laughter and the sound of fabric ripping.

Marisol Soltero awoke screaming. Fear wrapped around her like a vise and she sprang from bed, flinging her torn sheet aside. The room was cold and she was hot. Sweat beaded on her forehead and across her bare skin as she crossed to the window.

Moonlight and the fluorescent glow of streetlights came through the half-open slats of her wooden blinds and fell across her naked body. She turned abruptly at the window, scanning the shadows for dead enemies and absent lovers. She was alone, but the ticking of her living room clock echoed in the hollow space and the white noise of the Chicago streets swallowed the sound of her panting.

Marisol sighed as she opened the blinds to the city lights. Matching pale scars stood out on her golden-brown wrists. Her heart rate dropped to normal the moment she saw the row houses and apartment blocks of home. The bass from Club Alhambra's lively dance floor below hummed up through several floors, vibrating in Marisol's toes. A pair of unfamiliar cars slowed for a group of late-night partiers to cross the street. Marisol watched the cars drive out of sight. As her skin cooled, her eyes were drawn back to the line of scars.

It had been six months since her kidnapping. Since The Bishop, her enemy with money and power but no soul, had snatched her and Brin, flying them out of safety to his compound in Colombia. She'd been hung by her wrists from the rafters of a remote shack and tortured for hours. Brin had been forced to kill The Bishop's minion. They'd both been broken, but they'd both survived.

She reached out a shaking finger and touched the tortured skin on her wrist, her quickened pulse detectable underneath. Her pulse was in those scars. Her heart was in them. She had accepted these scars—those on her skin and those in her mind that disturbed her sleep—because they were a trivial price to pay for what had come after. For the sweltering heat of her single, blissful night with Brin. Marisol held her breath and counted, closing her eyes and allowing the scenes of that night to play across her mind's eye. Brin's pale skin in paler moonlight. Dust and sweat. Laughter and tears. Sweet, tender kisses.

"Five," she whispered into the night and opened her eyes.

Marisol had made it home from Colombia. Her faithful bodyguard, Gray, had been waiting at the rickety little airstrip on the edge of town. He'd hustled her aboard as the plane was taxiing to the runway. She'd cheated death by moments. They stopped in a dozen little airports between Colombia and Chicago, and made it back alive, her promise to meet Brin in these streets still ringing in her ears.

But Brin had not met her. Marisol had perched on the saddle of her motorcycle for more days and nights than she cared to admit, watching Brin's condo to see her home safely. Long after the media had left. For days, Marisol thought Brin had been recaptured. Her nightmares then had been of the woman she loved tortured all alone in a hot, stinking basement somewhere. Marisol had not handled those nights well, driving herself crazy with regret and anger. Gray had pushed her into a broom closet one day and demanded she explain, but she had refused—would always refuse—to endanger Brin by telling him the truth. She had been more cautious after that and Gray had backed off.

Marisol received her first report a week after her return to the States. Governor Sabrina Sloane was on a well-publicized tour of South and Central America, drumming up support for international business interests key to Illinois. Marisol had seen it on CNN. She nearly hit the floor with shock to see Brin, composed as always, no hint of her kidnapping and mental torture. She was the perfect politician. She visited hospitals, orphanages, and Indigenous settlements as often as she visited factories and corporate offices. Soon enough Marisol began to question her sanity. Had they really been kidnapped, flown to Colombia, and forced into a daring, deadly escape? Only the nightmares and the physical scars kept her sane.

Just as suddenly as the governor's tour had begun, it was over. Brin had boarded a plane and Marisol waited to find a way to contact her in Chicago. Only, Brin did not return as she'd promised. She was back in the Governor's Mansion in Springfield and she had not set foot in Chicago once in the previous six months. More evidence their trauma in Bogota had been real. Before the kidnapping, Brin had come home to her apartment in Chicago every other weekend. Now she was sending a clear message—she didn't want to be anywhere near Marisol.

"Can you blame her?" Marisol growled to herself.

The empty room and her empty life offered no argument. Before she could start another spiral, Marisol marched to the shower. It wasn't quite three a.m., but that was close enough to morning and Club Alhambra would be open for another hour. She still had a life to live and a bar to run, even if she didn't have the woman she loved.

CHAPTER TWO

Officer Hawkins followed three paces behind Governor Sabrina Sloane as she made her way through the Governors' Mansion Executive Wing. Officer Clarke waited outside her office door, his hands crossed at his waist, the bulge of a handgun visible through the tight fit of his suit jacket. She smiled and wished him a good morning, and he nodded, staring over her right shoulder. He had not once made eye contact with her in the six months he'd been assigned to her protection.

Sloane fished her office keys from her blazer pocket and fumbled for the right one. Clarke wore an ungodly amount of cologne, and she struggled to breathe while she fiddled with the lock. Once she'd finally opened the outer office door, Hawkins stepped into place opposite Clarke and adopted his same alert posture.

"Thank you, gentlemen," she said.

Neither responded. She couldn't blame them. They only took over the roles when her previous security team had all been murdered in the line of duty. The Illinois State Police had not lost so many officers in one incident in recent memory, and bitterness ran deep throughout the force. Ducking inside her outer office, she closed the door quickly to end the awkward silence. She grabbed the stack of her mail from her secretary's desk before unlocking her inner office door and getting to work.

She worked as the sun rose on another glorious spring day, but Sloane was none the wiser. She signed the final page of a long document and started reading an even longer one. This was a report she'd requested from the mayor of Chicago detailing the potential for economic recovery of a derelict industrial area in the heart of the city.

The mayor's—or more likely one of his assistant's—prose left a lot to be desired. While the report attempted to sugarcoat a hopeless situation to make it appear promising, they had failed miserably. As Sloane had suspected, the whole area was deteriorating rapidly and the omnipresent criminal element had already moved in. It wasn't the turgid prose that made the report hard to read. It was the intrusion of a husky, whispered voice and her own unkept promise.

I'll see you in Chicago.

Sloane shook her head and set the report down. If she closed her eyes, she could feel Marisol's closeness in the Colombian heat. She would be able to smell her skin and her blood. Taste her lips. Feel the way she set Sloane's body alive.

But Sloane did not close her eyes. She willed the memory away. To live with other memories. A leering face inches from her own and the unfamiliar weight of a gun in her hand. She tried to control those memories too, lest they take her close to madness. She pecked at her keyboard, bringing her computer to life, and began a memo to the mayor. She needn't read the entire report to respond to it.

Sloane was putting the finishing touches on the memo when there was an authoritative rap on her office door. She counted to three, a smile growing on her full lips.

Sloane's executive secretary was a formidable woman. She reminded Sloane of the nuns who terrorized her days at Woodlands Academy. She wore skirt suits to her knees in a variety of pastels, today's leaning toward shell pink. Her sensible heels matched perfectly. Her hair was neatly collected into a tight bun and the clasp of her rope of pearls was centered on the nape of her neck.

When Sloane had arrived for her tour several weeks before her inauguration, she had been introduced to this woman with a firm handshake from a remarkably soft palm.

"Madam Governor Elect, my name is Mrs. Lily Holmes. I am your executive secretary."

Sloane had been put off by the cold confidence. The appointment of executive staff was the domain of the governor or, more often, their chief of staff. Given the corruption and incompetence of the previous administration, Sloane had no intention of retaining so much as the cleaning staff.

"That remains to be seen," she'd responded. "Pleasure to meet you, Ms. Holmes."

"That's *Mrs.* Holmes. We'll discuss your office schedule when you've finished with Governor Holland."

Without giving Sloane a chance to correct the misapprehension, she had walked away. During her meeting with the outgoing governor, she'd told him she intended to bring her own personal assistant.

After a solid two minutes of belly laughs, Holland had replied, "Trust me, that's a battle you don't wanna fight. Keep Lily on or you'll regret it."

She did not trust him and she did not appreciate the warning. Her determination to be rid of Mrs. Lily Holmes had been greater than ever and she pointedly missed the appointment to discuss her office schedule. If she'd thought Lily Holmes a woman so easily dismissed, the next ten days were enough to teach her otherwise.

Lily had simply refused to be fired. She had emailed or called Sloane every three hours with requests and draft schedules. When Sloane had ignored them, she'd arrived on Sloane's office doorstep.

While Sloane had started the conversation with a curt dismissal, somehow it ended with her apologizing and promising to be more attentive in the future. Despite, or perhaps because of, their rocky start, Sloane had come to rely on Lily even more than the woman had initially implied.

"Did you have breakfast before you started working, Governor?" Lily asked, standing in front of Sloane's desk.

"Yes, of course. I had a…" Sloane waved her hand toward what she'd thought would be an empty breakfast plate. Instead, her fingertip bumped into a cold bagel. "Oh."

Lily was famous throughout Springfield for her sighs. They could communicate so much without a single word. She was only slightly less famous for the pointed way in which she smoothed her always wrinkle-free suits and picked nonexistent lint from her sleeves. Those gestures were rarely combined with each other and never, during Sloane's two years in office, had they been added to the aforementioned sigh. Not until this morning.

"Fortunately, I'm well-acquainted with your distractable nature. Breakfast is being delivered shortly."

"Distractable is unfair," Sloane replied, shifting some papers to hide her forgotten breakfast. "I've been busy."

"Yes, I've noted how busy you've been recently." Lily lowered herself into the straight-backed chair across the desk and crossed her ankles. "Might I have your full attention?"

Sloane's fingers stilled on the keyboard and she spent several seconds expecting the slap of a ruler across her knuckles. *Those damned nuns.* Laughing to herself, she looked up at her secretary. "I just need to review this memo."

"I'm happy to review it for you."

"No, thank you, Lily. I'm not quite finished with it."

"Then I'll review it when it's completed." A timid knock at the door interrupted them. Lily answered it and a waiter in a crisp white jacket rolled a cart into the room. "After you eat your breakfast."

Sloane suddenly felt the impact of her early morning and the previous late night. Her eyes stung and her hands ached where they hovered above her keyboard. While the waiter replaced her stale bagel with a plate of fresh fruit and a bowl of yogurt sprinkled with granola, Sloane rolled her head and shoulders.

Her neck cracked in a dozen places. One of them hurt quite a lot, forcing a hiss between her teeth that battled with the growl from her empty stomach. Looking up, she saw triumph in Lily's eyes.

"How do you do that?"

"It's my job." After a moment of thought, she settled more comfortably into the straight-backed chair. "Though I will admit that you have been the toughest nut to crack. Your predecessor never worked more than five hours a day his entire term."

"That's why I have to work twice as hard."

They both knew that wasn't the reason. She worked harder because it was in her nature to be thorough, which also set her apart from previous governors. This was an office that could either require little effort or it could work a person to death. The choice was entirely that of the occupant and she would always choose the latter.

She didn't wait for the waiter to set her coffee cup on the desk. With a warm smile, she took it from him and he blushed to the root of his graying hair before setting the steaming carafe next to her food.

Turning her attention back to Lily, she asked, "What's on my schedule for today?"

Lily didn't answer. She waited for the door to click shut behind the waiter, then her eyes flicked to the plate at Sloane's elbow. Sighing like a petulant child, Sloane dropped a napkin into her lap and grabbed the bowl of fruit. She settled back into her leather desk chair and ate, grabbing an unusual thin envelope from the stack of mail. While Lily tapped around on her tablet, Sloane opened the letter. Her blood ran cold.

It's time to get to work. I'm sending someone to help you. Keep your investigation quiet and don't tell her anything about our mutual friend. -A

Lily's voice broke through Sloane's shock. "Firstly, there is a Special Agent Tyler Graham from the National Security Agency requesting a priority meeting."

The piece of melon soured in Sloane's mouth. She forced herself to continue chewing, though she was certain Lily noted her hesitance. "Do we know what she'd like to discuss?"

Lily raised an eyebrow. "She said you would know. That someone from her agency had already contacted you."

Sloane set her fork down and flipped the envelope over. No name, address, or postmark. Sloane thought back through her morning. The office door had been guarded as usual. Yet here was this letter, hand-delivered, set innocuously amongst her other mail. Lily couldn't have seen the envelope. She would certainly have investigated something so mysterious. It had to have come after both of them had left the night before.

The signature of "A" and the mention of a mutual friend. It could only be from one person. The man who'd introduced himself as Anderson during their only meeting in the US Embassy in Colombia. He'd said he was from the NSA. That he'd recruited Marisol. That Sloane's presence in Marisol's life was a threat to the woman she loved. He was the reason she hadn't seen Marisol in six months and then he had a letter and an agent hand-delivered.

"Governor?"

Sloane shook herself. "Yes?"

Lily's second sigh carried a note of concern. "The NSA agent? Will you authorize a priority meeting with her?"

"Yes." Sloane yanked open her desk drawer and shoved the letter inside. "Yes, I'll authorize it."

"You have a slot open in your calendar tomorrow."

"I…" Sloane swallowed hard, closing her eyes and taking a deep breath. "Tomorrow isn't a good day."

"When might be a good day?"

Never. Sloane couldn't get away with that answer and the sparkle in Lily's eye made her wary. "Perhaps Friday."

"You are free any time after eleven on Friday. Unless, of course, you're planning to return to Chicago this weekend?"

"No." *I'll see you in Chicago*. Her final words to Marisol… She replied as evenly as possible, "Not this weekend."

Lily's glare was demanding, but Sloane focused on spearing a ripe strawberry quarter. "Very well." Lily's reply carried only a hint of judgement. "Shall I tell Agent Graham you will meet with her at eleven on Friday?"

Sloane swallowed both her pride and the strawberry. That would give her enough time to figure out how to work with her and also not let her know about Marisol. *Sure, that'll be easy to juggle.* "I suppose."

Lily nodded and scribbled a note. "Now, back to today's schedule. Your first meeting is with the Illinois Chamber of Commerce."

Sloane groaned and reached for her coffee. "Not them again."

"They're still quite upset about your trip to South America."

They aren't the only ones. The memories threatened to break through again, but with some effort Sloane kept tight control. Lily had no idea her trip hadn't been planned. Hadn't been *voluntary*. The cover story—that she had travelled to South America for a few weeks of glad-handing government and business interests—was the least innocuous explanation she could think of under duress. It certainly made for a better headline than the truth. That she'd been kidnapped by a human trafficker as bait to lure the one woman on earth no one would suspect of being an anti-trafficking crusader.

Sloane forced herself back into annoyance and replied, "It was six months ago and nothing came of it."

"They didn't like you before the trip, they'll never like you now. If you'd consulted me…"

"How do they keep getting appointments with me?" Sloane asked to forestall another lecture. "I thought I said to limit their access."

"I rejected two requests before taking this one. You can't be seen as anti-business."

"I'm not…" Sloane caught herself. There was no sense arguing this now, she'd have to do it again when the Chamber arrived. "What time is the meeting?"

"Nine forty-five."

Sloane spun the thin watch on her wrist to check the time. "You gave me less than an hour's notice?"

"How much notice do you need? You know how this will go. They'll accuse you of stifling capitalism, vocally threaten to pull the support they've never offered and make snide comments about your sexuality."

"What a wonderful start to my day."

"Just wait until I tell you about your second appointment."

CHAPTER THREE

Marisol sped along Lake Shore Drive, the few puffs of cloud hanging in the otherwise clear sky whipped past as her Ducati's wheels chewed up the miles. She darted through traffic, the engine whining as she topped out the speedometer. When she came to a particular section of highway, she dipped lower to the saddle and gunned the engine until it roared, keeping her eyes on the blacktop and the lake to avoid seeing the building that streaked past. She'd managed to steer clear of Sabrina's condo for months.

As the distinctive silhouette of the Palmolive Building came into view, she cut across three lanes of traffic to slip off the exit ramp. She felt the change in the road surface as she moved from highway to city streets. Her tires hummed at a different pitch and her body tensed as she scanned the sidewalks for watchful strangers. Parking in her usual spot, Marisol left her helmet on until she approached the elevator. Her eyes never stopped moving beneath the tinted visor.

The elevator moved with the glacial pace common to these historic buildings. Looking at the perfectly polished walls, she remembered her first trip. She had been in Chicago for less than a month and hadn't wandered over to the upscale Magnificent Mile until she'd received her summons from the great Dominique Levy, an actress and Goodwill Ambassador for the UN. She'd ridden this very elevator and the shiny walls had unsettled her. She had continuously checked over her shoulder, even though she was alone.

That trip had cemented her love of her new home. Fresh out of the lifer's wing of Huron Valley Correctional Center in Michigan, she'd walked into Chicago with no expectations. What she'd found was beyond her wildest dreams. She was still young enough back then to be blinded by its glitz. Everything smelled different. Cologne and leather and clean carpets. She'd had no business walking into a building like this back then, but her name had been on the list so they'd let her in. She'd felt smaller than herself and larger than herself at the same time, but she'd been certain that one day she'd walk into this building like she owned it. That's how it was now.

The elevator emitted a pleasant tone and the doors slid open. Marisol pushed off the wall and strode into the hallway, her boots sinking into plush carpet. Unwanted memories flooded in here, as always. She was powerless against the terror—this opulent hallway looked very much like Sabrina's.

The memory of gunshots echoed in her ears as she recalled frantically crawling through a dusty air vent. Bursting through a grate to find Sabrina's security detail dead and an assassin, moments from destroying the face Marisol had loved from afar. She'd saved Sabrina's life, but the governor had still been caught up in the web meant for Marisol.

Marisol's blood ran cold as the events flashed through her mind like a horror movie she couldn't stop watching. An associate she'd thought she could trust had warned her about the ambush. A new group in town was going to take out the Governor of Illinois as she came home to her Chicago condo for the weekend. Only it was a trap, not for Sabrina, but for

Marisol. Someone had put together the pieces of her secret life she'd hidden so well. They knew The Queen of Humboldt was also a spy, working for the NSA to combat human trafficking. They'd found one of the women Marisol had saved and learned of The Hotel, the safehouse where she sheltered the women she rescued. They knew everything but the location.

The Bishop—a major player in the international trade of women and girls—had kidnapped her and Sabrina, bringing them to his base of operations in Colombia, and had tortured Marisol for the information. She'd kept her mouth shut and managed to escape, but he wasn't the type of man to accept failure. Every day since her return, Marisol had looked over her shoulder, waiting to see his shadow at her heels.

Marisol didn't have to knock. Dominique's front door swung open as she arrived. A cameraman emerged, the logo of a popular morning talk show stitched into the chest of his fleece vest. The faintest smile played around his lips and his eyes were unfocused. Marisol caught the door before it swung shut behind him. He didn't even turn to look at her. The rest of the TV crew congregated in the foyer, chatting with the same unfocused ease. Even the TV host, a star in her own right, had the naked edge of awe in her gaze. Dominique wove her spell indiscriminately, ensnaring anyone who came into her orbit.

She lounged on her sofa across the room. A smattering of assistants, both hers and from the show, fluttered around her. The moment she spotted Marisol, she flashed a wide smile. She held out her hand and Marisol hurried to her side.

"Darling," Dominique cooed as Marisol dropped onto the cushion beside her and lifted her fingers to her lips.

The easiest way to hide their clandestine working relationship had been to pretend they were dating. It hadn't always been the easiest thing to manage, but they'd both discovered early on that there wasn't any attraction between them. But the feigned intimacy had given their relationship a closeness beyond anything Marisol shared with anyone else. Dominique was a tactile woman—hugging and touching everyone—and Marisol surprised herself by craving that touch. She'd risked her life so many times, it was nice to be held when she was safe. Besides, the smile Dominique gave her was unlike anything she'd ever seen.

The first time she'd seen that smile, Marisol's knees had turned to rubber. These days she just acted like they did. Tension filled the room, thickening the air and lifting the hairs on Marisol's arms. Even as she slipped an arm over Dominique's shoulders and bent to kiss her hand again, she noted the reaction of everyone around the room.

The morning-show star stiffened, her eyes on Marisol. She would know who Marisol was and the incongruity of this devil in the angel's space. Dominique's personal assistant gave Marisol a jealous glare. Her manager, a short, thin man with less hair than he believed he had, glowered. The rest of the crew looked like they were blinking themselves awake.

It wasn't such a surprise that they were under Dominique's spell. She was ethereal. Her dark hair flowed across slim shoulders and a long, graceful neck. Her face, heart-shaped and delicate, bore the signs of her fifty-five years with all the class and character of a leading lady. Her skin was a shade paler than Marisol's, contrasting beautifully with her dark eyes and darker brows. Magazines often compared Dominique to Rita Moreno, but that was little more than lack of imagination equating two women with similar features and matching ethnic heritage. Dominique's quiet reserve gave her more the air of royalty than Hollywood legend.

The crew filtered out while Marisol lavished Dominique with attention. When only her manager and assistant remained, Dominique swept up from the couch, bringing Marisol with her. She glided into her private sitting room, sliding the pocket doors shut behind them with the dignity of Scarlett O'Hara.

Once the doors closed behind the final sycophant, Marisol dropped Dominique's hand and paced to the window. Years of pretending to be a couple had taken off the shine off kissing Dominique Levy's knuckles long ago. Still, their friendship had deepened with time into something far more intimate than a love affair.

Dominique stretched, the flowing folds of her dressing gown spreading like wings.

"Sit," Dominique said, sliding into a leather armchair and reaching for the teapot at her elbow. "Tea?"

Marisol shook her head and marched to the piano at the back of the room.

"They'll be gone soon, but it's safe to talk now." Dominique added a splash of milk to her steaming cup. "They'll be too busy griping at each other to listen at the door."

Marisol grunted and circled the piano, trailing her fingertips across the curved profile. There wasn't a speck of dust on the highly polished surface.

Dominique hid her long, lean body in the many layers of her diaphanous dressing gown. This was her favorite way to fill out her form, though the long sleeves threatened to swallow her petite hands. She sat still, watching Marisol, and sipped her tea.

Marisol never withered under inspection. She shoved her hands into the tight pockets of her leather pants and straightened her spine as she retraced her steps to the window.

"I haven't seen you much since Colombia." Dominique's voice was a caress. A purr. "How've you been?"

"Fine."

"Sleeping well?"

Marisol thought back, trying to remember the last time she'd slept through the night. It had been a while. "Fine."

"Eating?"

Marisol always ate. Her long hours both running her Humboldt gang and the club, as well as spying for the NSA, required she fuel her body, and so she did. Even if she wasn't hungry. Even if the food tasted like ashes and felt like writhing snakes in her gut. "Fine."

"Can I get you to say anything else today? How's dear Gray?"

"Bueno."

Marisol spat the word and waited for the rebuke her sarcasm always earned. It didn't come. The room went quiet enough to hear the condo's front door close. She crossed to the sitting room doors and eased them open. She watched and listened for movement, but the door had clearly closed behind someone leaving, not arriving. She slid the doors closed anyway. Marisol heard the clink of a china cup on saucer but did not turn to look. She strode to the bar and listened to Dominique settle into her seat.

Marisol risked a glance at her as she crossed back to the piano. Dominique's brown eyes were tracking Marisol's movements. Her teacup rested on its saucer in her hands. Her lips, lacking the bow of youth she'd still had when Marisol had first met her nearly sixteen years ago, were a straight line.

"I'm fine," Marisol growled.

She leaned against the piano, her shoulders scrunching up to cup her ears. Her leather jacket squeaked and the lining bunched. A clock ticked in the depths of the condo, its echo dulled by distance. Dominique didn't speak.

"What?" Marisol roared, spinning again to face her. "What do you want from me?"

Dominique unfolded herself as she stood, then ambled to a spindly table topped with a marble chess board. She wrapped her fingers around a white pawn and slid it forward two spaces. She returned to her chair and lowered herself into it, her eyes never leaving Marisol.

The eyes did her in. Marisol had always been powerless against Dominique's soft, insistent stare. It had been that stare that had convinced Marisol to trust her all those years ago when she'd arrived in Chicago, still not believing her reprieve was real. She'd prepared mentally to spend the rest of her life bouncing between the general prison population and her frequent trips to solitary confinement when her anger got the better of her wisdom. She'd earned her freedom with a promise to work as a spy for the government, using her criminal pedigree to cover her efforts to end human trafficking. The man who had visited her in solitary had been a mystery. Dominique had been anything but.

On stationery sprinkled with rosewater, she'd sent Marisol an invitation to meet her for tea. Marisol had taken that as a sign this woman could be manipulated. Shaped to Marisol's will. How naïve a thought. Dominique had been assigned as her handler, the point of contact between her and the agency that pulled her strings. Whoever made the match had a brilliant mind. Someone must have foreseen that Marisol's desire to survive had been stronger than her desire to do good. Somewhere along the lines that had changed, and Dominique had been the one to do the changing.

Dominique and Sabrina.

They'd played their first game of chess that day. Marisol had never played before, but she'd watched others. In group homes and prisons, shelters and parks. She thought she'd known the game well, but more than a decade later she'd never won a game against Dominique.

Marisol snatched a black knight from the back row and deposited it facing the forest of white pawns. Then she dropped into the wingback armchair across from Dominique and accepted a cup of milky tea. She hated milky tea.

Taking a sip, she confessed, "It's been…difficult since Colombia."

"I can imagine."

She couldn't, of course, but that meant nothing. Marisol continued, "There are so many questions. There are cracks in my cover, but I don't know where they are."

"Have there been any issues since? Anyone following you?"

"No." Dominique didn't ask how she could be so certain. If anyone knew she could avoid a tail, it was Dominique. "But there are strangers in Humboldt. Similar model SUVs. I see them occasionally, but they aren't after me. More like they're running away from me."

"Someone new working in your territory?" Dominique never took notes of their conversations, but Marisol knew everything made it back to Washington. Everything. "Do you require assistance?"

Marisol gave her a hard look. "You know I can protect my own borders."

Dominique raised her hands and the corner of her mouth. "No offense meant. We know you've been under stress. If you need us to take some pressure off, we're more than happy to…"

"No. Stay out of Humboldt."

Dominique blinked but gave no other evidence that she'd been offended. Still, the point had been made. The outside world believed Marisol was the most wanton of criminals, so far outside the law she was above it. That belief was the only thing that maintained her cover. If the NSA sent in agents to clean out whatever was unsettling Marisol, that illusion would be ruined. No matter how professional the agents, they didn't have her legitimate pedigree of a hardened criminal. More lives than her own depended on no one learning the truth. Marisol Soltero was a government spy deep under cover.

"Any word on The Bishop?" Marisol asked to smooth the moment.

"None," Dominique replied, her manner snapping back to professionally neutral. "He vanished before we could get him in Colombia. Some of our analysts thought we might catch up with him in Mexico, but he never showed up there."

"What's being done to find him?"

"There's not much we can do except wait for a clue. Women and girls going missing in a place he's been known to operate."

"That's the big plan?" Marisol growled. "Wait for his victims to go missing?"

"It's the best method to find him."

"It's the best method to ruin a few dozen lives."

"We don't have any other options."

"You aren't trying hard enough."

"We have our best analysts on the job."

"And field agents?"

Dominique waved a hand in Marisol's direction. "The same."

"Oh no. Don't put this on me! I've been putting my neck out enough for you." Marisol pushed her balled fists out until her jacket pulled back, baring her wrists. Dominique's eyes sparkled as she reached out, laying her fingertips across the scarred flesh. Her skin was cool and too soft.

"Marisol," she said, her voice as silky as her skin. "That's not what I meant. You are not alone in this. You're one of many working on it. Believe me. I'm with you, dearest."

Marisol pulled back from her touch, but she did it slowly. Dominique was a mere cog, as she was, and Washington used her with the same lack of regard. It was easy to forget that she felt deeply and bruised easily. Dominique's success as an actress stemmed from her empathy, a well that never seemed to run dry.

"Is there anything else you'd like to report?" Dominique looked at her through hooded eyes. "Either to Washington or to me?"

Since Marisol's return from the horrors of Colombia, Dominique had dropped all pretense that she was ignorant of Marisol's feelings for Sabrina. They had not spoken of it directly, but there were times like this when Dominique asked without asking. She probably knew Sabrina's whereabouts better than Marisol, so she wasn't looking for an answer. She was looking for an explanation that Marisol had no intention of giving.

"Nothing."

Dominique nodded and poured herself another cup of tea. "Then your mission remains the same. I'll keep pursuing The Bishop, both with the tools Washington has given me and those they don't know about."

Marisol's eyebrow shot up to her hairline. "And what tools are those?"

Dominique's smile was coy, almost flirtatious. "If I told you, they wouldn't be a secret, would they?"

"I don't talk to Washington. I don't talk to anyone but you. Your secrets are safe with me."

"And yours are safe with me," Dominique said, her expression clearing. "You can tell me if you and Sabrina…"

Marisol stood. "Well use whatever tools you have to. We need to find The Bishop."

"It might not be that easy."

"It has to be."

"You think he'll come after you?"

"I know he will."

CHAPTER FOUR

"So what's it like living in this palace?" the reporter asked, waving a hand around the richly appointed conference room. "It must be wonderful to have all the domestic worries off your mind so you can focus on governing."

Sloane smiled and even managed a small chuckle. "It does seem like that, doesn't it? The décor isn't exactly my style, but my predecessors managed to make the place rather beautiful."

"Probably more the first ladies' doings than theirs."

"No doubt," Sloane replied, noting the softening of the reporter's gaze and the curve of her lip. She almost expected a wink or an eyeroll. Something tangible to acknowledge their shared, gendered burden. "I am exceedingly grateful for the Mansion's domestic staff. I quite literally couldn't do this job without them and they endure my eccentricities with remarkable grace."

The reporter stopped to jot down a few notes and Sloane took the opportunity to look her over. The smile and lingering looks were especially pleasant coming from such a beautiful woman. Tall, and rounded in many of the same places as Sloane, she looked to be in her mid to late thirties. Not more than five or six years younger than Sloane. Her skin was the deep, rich brown of precious hardwood and her hair, a shade darker than her skin, was beautifully twisted and studded with brass rings. Her legs were long and her skirt short and that fact might have been distracting to Sloane even a year ago. Now she looked on with an appreciative eye but nothing more. Only one woman could truly stoke her hunger these days.

"And you get to work from home, so your commute is better than anyone else's in Illinois."

Sloane's chuckle was louder this time and the reporter joined in. "I suppose you're right. Though I can't blame tardiness on traffic, so there are downsides."

This time the reporter did wink. If Sloane wasn't careful, this interview would turn into a puff piece.

"I can't imagine that would be a problem anyway. You had a reputation at the State's Attorney's office for long hours and punctuality. Haven't you continued that as governor?"

"Of course." She racked her brain for the reporter's name—Nia Hamilton—and caught it just in time to avoid an unnatural pause. "That's quite the compliment, Nia. I've always worked for the people of Illinois, both as a prosecutor and as governor. If my reputation is that I'm a hard worker and respectful of others' time, I'm doing right by my boss."

Nia tapped her pen against her chin while Sloane spoke, waiting until she finished to take notes. It was definitely turning into an easy, light interview. She should push it toward something more substantive, but Nia reminded her of a woman she'd dated years ago and it was hard to push with such happy associations so close to mind.

"Speaking of your time as State's Attorney," Nia began, her perfectly shaped eyebrow arching high. "Do you feel your past as a prosecutor leaves you ill-equipped to handle Illinois's battle with police brutality?"

"I...what?"

"You have a close relationship with both the State Police and several municipal police unions. Weren't you endorsed by the Fraternal Order of Police in your last campaign?"

"I was, yes."

"Couldn't that relationship hamper your ability to properly address police abuses of marginalized communities?"

"Excuse me?"

"I wonder that you don't recognize your own bias, Governor Sloane." Nia propped her chin in her hand and there was no hint of softness in her eyes anymore. "Do you even know how many Black Chicagoans you incarcerated in your years as a prosecutor?"

"I haven't analyzed my record. I treated each case individually."

"Do you think communities of color can trust you?"

"Of course."

"Why?"

Silence descended upon the room. Nia didn't push for an answer, but rather embraced the silence, her face and body still. A less seasoned reporter might have squinted and leaned in aggressively. Or followed up with several questions, each more provocative than the last, barking without waiting for a response. Or even felt the discomfort and tried to lessen it by moving on before Sloane answered. Nia did none of these things. She sat and waited.

Sloane cleared her throat, her eyes darting to the digital recorder on the table between them. "I've been hard on crime. I don't deny that because I'm not ashamed of that work. I have made the state a safer place for all its residents. Communities of color can trust me because I have fought to bring safety to their streets. As governor, I will continue that important work."

Silence filled the space left by her answer. Sloane had believed her words to be a good answer. A strong answer. As she looked at Nia's face, she knew she'd been mistaken. It was a stump speech. A political tag line. It worked with a crowd already disposed in her favor and it made for a good debate sound bite, but Nia was quite obviously unimpressed.

Another gut-wrenching moment of silence passed before Nia smiled and dropped her pen on the table. There was no flirtation in the smile now and Sloane wondered if she'd imagined it before.

"I think I've got all I need." Nia punched a button on the recorder and the whirring died. She stood and extended her hand. "Thank you for your time, Governor Sloane."

Sloane's fury bubbled, but she tamped it down and let the politician take over. She stood and shook Nia's hand. "It was my pleasure."

And then she was gone. Sloane looked around the room. The mahogany chair rail and striped wallpaper closed in and she leaned down, her fists on the table top. She banged a fist into the table and the crystal water glasses tinkled, laughing at her stupidity.

"One smile on a pretty face and you walk right into a trap," Sloane mumbled to herself, all too aware that these walls had ears. "Like a fucking rookie."

How could she have let this happen? Who was that woman? She hadn't looked closely enough at the reporter's credentials. And, of course, there'd been her assumption that her party affiliation would protect her in an interview with a Black reporter. How naïve could she possibly be? Lily would be furious with her. Then would come the call from her campaign manager. And the Democratic Party chair. As if she didn't have enough to contend with.

Sloane forced herself to stand tall, straightening her blazer and rolling her neck. She didn't have time to sulk. Judging that Nia was well on her way out of the building, she wrenched the door open and emerged into the hall. Rather than turn right, as she normally would, she turned left and marched toward the courtyard. Nearly every door she passed was closed, but there was the occasional glimpse into a cramped office. She studiously ignored the desks and their occupants.

The deeper she ventured into the Executive Wing, the more doors were open and the less she approved her decision to come this way. It was a longer route back to her office and there was less chance of running into Nia on her way out, but she didn't want to speak to anyone. Her head spun with their conversation and imminent fallout.

First, she had to figure out the publication. Depending on whether it was a newspaper or a magazine, the timing could be drastically different. Or, god forbid, it was a digital source in which case the catastrophe could come within hours. Perhaps Lily could cancel her next appointment so she could confer with her campaign team.

Rounding the final corner, her office in sight, Sloane's gaze fell on the figures outside her door. Clarke and Hawkins flanked her door and did not turn to watch her approach. Their body language, as usual, was stiff and their manner cold. In fact, contrary to Nia's words, she was unpopular with the State Police in general these days. When she was kidnapped, three of their officers had died protecting her and the story was far from settled as far as the State Police brass was concerned.

Anderson clearly had resources, and the media bought the story he fed them to cover up her kidnapping. But there were people inside the State Police who knew those officers were assigned to her person, not her condo. Someone knew the officers would only have been there if she had been there. Pressure or payment must have been applied to keep them silent, but cops were notorious gossips and Sloane had no doubt that rumors were swirling. With so many unanswered questions surrounding the incident, no officer was inclined to like her.

The third person outside her door was a stranger, but Sloane knew she must be the agent sent from the NSA.

"Good morning, Governor," she said, checking her watch. "I'm Special Agent Tyler Graham of the National Security Agency. I believe you're expecting me."

"Agent Graham." Sloane nodded to her, then turned to the officers. "Officer Hawkins. Officer Clarke."

The men nodded back, their expressions tightening.

Graham brandished a manila folder and jerked her head toward Sloane's office. "Shall we?"

In her early thirties, slightly tall for a woman and built like a marathon runner, Special Agent Graham was covered in lean muscle and had an air of respectful authority. Her eyes were pale blue with an unexpected depth.

It was that unexpected depth that made Sloane nervous. Thoughtful eyes were the surest sign of an insightful person, and Sloane could not afford an insightful NSA agent with whom she had to work but also lie to. The note from Anderson had been clear. Marisol's truth needed to remain a closely guarded secret and Sloane was not currently equipped to lie convincingly. Not after her disastrous interview with Nia. She needed time to prepare before she met with this agent.

"I'm afraid it's not a good time," Sloane said.

"I have an appointment," Graham replied. Her toothy grin was clearly an attempt to charm. "I just need a few minutes. It is important."

Shit. Eleven o'clock on Friday. Sloane checked her wristwatch and found that it was five minutes after eleven. "I know you have an appointment and I am sorry, but something extremely important has come up." She eyed the folder. "Something urgent. Perhaps we could meet on Monday?"

"With all due respect." Tyler's eyes narrowed and she was suddenly as cold as the officers on either side of her. "This is too important to wait."

Sloane opened her door and stood in the threshold. "I'm very sorry. I'll have Lily schedule a meeting first thing Monday."

She closed the door before Graham could protest, but the knot of anxiety in her gut did not lessen.

CHAPTER FIVE

As soon as her boot hit the cracked sidewalk, Marisol felt every eye on her. She ran a hand through the long bangs hanging in front of her eyes, pushing them back into the messy wave of black hair that faded neatly into the short, buzz cut on the side and back. Familiar faces nodded to her as she passed. She acknowledged half of them, gracing one or two of her admirers with a swift, barely perceptible nod. The rest shot jealous glances at the lucky ones. Nothing, not even the furtive glances shared between her subjects, escaped the notice of The Queen of Humboldt.

She walked for ten minutes, covering a small corner of her domain from the southern edge of Humboldt Park to the row homes of North Trumbull Avenue. The more rundown the neighborhood, the more respectful the nods she gave and received.

Marisol made it down to the corner of West Ohio, where a chain-link fence and a caution sign in Spanish sectioned off the whole corner of the block. The ground was churned up into a muddy mess around the freshly poured concrete pad on the spot where a crumbling laundromat had stood until recently. Marisol had quietly bought the lot months ago and donated it to a nonprofit organization. Their plans to build a community center included a two-year fundraising effort, but Marisol knew all too well the trouble a vacant lot could bring. She'd been the source of that trouble more than once. A few donations under fake names and some liberally applied pressure, and the construction had begun in earnest. Marisol scanned the lot, noted the lack of disturbance since her last check-in and continued.

She crossed the street and slipped into a nondescript bodega with a faded Puerto Rican flag hanging in the shopfront. A blast of aromas assailed her—good, rich coffee, cinnamon baking in bread, and the oily, starchy scent of plantains frying for the afternoon's tostones. Marisol smiled in anticipation.

Analise, who worked mornings here, loved to flirt. She was barely twenty, just a child in Marisol's eyes, and straight as a Midwestern highway, but she loved to bat her eyelashes at Marisol teasingly. This morning, however, the expected smooth, provocative notes of lilting Spanish did not come.

"Señora Soltero," said a gruff, male voice. "Buenos días. Café?"

"Please," she replied, filling a paper bag with conchas from a case on the counter. "Thank you, Justino."

While he poured thick, sweet coffee into a paper cup, she leaned over the counter and slipped a pair of folded bills into the drawer beneath the register. Analise always pretended not to notice when she did this. Justino really didn't notice. None of the businesses in her neighborhood, no matter how stretched, accepted payment from her, but she always found a way to pay nonetheless.

"Analise sick this morning?" Marisol asked as Justino turned, pressing a plastic top onto her cup.

"She better be," he said, scowling though the emotion didn't fit his round, kind face and fell off it quickly. "Didn't show up to open the store. My wife had to drag me out of bed to come down here when some of the regulars shouted up for their coffee."

"That's not like her."

Worry etched his face as he belatedly realized that Marisol might not be the person to tell about his employee's laziness. "She's a good girl. I'm sure she has a good reason."

Marisol considered his words for a moment, then went back to the case and added three more rolls.

"Of course. If she needs anything, let me know." After he nodded his acknowledgement, Marisol jerked her chin toward the construction across the street. "Haven't seen any looters at night, have you?"

"In your neighborhood?" He shook his head, his eyes scrunching in disbelief, and rested both hands on his ample stomach. "No one would dare. I'll watch for you, of course."

"Gracias, Justino." She shook his hand and he wrapped both his meaty paws around hers. "Take care."

On her way back to Alhambra, Marisol took a more circuitous route. Three blocks north of the bodega she cut into an alley and handed one of the rolls to a man with a curtain of beard covering his sunken chest. She knelt down to where he had wedged himself between a bent trash can and a concrete stoop, quietly asking him a few questions while he ate the roll. He answered in jerky, half-formed sentences, but his eyes were clear. He kissed her hand before she left.

Based on what the man in the alley had told her, Marisol took a detour one block west. Her next stop was a kid sitting under a basketball hoop with no net. She gave him a second roll when he devoured the first in two bites. After he answered her question, he scurried off. Marisol waited until he rounded the corner to march up to his front door and have a short but effective conversation with the boy's father. The father's eyes were a good deal less clear than the man in the alley, and there was fear in them when she left. A quick series of text messages to the contact she'd given the boy assured a hot shower, change of clothes, and a few hours of video games while his father followed Marisol's advice.

The rest of the rolls left her possession in a similar manner and she made her way back to Club Alhambra. Two of her men lounged on the bench across from the entrance and a woman who was far more useful than the other two picked her teeth as she leaned against the bus stop outside. They all acknowledged Marisol, but she went straight for Mel, the woman at the bus stop. Gray appeared at her side.

"Was Analise at Alhambra last night?" Marisol asked without preamble.

"She's underage," Gray said.

Before Marisol could give him a withering look, Mel did it for her. "We expected her, but she didn't show. I can check with Isabella and Margie. They usually hang together."

Marisol nodded. "She wasn't at work this morning."

Gray crossed his arms and said, "That makes three in the last week."

"Three what?"

"Never mind, Mel," Marisol said. If she needed to warn the girls, she would, but no need to spook them yet. "Just talk to Isabella and Margie and get back to me."

Mel pushed off the sign and headed down the block, a strut in her walk that caught the attention of the guys across the street. Gray snapped his fingers once and the guys went back to their studied nonchalance, their ears going red at the rebuke. Marisol followed Gray into the club and up to her office on the third floor.

Marisol threw herself into the leather desk chair and propped her boots on her desk. Gray opened the blinds so he could watch the boys across the street for a moment, then dropped into the couch in the corner. Leather groaned beneath his bulky frame.

"The Vasquez girl…" Gray began.

"Caroline," Marisol provided.

"Caroline Vasquez," Gray started again. "Left her shift at the hotel around ten p.m. last Monday. Didn't make it to her boyfriend's house on North Drake."

"He's one of ours," Marisol said, pinching the bridge of her nose. "Guns?"

"Cars. She helps him sometimes."

"But she doesn't have an obvious connection to us?"

"Not obvious, no." Gray crossed his ankle over his knee, a flash of navy-blue sock appearing before he pulled his pants leg down. "Then there's Sofia Hart. She dropped her daughter off at daycare and was heading to visit her grandmother at the nursing home. It was daylight but early. A long walk, maybe a mile depending on her route."

"And no one saw anything." Marisol sighed, wishing she had another cup of Justino's excellent coffee. "No one saw Analise last night. Her mother works nights at the hospital so it's hard to pin down when she went missing. We'll see what Mel's girls know."

Gray fired up the espresso maker. Marisol didn't remember asking for coffee. Gray was either getting better at reading her or her lack of sleep was more evident than she thought. Gray had hooked onto her when they were both kids and together they'd grown smart and hard running the streets of Detroit. When an increase in fortunes brought her to Chicago, she didn't even have to ask, he just came along. He was like her—calculating and ruthless. It's what made him the perfect right-hand man.

"It might all be a coincidence. Three girls is a lot in two weeks, but this is Humboldt. Anything can happen here."

"The bad things that happen here are my doing and this," Marisol said, waving an arm at the window, "is not my doing."

"Sofia used to run drugs near the Auto Pound."

Gray foamed milk and the hiss of steam made Marisol's head scream.

"I remember." Marisol's jaw clenched, but not from the headache. She'd caught Sofia selling coke to a high schooler. Normally she'd kill anyone selling in her neighborhood, especially to kids, but Sofia had been pregnant and the father was in prison. Marisol didn't kill scared, pregnant women. "Where's her daughter?"

"With her father. He's a good kid. An idiot, but a good kid."

"Make sure he stays out of jail."

He slid a latte in front of her. "Already on it."

"Everyone knows Sofia's not ours. So this isn't an attack on me." Gray was silent too long, so Marisol barked at him, "What?"

"You let her live and you've been looking out for her ever since." He settled back onto the couch but stared into his coffee rather than at her. "And there are rumors about you sleeping with Analise."

"She's a goddamn kid, Gray. I would never do that."

"She's twenty, boss."

"Like I said." Marisol knew her anger was getting the better of her, but she let him have it anyway. "A goddamn kid."

Gray put up a hand in surrender. "I know how you roll, but you play your part a little too well sometimes."

Shock made Marisol's vision go blank for a heartbeat, then two. Gray couldn't possibly know about Washington. She'd been careful. She'd never slipped around anyone, even Gray. She kept her voice level. "I don't play parts, Gray. You know that."

"Look, I don't need to know why you stopped bringing women upstairs. I know something went down in Colombia and you don't have to tell me what, but I might not be the only one who's noticed your recent self-imposed dry streak."

Relief flooded Marisol, but it was tempered by concern. Gray was right, she hadn't been hiding her extraordinary celibacy. How could she even pretend to sleep around after her night with Brin? She'd cultivated the reputation as a stud, but she didn't care about that anymore. He didn't know she'd gone to bed with a goddess. He didn't even know Brin had been with her in Colombia. Now wasn't the time to let anything slip, though. Gray was too smart to be fooled without monumental effort and she had a much bigger secret to keep from him than the occupants of her bed.

"I wasn't screwing Analise, but you're right, someone might've thought I was. She certainly wanted people to think I'd nailed her."

Marisol was already talking about her in the past tense. She hated herself for it, but she had no doubt that she'd never see that lively, beautiful young woman again. Her other hidden life involved too many stories that started how Analise's did. Very few of them ended well, and none of them ended happily.

If they were lucky, the women Marisol saved in her undercover work went to her safehouse, a place she called The Hotel. The original intention had been to keep them hidden there until it was safe to return them home. Over time, more and more of the women she saved decided to stay. Sometimes it was because they had no home to return to, sometimes it was because they were afraid their families would see the haunted look in their eyes. The more women who stayed long-term, the closer Marisol guarded The Hotel's location. Their captors, most often The Bishop, would risk a lot to get them back. Marisol hadn't quite worked out if he wanted them for the profit they brought him, or to keep them from testifying one day.

"So all three of them could be hits at you." Gray sipped his cappuccino and studied Marisol's face. "You think that's what this is?"

"If someone is after me there are more direct ways."

"Except any attack on Humboldt is obviously an attack on you."

"You think one of the other gangs?"

Gray laughed and set down his empty cup. "None of them are strong enough or dumb enough. If it's a hit on you, it's a new player."

Marisol eyed the dregs of her coffee. If there was a new player, who were they after? Marisol The Queen of Humboldt or Marisol the undercover agent trying to wipe out human traffickers? The image of The Bishop, a shadowy face seen through a cloud of dust and a dirty car window flashed in her mind.

CHAPTER SIX

"You've managed to feed yourself this morning," Lily said, settling into her usual chair across from Sloane's desk. "And I understand that you did not enter your office at all yesterday. Congratulations. That marks the first Sunday you've taken off in three months."

"I do occasionally relax."

"I've yet to see it."

"You don't work weekends," Sloane retorted.

"My spies are everywhere."

That Sloane didn't doubt. Not a single member of the domestic staff at the Governor's Mansion was free of Lily's influence. Sloane had seen her approaching employees on their first day of work, whether they fell under her purview or not.

Sloane leaned back in her chair, letting the leather wings hug her aching shoulders. "And what have your spies told you?"

"That you spent most of yesterday morning reading in your apartment and you watched a movie after yoga in the afternoon."

"Your informant was mistaken. It was a TV show."

"I'll relieve them of their duties."

Sloane tipped her head back and laughed. Lily graced her with a rare grin.

"In their defense, I binged three episodes so it probably seemed like a movie."

It may have been four. Sloane wasn't quite sure. She hadn't watched more than a few frames and the dialogue had faded into the background easily enough. Her mind had been elsewhere. Several elsewheres, in fact. She had enough worries and regrets to chase through her mind for a week of Sundays. The day hadn't been relaxing, but at least she had been lying on the couch, giving her body the break her mind wasn't destined to enjoy.

Lily cleared her throat and flipped open her notebook. The thick, fabric-bound cover creaked as she opened it to the marked page. "You have a relatively light day, though the trend doesn't continue for the rest of the week."

"It never does."

"Oh, before we get started." Lily propped her tablet on top of the notebook and scrolled through a few pages. "You received a lovely note from the reporter from last week, thanking you for your time and informing you the story will be released soon."

Sloane had determined that Nia wrote for a lifestyle magazine, meaning she had a brief reprieve before the article dropped. That was all she'd managed to find before yet another distraction tore her away. She hadn't alerted Lily or her campaign manager, but now was as good a time as any.

"Warning me, you mean."

"How so?"

"It was not a pleasant interview."

Lily's eyes focused on her, cold concentration evident in every movement. "Will it require damage control?"

"Potentially."

Lily turned back to her notebook, flipping to a fresh page in the back. "Explain your concerns so we can craft a response. I can have your press department on it within the hour."

"Hard to say how she'll frame it."

"They'll need something to go on."

Sloane ran a hand through her hair. It was getting long and felt brittle. "I know, Lily. I'm sorry. I just don't quite know what to expect."

Sloane couldn't explain even to herself why she was hesitant to recount the disastrous interview. It had been that hesitance more than the inevitable distractions that kept her from informing anyone on Friday. Her stomach squirmed each time she thought about the encounter and she found herself avoiding the memory.

When she did not elaborate, Lily flipped her notebook shut. "Well at least we're forewarned. I can put them on alert. They're good on their feet."

"Thank you, Lily."

Standing to go, Lily replied, "I'm merely doing my job, Madam Governor. As are you."

Coming from Lily, that was the height of praise. Sloane nodded her appreciation and Lily marched across the room. When she opened the office door, she revealed a familiar face waiting in the visitor's chair.

"Special Agent Graham." Lily stepped aside to admit her. "Right on time for your appointment."

Lily shot Sloane a look that held no remorse and a great deal of satisfaction. Sloane had forgotten to reschedule the appointment she'd skipped Friday. Apparently, Agent Graham had ensured she got that meeting first thing instead of counting on Sloane to arrange it. It was presumptuous but admittedly efficient to remove Sloane from the process. And Lily appeared to favor Agent Graham, if her warm smile was any judge.

"Before you go, Lily." Both Graham and Lily turned to look at her, but Sloane focused on her secretary. "Can you pull my prosecutorial records?"

"Full case files or summaries?"

"Summaries should be sufficient. If you don't mind?"

"Certainly." Lily flipped open her notebook again, balancing it in one hand. "Which year?"

"All of them."

Lily's eyebrow jumped. "Including when you were Assistant State's Attorney?"

"All of it."

"It'll take some time."

"Thank you, Lily."

She nodded and turned on her heel, leaving it to Graham to close the office door. Sloane would have given just about anything for the agent to leave too, even another meeting with the Chamber of Commerce. She wasn't that lucky.

"That sounded serious." Graham remarked as she marched into the room.

"Just damage control. It's a constant part of the job when you're a public servant." Sloane rounded her desk and held out a hand. "Special Agent Graham, please accept my sincere apology for Friday."

"Of course. I understand you're a busy woman." She smiled charmingly and continued, "Please, call me Tyler. I can't stand titles."

Sloane appraised Tyler as she crossed the room. She moved with unsinkable determination, but she was ostentatiously gentle with the manila folder she juggled between hands in order to shake Sloane's. Sloane had been a politician for a long time now, but she would always be a prosecutor at heart. Looking at Special Agent Graham, she saw the perfect witness. She was the sort of woman in law enforcement that would have the jury eating out of her hand. State's Attorney Sloane would have made it a point to hand her a file to read from as soon as possible. That way the jury could see her care and hear the calm power of her voice.

She wore a tight-fitting men's suit and she wore it well. Her brown hair was short and stylishly groomed, speckled with just enough premature gray at the temples to give her an air of experience that was only partially earned. Male jurors would respect her confidence and composure. Female jurors would respect her empathy and thoughtfulness. Everyone would appreciate the fact that she was incredibly attractive in an androgynous way.

Even her most noticeable feature would be an asset, given her profession. It was certainly the first thing most people saw when they looked at her. A pale, puckered line of scarring curled from the edge of her right ear down to her chin where it picked up again on her neck, dangerously close to the point where her pulse fluttered under her skin, disappearing under her shirt where it met her collarbone. Tyler's white skin was richly tanned and the scar stood out all the more for the contrast. While Sloane was sure it caused her embarrassment in her everyday life, there was nothing a jury loved so much as someone in law enforcement who could prove their commitment to their work with a scar like that.

"You're at work early," Tyler said, nodding toward the large stack of completed work on her desk.

"I'm always here this early, Special Agent Graham. The business of government does not end at five, nor does it begin at nine."

"Of course. But I did ask you to call me Tyler."

Her smile was kind and the words were spoken politely, but Sloane wondered whether the politeness would last if she refused the request. Or neglected to offer the same concession. She decided it would be best to give in on this point. Tyler could be trouble, both for herself and for Marisol, if Sloane didn't manage their relationship.

"Sorry, Tyler." Sloane tried out a chummy smile. It usually worked on the campaign trail so it might work here. "Call me Sabrina. Please sit."

Tyler had waited to be invited into the chair across from the governor's desk, but she dropped onto the hard, wooden seat with obvious relish. "Lucky for me few of your constituents are clamoring to meet with you so early."

Sloane settled into her desk chair and finally dragged her eyes away from her guest. She knew all of her own strengths and weaknesses, so she knew her unguarded eyes could give her away to a thoughtful observer. After just a few moments in her presence, Sloane knew Tyler would be a thoughtful observer.

"What brings you into my office so early?"

"It seems we have similar interests." Tyler leaned back in her chair, exuding confidence and ease.

"Do we?" The confidence and overfamiliarity should have annoyed Sloane, but she had a weak spot for confident butch women. Not to mention the request from Anderson to let Tyler help her. "And what interest is that?"

"Your trip to South America ended with a bang."

Sloane couldn't keep herself from flinching. *If only she knew how the trip to South America had started.* But Tyler couldn't know that. While Anderson worked at the NSA and knew about Tyler's assignment, Sloane suspected he hadn't sent her. After all, if he had, he wouldn't have told Sloane to keep Marisol's involvement with his agency a secret.

No, Tyler believed the official lie. According to that official lie, Sloane had seen firsthand the devastation caused by the trafficking of women and girls from poor communities. She had given an impassioned speech on the tarmac in Bogota about her commitment to stopping the trade. The American ambassador had stood behind her, flanked by his wife and his Colombian counterpart, a look of shock and incredulity painting his weak features. Watching the news footage later, Sloane had laughed at his discomfort. Now she wondered whether his pressure was responsible for Tyler's presence in her office.

"I'm sure Ambassador Perry has recovered in the last six months," Sloane replied with a wink. Tyler's chuckle in reply made her continue, "Is that why you're here? To help an embarrassed politician save face?"

"He did call, but he doesn't have enough clout to make the NSA respond."

"Who does?"

Tyler met her eye. "You."

"I didn't ask for this meeting."

"No, but you caused it nonetheless. The NSA has been working on human trafficking in and out of the US for many years. Your speech…hell, your whole trip made it look like we've been sitting on our hands."

"Haven't you been?" Sloane leaned forward, her arms on her desk. "Apart from the signs in airport bathrooms, what work has the NSA truly done to crack down on these crimes?"

Tyler's charming grin vanished and her eyes went cold. *She doesn't like being challenged. Interesting.*

"Just because you don't hear about our work on the evening news doesn't mean nothing's being done."

I'm well aware. Only you aren't the one putting your life on the line.

"Enlighten me."

"Our task force is one of the largest at the agency. We have a presence in every major city and every state, gathering intelligence and making arrests. I assure you…"

"What about our territories?"

"Excuse me?"

"How much of a presence do you have in the United States territories? American Samoa, Guam, the US Virgin Islands. That's the avenue most trafficked women take to arrive on the mainland."

"And we have a significant presence there, but not all trafficked women come from outside our borders. Many are US citizens taken from our own streets."

"Doesn't local law enforcement handle those cases?"

"Local law enforcement has neither the manpower nor the expertise to identify or stop human trafficking."

"And does the NSA conduct training for…"

A loud rap on the office door was followed promptly by Lily's entrance. She carried a large silver tray to the sideboard and turned to Tyler.

"Special Agent Graham, coffee?"

The interruption had clearly unsettled Tyler. She peeled her eyes off Sloane, shaking her head a fraction and releasing the tension from her mouth.

"Sorry?"

"How do you take your coffee?"

"Oh. Black. Thank you."

While Lily poured, Tyler returned her angry stare to Sloane. Her jaw was set and there was a fire in her eye. Sloane wondered if it was wise to challenge her. There was clearly fight in this woman and she didn't necessarily want it focused on her. But if she was disagreeable enough to send Tyler back to Washington DC, Sloane could get on with her work. She had precious little free time and she spent all of it trying to track down The Bishop. If she had to split that time between tracking down The Bishop and lying to Tyler, she could end up overwhelmed quickly.

"Cream, no sugar, Governor Sloane."

Lily set the cup on her desk and lingered long enough to catch Sloane's eye. She flashed a squinty-eyed, disapproving glance, then returned to her tray. Again, Lily's ability to communicate a host of emotions nonverbally sobered Sloane. She glanced over at her desk phone, noting the open intercom line. Lily's desk phone was no doubt on the other end.

So that's why she brought in refreshments I hadn't requested.

Sloane took a sip of her coffee and casually dropped her free hand to the phone. Lily held her head high as she marched out of the office with the tray, but Sloane had caught the flinch as she'd disconnected the open line. If Lily had risked missing out on the rest of the meeting just to warn Sloane to behave, she must've been too rude.

"Forgive my bluntness," Sloane told Tyler when they were alone again. "I'm very passionate on this subject."

Tyler's whole body relaxed. "No need to apologize, Sabrina. I'm equally passionate. I think we can work well together."

"And what is it you want to work on with me?"

"My commanding officer thought this would be a good opportunity to…firm up relations between our agency and an important state government." Tyler was all business again, brandishing her folder. "A joint venture. Make Illinois the center of the fight against trafficking in the US."

"What would that entail?"

"Two main areas. The first would be fact finding. There seems to be a dramatic increase in suspicious disappearances in this area recently. We suspect a new player here in Illinois."

Sloane's gut turned to lead. *A new player or an old player with a new target?* "Can you give me more information on that?"

"My investigation is just beginning and it won't be my primary focus. I'll keep you updated but I'm not here in a law enforcement capacity."

"No? What capacity then?"

"Policy advisement. That's the second area we can work on together. I want to be a resource for your administration. You promised a bill to crack down on human trafficking. I'm here to help you write it."

"That's presumptuous of you. Writing bills is my area of expertise."

"And human trafficking is mine," Tyler answered quickly. "You need an expert and I'm here to help you make the most effective law possible."

Sloane couldn't help smiling. Tyler may think herself an expert on human trafficking, but she couldn't hold a candle to Marisol. *I'll see you in Chicago.* The smile melted off Sloane's face. Maybe Tyler would be useful after all. If she really could help catch The Bishop, maybe Sloane could get back to Marisol before their relationship was ruined completely.

"I think this will be an excellent partnership, Tyler."

CHAPTER SEVEN

Three days after Analise failed to show up for work, her friend Isabella turned up at Club Alhambra. It wasn't an unusual occurrence to see her there, and although she'd been less than forthcoming with Mel, Marisol hoped it was a sign she was ready to talk. With a flick of her fingers, Marisol sent Gray down into the crowd to fetch her. Another flick brought her personal waitress scurrying to Marisol's side, an unopened bottle of tequila in one hand and a pair of thick crystal tumblers in the other. By the time she'd poured a pair of generous servings, Isabella was sauntering into Marisol's Throne Room, desperately pretending that she'd been afforded this honor before.

"Welcome to Club Alhambra," Marisol said in her smoothest purr. She leaned forward, putting her lips against the shell of Isabella's ear as she spoke. "Will you join me for a drink?"

Marisol couldn't help but smile as a shiver passed through Isabella's body, from the tips of her peep-toe heels to the pile of permed curls on the crown of her head. She nodded, her mouth open and her eyes hungry. Marisol trailed her fingertips down the girl's arm, leaving goose pimples on the exposed, golden-brown flesh, and pressed her hand into the small of her back. Isabella lurched in her too-high heels, but made it to the couch without incident. Marisol made a show of falling a step behind to watch her backside as she walked. Isabella flashed her a grin that stated quite clearly that she knew she was being watched and liked it. Marisol sat first and Isabella slid in next to her, practically in her lap already. It was just too easy.

Gray kept an eye on them throughout the night. Marisol thought she saw his approval in the way Marisol pawed at her, feigning drunkenness and desire. She felt neither, but if Gray thought she did than she was certainly convincing everyone else. Isabella made it easy. She drank enough for both of them and kept up both sides of the slurred conversation. Marisol guessed she wasn't gay, since she never had to redirect Isabella's hands away from anywhere in particular. The ones who really wanted her had their hands down her pants from the moment they sat down and Marisol had a hard time deflecting their attentions without drawing their suspicion or anger. Those who just wanted to be seen with her carefully avoided sexual contact. Since Marisol had no intention of sleeping with any of them, she preferred the straight ones.

Around midnight a pair of beautiful young women wearing very little stumbled up to Marisol and Isabella and made clear their interest in joining them on the couch. Marisol had to entertain the idea for longer than was comfortable before Isabella got jealous enough to shout at them. Finally, Marisol was able to step in to cool the situation and offered to walk Isabella home. The new couple practically wept with jealousy, but Isabella turned green. Flirting was one thing, but she had no more interest in going to bed with Marisol than Marisol had in going to bed with her. But they both had appearances to maintain, and Marisol was happy to note that the bottle of tequila—an excellent añejo she hated to waste on a woman who would have been content with Jose Cuervo—was almost dry.

Since only one glass made it past her lips, Isabella would be ripe for Marisol's questions.

Unfortunately, Isabella was not very useful. It only took two blocks for Marisol to realize she knew nothing about Analise's disappearance. She hadn't seen Analise the night she disappeared, Isabella told her as a black SUV with tinted windows rolled slowly past before gunning its engine around the next corner. If the driver intended to impress the two women walking in the moonlight, he only succeeded in impressing one. Isabella's eyes followed the car with obvious hunger, the chrome rims flashing in her wide eyes.

Her night a bust, Marisol allowed her mind to wander as Isabella prattled on inanely. The moon hung heavy and full just over the line of buildings before them. The streets of Humboldt, normally bustling and loud even at this hour, were subdued enough to melt into the night.

Marisol let her mind wander to another night. Another full moon. The danger had still been close, even if Marisol and Brin had escaped their enemy's clutches. She had never expected Brin to come to her that night.

She had been in love with Sabrina Sloane for the better part of her life. Or at least the part of her life that was better. The weekend they'd shared a decade ago had blown up in her face. Had Brin known she was a criminal, she'd never have gone home from that bar with Marisol. But lying about her identity after they'd been intimate had led to years of hatred. All the while, Marisol's feelings had deepened. She had loved this incredible woman from afar knowing that there was nothing she could ever do to win her heart. Marisol's lies and her lust had ruined everything once before. Yet Brin had come to her in Colombia.

Had she come out of obligation or out of fear? Would she have come if they had been in Chicago, without the danger? Would she have come if she had known from the start that Marisol's life—the façade of The Queen of Humboldt—was only a partial truth? What had brought her into Marisol's arms and what would keep her there? These were questions Marisol had intended to ask when they were reunited in Chicago. But

Brin had not come. A brief delay could be expected. Six months was nothing short of a proclamation. Governor Sabrina Sloane had rejected Marisol Soltero, regardless of her worthy secret life.

Without warning, and interrupting Marisol's reverie, Isabella launched herself forward. She wrapped willowy arms around Marisol's neck and dragged their lips together. Had she time to consider, Marisol would have done as she'd done countless times before—she would have gently held Isabella at bay. But now Isabella's lips were on her when her mind was still full of Brin.

For a moment that Marisol allowed to stretch far longer than it should, she kept Brin close. Isabella's lips became Brin's lips and Marisol, in her wild need, kissed her back. Not just kissed her. Devoured her. Isabella had stopped them beside a brick row house and before she could stop herself, Marisol was pressing Isabella's body against the wall. She slid her fingers into Isabella's hair, felt her scalp under clawing, needy fingertips. Pressing forward with pelvis and tongue, Marisol melted into this warm, inviting body.

It almost worked.

She knew she should stop it—knew the moment the kiss started it should end. But she didn't want to stop it. Just for a moment, she wanted the feel of someone else's lips on hers. For a moment her mind forgot that Brin was miles away. She grabbed Isabella's thigh and wrapped it around her waist, swallowing the girl's surprised, delighted chirp. Then reality began to come home. As she slid her tongue into Isabella's mouth, she tasted her lips. They were glossed with the peppery, overripe fruit flavor of aged tequila. Brin's lips had tasted nothing like this. They never would. She didn't drink tequila. She liked French wine and Scotch whiskey.

It wasn't just the taste that was wrong. Brin had not kissed like this. This kiss was desperate, whereas Brin's had been hungry. Isabella was furtive while Brin had been confident. She had moved with intent and skill. Isabella, for all her enthusiasm, had a good many things to learn about how to kiss. This was a kiss meant to give pleasure rather than to share it.

With a sigh, Marisol forced herself to pull away. She wanted to run. To scream. To find Brin and tear her own throat out begging for one more kiss like the one they'd shared under the South American moonlight. Instead, she reminded herself that she was Marisol Soltero, The Queen of Humboldt, and this woman wanted a story to tell.

"Nice start," she purred, keeping her face close to Isabella's and her body even closer. "But part two requires a little more privacy."

Isabella giggled and slumped against the wall behind her. When she spoke, Marisol turned her mind to Spanish, wanting to translate the words flooding her ears. It didn't take long to realize they were another language all together. One invented at the bottom of a liquor bottle and thus indecipherable. Isabella's head lolled back, and it was only with a quick slip of her fingers through her hair that Marisol saved her from a bloody scalp. Isabella would not remember anything after the kiss.

Much to her relief, she discovered that the brick row house was where Isabella lived with her grandmother and three younger brothers. Isabella wasn't capable of wrestling her keys from her purse, but on her third attempt Marisol found the one that opened the front door. The rest of the family was in bed, and thus missed Marisol dragging a barely conscious Isabella into her bedroom. She murmured happily as Marisol removed her clothes, but she was snoring by the time she was naked. Once she was under the sheets and safely on her left side, Marisol slipped out through the window into the backyard. Isabella had giggled and whispered loudly enough that her family would corroborate a wonderful night with the neighborhood's sexiest lesbian crime lord. Hopefully that would be enough to satisfy Gray's concern for a little while longer.

She slipped through the shadows, her steps light and soundless. Headlights bloomed at the end of the alley, painting its gaping mouth with the blinding blue-white light of halogen. Marisol slipped behind a crumbling fence and watched the car roll by. It moved slowly, like the less subtle drug dealers from other parts of the city. No one Marisol employed would be so obvious. Marisol saw a dark SUV with dark windows. It passed beneath a flickering streetlight, and the color flared from black to royal purple, then back to black when the angle of the light above changed. She'd noticed the same expensive paint job on an SUV that had slowed when it passed her walking Isabella home. That was the only time she'd seen it before. It had to be the same vehicle. No one in Humboldt would dare get such a flashy paint job unless they worked for her.

Marisol waited on itchy feet while she counted to five in both English and then Spanish, slipped out from behind the fence, and risked a jog down the alley. Her boots didn't make much noise on the pot-holed street. She only slid around the corner far enough to let one eye scan the street. The SUV was gone.

Reverting to her casual stride, Marisol turned the corner and strutted off in the direction the car had vanished. Alhambra's bright lights faded into the distance behind her.

CHAPTER EIGHT

Sloane had no room in her official schedule, so she and Tyler met to write their groundbreaking new law in the evenings after everyone else had gone home. For an hour each night they hammered out the details, starting with a draft with such strict limitations and punishments that Sloane knew it would never pass through her moderate legislature. Surprisingly, it was Tyler who convinced her to water down some sections. Sloane hated watering down anything, but pragmatism was a necessity in government and she was slowly accepting.

On their fourth evening of collaboration, Tyler entered her office with the slightly sheepish look of a woman fresh from a Lily Holmes lecture.

"Why don't we…um…work in the dining room this evening," Tyler said, hovering near the doorway. "That way we can eat dinner at a reasonable hour."

Sloane laughed as she gathered her files and tablet. "Don't mind Lily. Whatever threats she used, she's not capable of carrying them out."

"I don't believe you. I've met hardened criminals without that much anger in their eyes."

The chef served a simple meal of salmon and asparagus swimming in a perfectly tart lemon dill sauce. Sloane would've done anything for a nice crisp New Zealand Sauvignon Blanc to pair with it, but they were so close to a reasonable draft. Wine would have spoiled any chance of finishing.

"I doubt any Republicans will sign on with this amnesty clause," Tyler said, sliding her empty plate away.

"We won't need them," Sloane answered. "And I refuse to allow the victims to be deported or imprisoned. That's what always happens in these cases. The traffickers get away with no punishment and the women go to jail for prostitution."

"Not to mention the johns going unnamed and unpunished." Tyler sneered. They'd been over this ground before, but it was a sore spot for them both. "But prostitution is a crime."

"A crime that's forced on them by…"

Tyler held up her hands. "I know. I agree with you. I'm just here to advise and I'm advising this will be a tough sell, especially in your Senate."

Sloane sighed and leaned back into her chair. "You're right, I know. It's just…" Failing to find the words for her frustration, she threw her arms into the air.

Tyler leaned her elbows on the table, shrewd eyes searching Sloane's face. "If I may be bold, Sabrina. It feels like your heart isn't in this tonight."

Sloane turned away from the searching gaze to stare out the window. The view was uninspiring. A few trees. A swatch of lawn. Nothing to hold her interest. Not like the view from the dining table in her condo back home in Chicago. That view was always vibrant. Glass and steel and concrete. A city broken into its most basic elements. And people. Always people moving through the scene far below. She missed the city.

Being away from Chicago was an empty ache, but she knew it was the only course of action. The Bishop had used her against Marisol once before, and he wouldn't hesitate to do it again. Marisol's safety was paramount and the best way to ensure it was to stay away and work to get rid of The Bishop once and for all. Then she could relax. Then they could be together.

Taking a cue from Tyler's boldness, Sloane replied, "I'm less interested in this bill than the investigation you're running. How's that going?"

Tyler perked up. "I didn't think you would be interested in that aspect."

"I'm very interested."

"Why?"

Sloane realized her mistake too late. She supposed most governors wouldn't care, but then again most governors weren't trying to protect someone like Marisol Soltero. "You forget I was a prosecutor in Chicago. Keeping my city safe will always be an interest."

"Were you? I had no idea."

"You don't have a file on me?" Sloane asked, leaning in and smiling. "How disappointing. I thought the NSA keeps tabs on all of us."

Tyler laughed and tapped the bottom of her pen on the table. "I'm sure we do have a file on you, but I didn't bother to read it." She shifted her gaze to Sloane, her eyes shining in the muted light. "I'm starting to think I should have."

A flutter in her chest reminded Sloane it had been a long time since a woman looked at her with that interested gaze. Too bad it was the wrong woman. She kept her eyes trained on Tyler's and her expression light, avoiding the clichéd averted gaze and widening grin that might lead Tyler to think flirting was an option. She had no interest in flirting, but a friendship seemed more and more likely the longer they spent in each other's company.

Tyler was an anomaly. She worked for the most clandestine intelligence organization in the country, and yet there was nothing underhanded or secretive about her. Not for the first time, Sloane wondered how she'd landed at the NSA rather than the FBI or even the military. The way she carried herself, Sloane thought she would fit in well at the Pentagon.

"As to the investigation," Tyler continued with obvious bitterness. "It's hit the stone wall of jurisdiction. The Chicago PD doesn't like feds much."

"In my experience, Chicago PD doesn't like anyone much."

Tyler laughed and ran a hand over her jaw, weariness settling into her features. As she propped her chin on her hand, Tyler's fingers settled against the scar on her cheek. Sloane stared at them, thinking, as always, of Marisol. Had she gained any scars from their time in Colombia? She must have. What they'd done to her had been sadistic.

Sloane doubted Tyler had acquired her scar the same way. No doubt it was a heroic event. Something she could tell her grandkids about. Nothing like the shadowy secrets that left their mark on Marisol. Sloane had always thought nothing good could come of working in the shadows, but Marisol had shifted her thinking.

Tyler and Marisol both worked to free women and girls from traffickers. Tyler did it Sloane's way, but how could that be considered better? Marisol worked in the shadows, and yet she had The Hotel. She saved women and then took them away to a secret location where they could be safe. Meanwhile, here was Tyler, advocating for arresting the victims for prostitution as a compromise. Looking at it that way, Sloane had no doubt which person did more good.

"May I ask you a personal question, Tyler?"

"Sure."

"How did you get that scar?"

Tyler tensed, her gaze locked on Sloane. There was a depth to her gaze. A vulnerability Sloane should have anticipated.

"I'm sorry," Sloane stammered. "That was rude of me."

"No, it's fine." Tyler broke eye contact, looking down at her fountain pen. Slowly, she picked up the lid and settled it into place over the nib, but didn't click it shut. "That's...a story I don't tell just anyone. Only a certain type of woman is ready to hear it." Tyler looked back up and met her stare. "I doubt you're that woman, Sabrina."

"No, I'm not," Sloane replied without hesitation. "Not for you, Tyler."

"I thought not." Tyler's smile held no hint of malice or bitterness, just unmistakable kindness. "I'll save the story for her, if you don't mind."

"Of course. I'm eager to meet the woman worthy of the story." Tyler nodded and Sloane continued, "In the meantime, I have a knack for knocking down stone walls. Who should I call in the Chicago PD?"

The name Tyler gave was unfamiliar, but Sloane wrote it down so she could make the call first thing in the morning.

"You think he'll listen?" Tyler asked.

"I am the governor. He doesn't have much choice." She decided now was a good time to set ground rules. "I hope you can keep your investigation and any arrests it leads to quiet."

Tyler's eyebrow shot up. "We try not to alert the news when we perform a raid. It's not the NSA way, if you catch my meaning."

"I do and I approve. The fewer agencies involved in this, the better."

"You don't want a splashy arrest to coincide with your policy announcement?"

"That would be the last thing I want." Sloane left it at that, allowing Tyler to come to her own conclusion.

"My superiors will be pleased to hear it. The less the public knows, the less our targets fear capture. That always works to our advantage."

As they got back to work, Sloane mused over the benefits of working with an organization that valued secrecy. With Tyler on her side, doing her work quietly, Sloane could get back to finding a way to save Marisol from The Bishop.

CHAPTER NINE

Sloane paced her office, her tablet in one hand, the other gesticulating as she emphasized certain phrases in her speech. It was a decent speech. It wouldn't be remembered in the annals of great political messages, but it would give her a sound bite on the evening news. She highlighted a phrase and made a note to share with her social-media team. Something to tweet out and keep her accounts active.

She flubbed a paragraph and went back to try again just as the murmur of voices filtered through her office door. The distraction made her trip over a particularly complex sentence again. Ignoring the increasingly loud voices in the hallway, she repeated the line ten times. With each repetition, her lips wrapped more precisely around the syllables. By the tenth recitation she could read the line with ease.

Pausing, Sloane listened hard and distinguished Lily's lilting tones and Tyler's deep rumble. At first she thought they were arguing, their voices were so loud, but Lily rarely argued with anyone. If anything, she conspired with any willing partner. This particular comradery was deeply inconvenient. Lily alone could overpower just about anyone. When combined with Tyler's steady charm, Sloane didn't stand a chance. But she needed to keep the upper hand with Tyler if she was going to use her and protect Marisol at the same time.

Tyler's melodic chuckle broke any hope Sloane had of Lily being an ally. They hadn't been arguing but joking. She sighed and wandered back to her desk. She briefly considered trying to escape, but the only other exit was into her private bathroom and she could only hide in there for so long. Tyler would wait her out.

Lily's bark of laughter joined Tyler's as she pushed open the office door.

"Not even a presumptive knock this time," Sloane grumbled to herself.

When Tyler tried to enter behind her, Lily held out an arm to block her. "Don't make me call security, Special Agent Graham. You don't have an appointment this afternoon."

Neither of them looked at her, so Sloane eyed the bathroom door again.

"Oh no," Tyler said. Sloane looked back to see her pointing an accusatory finger. "Don't you dare think about hiding."

"I…"

Lily ignored her spluttering boss and crossed her arms. "You thought I could be distracted, did you? You aren't as charming as you think, Special Agent Graham."

"I asked you to call me Tyler."

"And I told you that line won't work with me either."

Tyler smiled and leaned close. "I'm not trying to charm you, Lily."

"Excuse me," Sloane growled. Neither woman spared her a glance. "This is my office and I'm very busy."

"No you aren't," Tyler and Lily said in unison.

Tyler held up her folder. This wasn't the same folder she'd had at their first meeting. "We need to get to work on this, Sabrina."

Sloane avoided Tyler's eye, focusing on her desktop. They'd spent every night last week at work on the bill and she was thoroughly and completely over it for the moment. "I don't really have time to draft policy at the moment, Tyler. Perhaps we can put you on the schedule for…"

"This isn't about the bill," Tyler interrupted. She cut a wary look at Lily and continued, "It's the…other thing I'm here for."

The suspicious disappearances. It had only been yesterday morning that Sloane talked to the Chicago PD contact and yet here she was with a case file already. Sloane wasn't shocked to discover Tyler had made progress already. She was a field agent, after all, and had clearly been more interested in the investigation than the bill. But as little as Sloane wanted to dive into a policy discussion again, she was less interested in discussing missing women with Tyler. She still wasn't sure how to avoid the topic of Marisol.

Tyler had been given a carefully crafted story about a school for young women outside Bogota that Sloane had visited in her South American tour. A school she'd returned to later to find abandoned. Stories told by weeping mothers of a man who came in the night and stole their daughters to sell in the United States. The fairy tale of Governor Sloane swearing to stop the horrors of human trafficking.

It was a reasonable enough story and the fiery speech that embarrassed Ambassador Perry capped it well. It was the justification for an American military unit storming a notorious compound in the mountains surrounding Colombia's capital. But eventually Tyler would discover Sloane knew far too much, even for an interested politician.

Rather than rescuing Sloane, Lily left her to fend for herself. She stood by, quietly waiting for her boss's decision. Sloane sighed and slumped in her chair.

Sloane forced every muscle in her body to go perfectly still. Would there be photographs in that folder? Of missing women and evil men? Would there be a photo of Marisol? Sloane wasn't ready for that. Not yet. She forced herself to breathe, focusing on the movement of air in and out of her lungs. When she was sure her voice wouldn't give her away, she replied, "I'm in the middle of something here. Can it wait until tomorrow?"

Tyler's face hardened. Despite the scar curling across her cheek, it was not a face built for anger. "This is important, Sabrina."

"So is this speech. I need to prepare."

"Can't we discuss…"

"Tomorrow." The snap of Sloane's voice cut off any discussion and the anger did not recede from Tyler's features. "We can discuss it tomorrow."

CHAPTER TEN

Forcing herself to sit through a few hours in her Throne Room, Marisol chewed the inside of her cheek. She knew all too well the importance of being seen, but the longer she sat here, pretending to get drunk, the more chance another woman could go missing. Another of her people could drop into the hands of her enemy.

She poured another measure of booze, being sure to slop some over the side of the glass. Thinking of The Bishop made her grind her teeth, but fortunately she had a reputation of surliness and introspection. It allowed her to be thoughtful as she gulped down her drink. It really was tequila, but the dim lights and dark bottle allowed her to water it down to the point that she could keep her wits about her.

Crossing her ankle over her knee, Marisol's thoughts turned again to the evil man from Colombia. She didn't like naming him. Naming him gave him power, and her wrists were proof that he'd had power over her once. In Colombia his goons had tied her up like a side of meat. Helpless as they'd tortured her. It wouldn't happen again.

It had to be him, though—the man taking women off Marisol's streets. He knew about her covert life and he knew about The Hotel, even if he didn't know where it was. For a brazen, sadistic man like him, shifting his target to her people would be sweet revenge. Marisol squirmed on her couch, the leather of the seat and the leather of her pants groaning as they rubbed against each other. His attacks had been well-designed. She could feel the itch under her skin. The need to find him and destroy him. The desire to tear Humboldt apart looking for him.

She wanted to be reckless, but she had ample practice in denying herself what she wanted most. He wanted to make her angry. He had. Unfortunately for him, she didn't let that make her vulnerable. On the contrary; she knew he had made a fatal error. By taking her people, he had revealed his new base of operations. He was in Chicago, in Humboldt, which meant he was in Marisol's crosshairs. Now she just needed to pull the trigger.

Marisol snapped and Gray was at her side. "I'm going to find a friend for the evening." She flicked her eyes to his and he nodded almost imperceptibly. "Keep an eye out."

As he moved away, bringing his phone to his ear, Marisol slithered off the couch. She'd been watching the dance floor for an hour, and everyone on it knew they were being seen. It made some lose themselves in the velvet rhythm of the music. It made others seem nervous.

Marisol descended the stairs to the main floor, and the whole world turned to watch her. Her target was no exception. She danced a hair off the beat and smacked an elbow into the person beside her. Her target tensed, ending any pretense of dancing.

She was cute, objectively speaking, though nowhere near Marisol's type. She would do. She had a fresh face and the big, frightened eyes of a doe when Marisol draped her forearm across the woman's shoulder. Her body was an inferno on the crowded dance floor, the heat radiated through Marisol's leather jacket.

Marisol watched her target's throat bob as she swallowed anxiously. Marisol leaned closer, her body sliding in rhythm against the strangers.

When her lips brushed against the woman's ear, she hissed, "Dance."

As though Marisol was a puppet-master pulling her strings, the woman burst into life. She dipped with Marisol, her knees bending but her feet cemented to the floor. Marisol leaned back, throwing her fake smile to the ceiling. She grabbed the stranger's hand and guided it to her hip. Eventually, her target came to life, moving in time with the music. She even glided closer. Given enough time, she might figure out how to dance.

Marisol didn't have time and she didn't have patience, so she grabbed the wrist of a much more enthusiastic partner. Her original target's face fell but brightened again when Marisol placed herself between the two. As the song continued, more women joined the group. Bodies pressed in close. The stink of sweat and booze wrapped around her and Marisol relaxed. She turned to one dancer then another, never giving anyone too much time. The crowd swelled.

When she heard the first cry of pain from a crushed toe, Marisol made her move. She slipped around one dancer, pressing her breasts hard into her back. When the women reached back, she was gone, grinding into someone else. There were too many people to see who was touching whom. The lights dimmed and flashed red and purple.

The song ended, a new one began, and no one realized the woman they had all crowded around was gone.

Gray had done his job well. The back alley was empty, though it was usually a popular place for quick liaisons. She kept to the shadows for the first few streets, but once she arrived on Evergreen, a multistory apartment block made the roof a safer option. Scaling the fire escape, she made sure to avoid its northern corner on the second floor. The grating there had come loose and squeaked. On the next floor she had to hop over the fourth step and her motorcycle boot landed a little too loudly. She froze, crouching on her perch and listening hard. When the only sound that came to her was the rhythmic, muffled squeaking of bed springs, she continued up to the roof.

On her first trip up here, Marisol had loosened the bare bulb hanging over the exit door. Someone had been up here in the three nights since, because the bulb burned again in the darkness of the night. Vaulting over the lip of the fire escape, Marisol dropped onto the roof and hurried across to the door. She unscrewed the bulb until the light flicked out, then pressed her body to the wall and listened. Laughter cut through the distant rumble of traffic and thump of bass from a house nearby. Marisol slid her pistol from the holster under her arm. The murmur of low conversation covered her footfalls as she slipped across the smooth surface of the tar roof.

This corner was blanketed in shadow, the only light coming from the moon. When the murmuring stopped, she dropped into the shadows. A sniper was unlikely unless her enemy knew she'd been prowling. Marisol was certain no one had seen her, but she couldn't say the same for Mel and the other scouts. They were meant to be seen.

Peeking around the massive air handler, Marisol caught sight of a tall, slim form near the roof ledge, clearly outlined in the moonlight. If he was an enemy, he wasn't nearly as smart as her. Marisol took a moment to check around her, in case this man was a distraction. Nothing. The man spoke again and his voice gave him away. Not a man at all, just a teenager. Two teenagers, actually. The other boy reached up, using a long, passionate kiss to silence his boyfriend's voice.

Marisol cleared her throat and they jumped apart like they'd been electrocuted. She kept herself in shadow as she spoke. "A little late to be out, isn't it, boys?"

One of them spoke, his voice a tight squeak. "Who is that? Who's there?"

Marisol slipped a little further out of the shadows, her favorite chrome-plated Colt 45 flashing in the moonlight. The boys jumped again, the taller one slipping in front of his boyfriend protectively.

"Get your asses back downstairs and go to bed."

One of them whispered, "Marisol Soltero?"

"Downstairs. Now."

They scrambled to obey, nearly knocking each other over as they jogged to the roof door. As they passed, Marisol snapped her fingers, bringing them both to a skittering halt. She grabbed a string of condoms out of her back pocket and tossed them into the taller boy's chest. "Be safe."

The door slamming shut behind them was their only reply, but hopefully they'd be too afraid to return. She needed this roof. If she was lucky, they'd use the alley or laundry room for their next hook up.

Marisol hopped onto the roof ledge and crouched, her eyes scanning the streets below. This view made it her most useful rooftop. Apart from the neighboring building, which was an easy jump away, everything else nearby was only one or two stories. She could see every street and alleyway for a mile around from up here. Including the black Chevy Suburban with dark tinted windows and halogen headlamps that rolled slowly around the corner in front of her building.

"¡Ganadora!" Marisol whispered.

She shuffled around the ledge as the Suburban jerked to a stop in front of the building. The back half of the vehicle shimmered purple under the streetlight. Two men and a woman lounged on the steps across the street. Something about the vehicle must have caught their attention, because the men turned toward it. Cigarettes, or perhaps something else, flared between their lips as they stared, smoke curling up around their faces.

In this neighborhood, attention like that was as good as a warning, but the Suburban didn't move. One of the men stood and squared up to the street. The Suburban waited.

"Not from around here," Marisol murmured, sliding binoculars from her jacket pocket. "Unless you're itching for a fight."

The man hopped down from his stoop and stomped toward the SUV. His words didn't make it up to where Marisol crouched, but his body language was clear enough. So was the shrill laughter from the woman back on his stoop. Finally, the Suburban's driver took the hint and gunned its engine. The man stepped out into the street and grabbed his crotch, throwing up his middle finger at the departing vehicle. Marisol kept her binoculars on the SUV's license plate. A dirty, nearly opaque cover obscured most of the number, but she got enough to start a search.

Marisol waited until the man had settled back onto his stoop and accepted a congratulatory kiss from the woman behind him before climbing back down the fire escape. When she approached the group, he showed none of the swagger he'd thrown at the Suburban.

An hour later she eased back onto her couch in her Throne Room and Gray handed her a bottle.

CHAPTER ELEVEN

Three days passed before Sloane finally allowed Lily to schedule a meeting with Tyler to discuss her investigation. She spent most of that time agonizing over every aspect of Tyler's presence. What exactly Tyler was investigating and where. The contents of the file she'd carried into Sloane's office. Her ability to help craft meaningful legislation. But mostly, how to use her to protect Marisol from The Bishop.

It was clear enough that something major was happening in her state. The new player Tyler had mentioned must be making a lot of trouble for the NSA to send an agent to her office. Was it naivete in thinking he was the only trafficker at play, or intuition that made Sloane certain it was The Bishop? After all, he had made a big move here before when he had targeted both Sloane and Marisol. But he'd been thwarted. She had no doubt he would keep trying.

The distraction of not knowing was becoming a problem. Despite her practice, she had flubbed her big infrastructure speech. The evening news had focused on the blown lines rather than the contents and she would have to work hard to sell the plan to the voters. She didn't have time for endless town halls, so she needed to get her head on right.

Putting Tyler off longer would only mean a larger file and more distractions to her overburdened mind. Besides, the sooner she got to work with Tyler, the sooner she could free herself and Marisol from the threat of The Bishop. At some point in the last six months, she had started avoiding anything to do with Marisol. It had been the only way to stop the dreams—both the nightmares and the far more painful fantasies. But avoidance wouldn't work forever.

To her credit, Tyler didn't gloat over her victory. She arrived on time for her appointment and didn't waste time with pleasantries. She marched directly to Sloane's desk, flipping open the folder. As she looked at it, Sloane's nerves got the better of her. She hopped up out of her chair.

"Do you want a drink?"

"What?"

"A drink," Sloane said, crossing to the liquor cabinet in the corner. "Whiskey?"

"It's two o'clock."

The governor's liquor stash was stored in an armoire. Sloane wrenched it open and snatched the nearest decanter. She had no idea what was in it, but it didn't particularly matter.

"Am I going to like what's in that folder of yours?"

"Definitely not."

"Then I'd like a whiskey. You may judge me but do it silently."

"I'm not judging."

Sloane didn't much care if she was or not. She had to search several nooks before she found a tumbler. The warm burn of smoke and oak filled her nostrils as she poured. The rustle of Tyler's papers joined the clink of crystal as she replaced the stopper in the decanter. Rather than returning to her desk, she took her drink to the far end of a Regency settee and perched on the edge. She sipped, discovering too late that it was bourbon rather than whiskey. She took another sip anyway, trying to ignore the unwelcome sticky sweetness.

Tyler laid her file on the coffee table, spreading out several photographs. Sloane picked up the one closest to her. It was a candid shot showing a Latinx woman—a girl really—smiling through heavily painted lips with springy curls framing her cheeks. Sloane set it down next to her drink.

"Who is she?"

Tyler hadn't looked at the photo but Sloane couldn't take her eyes off it.

"Analise Romero. Twenty years old. High school dropout. Father dead. Lives with her mother in the Humboldt Park neighborhood of Chicago. Word around town is that she's been sleeping with Marisol Soltero."

Sloane spread her hands out on either side of the photo to feel the heavy polish of the table beneath her fingers. She took a few slow breaths. The woman was so young. Sloane tried not to think about the young, lithe body attached to that smiling face or her own, much less lithe one. The swell of belly beneath her navel and the weight around her hips.

Stop it. Marisol isn't sleeping with her. She's just a child.

"I believe you're familiar with Soltero," Tyler said. "From your time as a prosecutor?"

Sloane fought the urge to laugh. She and Marisol had certainly sparred when Sloane was State's Attorney. She'd hated Marisol for so many years, fighting her attraction because she thought Marisol was nothing more than the scum gang leader she pretended to be. *So many years wasted. And now I'm wasting more time.* She'd make The Bishop pay for that eventually.

"Her name came up many times. She runs a gang in Humboldt." Sloane picked up the picture. "You said this girl is from Humboldt?"

"She was. She's missing. One of several women who've disappeared recently. There's been a lot of buzz around the neighborhood. A lot of questions asked and only one person in that neighborhood asks questions."

Tyler laid out a glossy eight-by-ten candid shot of Marisol strolling down the street. Sloane purposefully did not look over at it. Tyler's implication was clear. Anything that happened in Humboldt happened because Marisol ordered it to happen.

"How did you hear about this?" Sloane asked, at last looking up from the photograph of the missing girl. Tyler was sitting on the edge of the settee, watching her closely. "You said the day you arrived that there had been disappearances. How did you know?"

"I've been investigating this for a while."

"Before you were sent out here?"

"This is *why* I was sent out here."

"I thought you were supposed to be helping me write an anti-human trafficking law."

Tyler pinched the crease in her pants leg. "That too."

Sloane laughed and sipped her drink. "Are you using advising me as cover to run your own investigation?"

"Not how I would put it." Tyler shrugged. "I'm a field agent, Sabrina. I do what my boss tells me, but you can't keep me from an active investigation for too long."

"I should be offended."

"Are you?"

Sloane took a moment to look Tyler over. Her jaw was set and there was a compelling determination in her eye. If she wasn't careful, she might grow to like this Special Agent Tyler Graham of the NSA. "No."

"Glad to hear it."

"Why don't you fill me in on the whole investigation?" Sloane set her drink on a side table, focusing on the still bulging folder in Tyler's hand. "What started all this?"

"Sofia Hart." Tyler flipped through her folder for the photograph at the very back. "She was last seen dropping off her kid at daycare three weeks ago. Also in Humboldt Park. There have been several since. Similar age, socioeconomic status, and neighborhood. All centered around Humboldt Park. You can see the pattern as well as I can."

The prosecutor came out before she could stop it. "A pattern isn't evidence."

"No," Tyler responded, poking a finger at the shot of Marisol. "But nothing in Humboldt happens by accident."

Sloane finally allowed herself to look at the photograph. Strong shoulders. A confident stride. A jaw like the statue of a Greek hero. Those arms. Arms that had held her in the moonlight. She'd let her hair grow out. Though the back was still short, her bangs covered her eyes. Those eyes. Sloane couldn't catch a shiver that passed through her whole body and she hated herself for it.

"How many?"

Tyler finally looked away, sorting through the pages. Sloane doubted she really had to check her notes. Tyler didn't strike her as the kind of agent to forget the big picture. She was the kind of woman who prepared herself for interrogations.

"Ten total in the last month. Seven in Chicago. Two male, five female. All in Humboldt."

"The men are important, but they aren't involved in this."

"With all due respect, Sabrina, human trafficking isn't restricted to..."

"The individual we're looking for will only be taking women."

Tyler's voice was low, smooth—calming by design. "You're talking about the man from Colombia? You think it's him?"

Sloane shuddered again, but this time it was because a different face came to mind. One of pure evil. The shadow of a face she last saw as she zoomed out of hell, car tires crunching in gravel. She had looked back as Marisol whipped them through the gates. She had looked over her shoulder as a man in a white linen suit stepped into their tracks and into the circle of light from an overhead lamp. She'd seen The Bishop's face and he'd seen hers.

Worse had been what came after. The day she learned all the things Marisol hadn't told her. The whole truth about the man who had kidnapped a United States Governor and flown her to a foreign country to die only because she was the bait. The target was Marisol. A man like that was a man to be feared and Sabrina Sloane feared him. She didn't like being afraid, and so she would be the one to destroy him.

"It is him."

"Marisol Soltero is a far more likely suspect."

"It isn't her." *If only the rest of the world knew what I know about Marisol.*

Tyler sighed and crossed her arms. "I know you can't be objective on this."

Sloane looked back down at the photograph of the missing girl just to avoid Tyler's eye. Her heart pounded as if she'd been running. She had been running. Ever since she'd left Colombia she'd been running and now Tyler had caught up. Discovered the truth about her and Marisol. It wasn't surprising. She was an intelligent woman. She read rooms well and people even better. Somehow she'd discovered Sloane's secret.

Still, Sabrina Sloane wasn't a fool. She said slowly, "I'm a prosecutor. I'm objective about everything."

"There's a reason prosecutors sometimes have to recuse themselves," Tyler said, sliding closer to Sloane on the narrow settee, leaning in and speaking softly. Trying to gain the confidence of a hostile witness. "You saw what he did in that village and it haunts you. You see him everywhere and I understand, but the bad guy isn't always the boogeyman. Sometimes it's just the local gang leader."

Sloane's mind whirled and it took her a moment to find her footing. Tyler wasn't talking about her relationship with Marisol. She was talking about the man in Colombia. The man the locals called The Bishop because of his dark shirts with straight collars. And because when people saw him coming, they started praying. Praying he wasn't coming for them.

"You forget that I investigated Marisol Soltero for years," Sloane said. She swallowed hard and continued, "She's like the Godfather for her neighborhood. They let her rule because they respect her as much as they fear her. She wouldn't ruin that by kidnapping her own people."

"Maybe she isn't kidnapping them. Maybe it's revenge?"

Even Tyler didn't believe her own explanation, that much was clear in her hesitant, halting words. Sloane smiled. *I've got her.*

"It would be immensely stupid for her to piss where she sleeps. Whatever else Marisol is, she isn't stupid."

"I'd argue with that," Tyler said, then sighed, falling back against the cushions. "But I'll admit it would be impossible for her to abduct them and remain anonymous. Her people are known all over Chicago and in Humboldt especially. Someone would ID them for sure."

Sloane congratulated herself on the near escape. It wasn't just keeping the heat off Marisol. She needed Tyler if she had any hope of catching The Bishop.

And catching The Bishop was the only thing that mattered.

CHAPTER TWELVE

Marisol lay across Dominique's white, L-shaped sofa, her boots dangling off one arm, her eyes fixed on the sky over Lake Michigan. The clouds were just as heavy and dark as they had been for the last three days, swollen with rain and lit by the occasional flash of lightning. The rain had made her nightly surveillance uncomfortable. The absence of the black Suburban had been frustrating. She raised a half-eaten apple to her lips and contemplated changing her route through Humboldt's streets.

Keys rattled in the hall and Marisol's eyes flicked to her phone. Dominique's security system was far from state of the art, but that had only made it easier to hack. The entryway camera was an older model and the image was pixelated and jumpy, but clear enough to show Dominique was alone. Marisol tossed the phone back to the cushion and finished her apple.

"So you are eating," Dominique said, dropping her key onto the coffee table. "And fresh fruit to boot."

She leaned over, sweeping aside Marisol's ever-lengthening bangs to press a kiss onto her forehead. Marisol cradled her hand, bringing diamond-encrusted fingers to her lips. She didn't notice the blood until it coated her lips.

"They finally killed you off," Marisol said, pushing herself upright to get a better look at her handler.

Dominique wore a shimmering, floor-length evening gown covered in black sequins. A diamond solitaire necklace hung between her modestly covered bosom, and diamonds adorned her wrists and several fingers. The way they glittered in the afternoon light proved them genuine. Her hair was piled into an elaborate updo, held in place by glittering combs. A dark line of red slashed across her elegant throat and dripped down her chest and limbs. Marisol licked her lips and tasted the artificial cherry and cloying sweetness of stage blood.

Dominique held out her arms like a supplicant. "Subtle, don't you think?"

"Will you be back next season as a vampire or are you really dead?"

"That depends on my agent's ability to negotiate."

"Then you'll definitely be back."

"He is quite the bulldog when it comes to contracts. And if they kill me off, the uproar on social media will help his cause."

"Ah." Marisol threw an arm across the back of the couch and leered. "You told Maddy you love her. Let me guess, right before they killed you off?"

"We were kissing when The Coven attacked."

"This is gonna be a great season."

Dominique turned and looked over her shoulder. "Get me out of this thing, would you? I need a bath."

Marisol popped up and jammed the apple core in her mouth. The zipper was miniscule and required both hands to maneuver. "You could've asked Maddy to help you with this, ya know."

"Madeline is twenty years younger than me and might be my costar for years to come." Dominique sighed as the dress released her. "It would be wildly unprofessional to make a pass."

"Stop pretending I don't know your type. Twenty years is your ideal age gap." Marisol followed her toward the bathroom, scooping up the dress when she let it fall. "I can't believe they let you leave the set still in costume. Don't they want this back?"

"Probably," Dominique shouted over the roar of water into her soaking tub. "I have to maintain my reputation as an eccentric woman of stage and screen."

Padding back into her bedroom wearing nothing but her shapewear, Dominique turned her back to Marisol again. While battling the necklace's delicate clasp, Marisol murmured, "They even let you leave with the jewelry? There must be half a million worth of diamonds on you right now."

"Please," Dominique scoffed. "These are mine, darling. They wanted me to wear some fake nonsense. I refused. My collection is far nicer than anything they could afford anyway."

"Pity," Marisol laughed as she started on the bracelets. "Swiping jewels from the set of my girlfriend's TV show would make for a nice reputation-maintaining headline."

"We'll come up with something better for you," Dominique said as she peeled down her top. "Besides, maintaining a fake relationship is tedious enough without such obvious criminality."

Marisol took her time tucking the rings and bracelets into Dominique's jewelry chest. She then retreated to the kitchen and poured Dominique a tall glass of detox smoothie. She didn't venture into the bathroom until she heard the faucet stop and the splash of her friend stepping into the tub.

Dominique's head was just visible over a mountain of bubbles and her eyes were closed. Marisol set the glass on the tub's tile surround and dropped into the chair in the far corner.

"What've you found?" Dominique asked.

"A black Chevy Suburban's been hanging around where it doesn't belong."

"Plates?"

"Partial. Not enough for a match, but I'll get the rest." Marisol uncrossed and recrossed her legs. "I'm certain I've seen it before."

"The one that was avoiding you?"

"No one can avoid me for long. Not in Humboldt."

Dominique opened her eyes. They fixed on her and held. "That's occurred to you as well."

Marisol cocked her head, turning the comment over in her mind. "What do you mean?"

"I mean if they truly wanted to avoid you, they'd be in Schaumburg." She leaned forward to grab a massive sponge, plunging it under the water. "Or better yet, Detroit."

She ran the sponge along her long arm and Marisol stiffened. "You think they're setting a trap?"

"I think they want you to know they're there." She pushed forward in the tub, draping her arms over the side. Marisol knelt beside her and took the proffered sponge. While Marisol washed her back, Dominique said, "I don't know what they're after, but you have a lot to lose."

"That's why I have to stop them, whatever their motive."

Dominique turned enough to still Marisol's hand. Their eyes met and the question in Dominique's gaze held an edge of pity. Part of her screamed to answer the unasked question. To confess her loneliness and her confusion and beg for an explanation of Sabrina's absence. To confess that, yes, she had so much to lose but she'd already lost it. Instead, she handed the sponge back to Dominique and retreated to her chair in the corner.

"Give me what you've got on the Suburban and I'll pass it along."

"I don't need Washington's help on this."

"I didn't offer it." She slid back against the tub and closed her eyes again. "I have reports to file."

Marisol nodded but didn't say anything more. She'd decide later whether she'd hand over what she had.

Dominique must have felt her reluctance, because after a long moment of silence she said, "He does care, you know."

Marisol fixed her eyes on the grout lines at her feet and did not move them. They had never spoken of the man that pulled both their strings. They spoke of "Washington" as though it were the city itself that commanded them and not the man who called himself Anderson. Marisol hadn't seen him since the day he'd appeared in her prison cell and convinced her to spy for him. Had she not seen ample proof of the power he wielded in the years since, she might've thought he was a figment of her imagination.

"Not just about the mission," Dominique continued. "About you, too."

Marisol was up and out of her chair before Dominique finished the last word. Anderson caring about her? What bullshit. How could Dominique possibly believe it? Friendship was one thing, but they would never agree on Anderson. Dominique thought him a saint, Marisol knew he was a sinner. What other kind of man could trap her into living this sham double life? Where the only people who knew who she really was were destined to disappoint her. Or leave her.

Marisol stomped out of the bedroom. She stopped in the sitting room to collect herself and found another white pawn, shoulder to shoulder with the first. Marisol's pulse still pounded in her ears. She couldn't remember this dynamic in any of their previous games and didn't know how to respond. She looked at her black knight, standing alone in the line of fire, and decided to move the other out to stand with it.

Her knight was still rattling from its impact with the board when she pulled the front door shut behind her.

CHAPTER THIRTEEN

"A little late for dinner, isn't it?"

Tyler strode into the Executive Dining Room, tapping a manila file folder against her thigh. Sloane looked up from her stack of papers, her eyes slow to focus on the newcomer.

"Is it? It's only eight o'clock."

"Most people are home with their families, fed, and settled onto the couch in front of the TV by now." Tyler leaned over the back of a chair several seats down from Sloane. "Or hanging out with friends. Doing yoga? Winding down?"

Sloane grunted and turned back to her papers, shoving a forkful of arugula salad into her mouth. "I practice yoga on Sundays and Thursdays. The people of Illinois are my family and these…" With a sweep of her arm, she indicated the assorted papers on the polished tabletop. "Are my friends."

"Sounds lonely," Tyler responded in a soft, almost apologetic voice.

"Sounds like the life of a politician." Sloane set down her pen and turned hard eyes on Tyler. She didn't need this woman swooping in from Washington with her judgement or her pity. Sloane was happy with the life she had chosen. "Was there something you needed, Special Agent Graham?"

"Ouch," Tyler said, grabbing the chair next to Sloane's and dragging it to the end of the table so they could sit facing each other. There was no space on that side of the table anyway, covered as it was with the day-to-day workings of government. "I really screwed up if you're using my last name."

When Sloane did not respond to her wide grin, she sighed and tried again. "I'm sorry. It's not my place to intrude in your personal life."

Sloane stopped herself from uttering the usual joke. *What personal life?* It sounded less funny these days, even in her own head. She turned to Tyler and said, "Apology accepted."

She swallowed hard and let her eyes drift to the folder Tyler brandished. She'd avoided these conversations for too long, and now seven women were missing. She needed to assume this responsibility or Marisol's picture would be in that folder for a very different reason. The thought sent a spike of fear into her belly. "What's in there?"

For a moment Tyler looked like she wanted to say more, but Sloane's scowl clearly communicated it was wise to stay away from any more personal inquiries. She flipped open the file and pulled out a stack of glossy eight-by-tens. The top one was a timestamped photo of a dark SUV on a poorly lit street. The vantage point was high and at an oblique angle, most likely from a building's security camera. Sloane squinted at the photo, pushing aside the remnants of her salad.

"Looks like an Escalade? Maybe a 4Runner. Black?"

Tyler nodded. "Suburban. With tinted windows."

Sloane slid the photo back to her. "Well, that narrows the field to a few thousand vehicles. Plates?"

"Obscured."

"Of course they are," Sloane replied. No good criminal left their license plate fully visible at night. "And no image of the driver because of the tint?"

"Correct."

"So we have a useless photograph of an untraceable vehicle."

"No," Tyler responded, her confidence undented. "We have a dozen photographs of the same vehicle. But it has a fancy paint job that changes color in different light, so that narrows the field."

She laid out all the photos, but Sloane didn't bother to study them. ATM cameras, traffic cams, and everyday security footage. Another pattern, but still no evidence. But there was more in the folder than what Tyler had laid out.

"There are more missing women, aren't there?"

Tyler nodded, looking as grim as Sloane had seen her in their brief acquaintance. "Three more since we talked last week. Well, I should say three more that we know about. You know how a big city like Chicago is—people can disappear and no one is around to miss them."

Sloane did know. Young girls who had already lost everything. With no one to look out for them when the bad guys come wandering around the alleys where they live or the restaurants where they work. Women and girls who vanish without a trace. No one tells the cops because they're either scared of them or, more likely in Chicago where the rich and poor live too close for anyone's comfort, they're relieved that the eyesore is off the street. Never mind that the eyesore is a person.

"All in Humboldt?"

Tyler squirmed and her discomfort on this matter lessened Sloane's. "Two in Humboldt. The other nearby. But one thing is for sure—Chicago has a problem."

Sloane thought of the haunted looks in so many eyes all over Peru, Nicaragua, Brazil, and Colombia. There was a problem all around the world, but she only knew of one woman who had cared about that problem before it hit American shores.

The next photo dropped in front of her with the weight of a nuclear bomb. It sounded just like a sheet of paper landing on top of others, but her heart cracking down the middle at least matched the gravity. It was another photo of a poorly maintained city street at night, but it was less grainy. Less obscured. It showed a woman, barely old enough to warrant the term. She looked dressed for a night out, but it was hard to tell for sure since the other woman's body was entwined so tightly to hers. The other woman's face wasn't visible, since it was tilted to give her lips better access to the woman she was pressing against the cracked brick façade of a row house. They were locked in a kiss. Not a polite, end of the first date sort of kiss. A hungry kiss. One that was the beginning of something the end of which Sloane did not want to know.

Marisol should really get a jacket that was less recognizable. A golden crown and Moorish arch. The logo of her nightclub and gang was airbrushed onto the back of her leather motorcycle jacket. Sloane knew that jacket well. It had been draped over her as she slept while Marisol drove them through the Colombian mountains. Sloane had peeled it off her shoulders before they'd made love. She wasn't likely to forget that jacket.

"Her name's Isabella. She went missing two days after this photo was taken." Tyler's voice cut through the ringing in Sloane's ears. "Her best friend went missing the week before. Analise. Also rumored to be intimate with Marisol Soltero."

Sloane had been analyzing how the woman's thigh was wrapped around Marisol's hip, but she forced her eyes back to the woman's face. *Missing*. Tyler had never said presumed dead. They both knew she wasn't dead. Sloane held out a glimmer of hope that she would end up in The Hotel. As far as Sloane knew, The Bishop was still unsuccessfully searching for its whereabouts.

"Seems like keeping her on the street would be in Soltero's best interests," Sloane responded, pleased to hear that her voice was steady. She handed the photo back to Tyler. "Given their relationship."

Tyler took the photo but didn't return it to the folder. Rather, she dropped it back on the table, letting it join the photos of the SUV. "I don't think Soltero hangs onto women that long as a rule, but I'm starting to agree with your assessment." She gave Sloane a conciliatory shrug and picked at the corner of the folder. "I'm not going to say she's innocent, but it seems less likely she's involved. She would be implicating herself and there's no reason to believe she has suddenly decided to eliminate her many conquests."

Sloane clenched her jaw at the "many conquests" comment, only loosening it to reply, "It would certainly be out of character."

"Precisely. Unless something catastrophic happened to her or her business in the last few months, she'd have no reason to suddenly change her habits so drastically."

Something like being kidnapped and tortured by a sadist, followed by a broken heart. As she so often did these days Sloane pushed the thought away. The fear evoked by those memories was only surpassed by her constant fear for Marisol's safety.

Tyler continued, "It looks far more likely that someone is going after her specifically. Not her territory since there's been no disruption of her business interests. Only to her personally."

Sloane went cold. *The Bishop.*

"So," Tyler said, slapping her knees as she stood. "Maybe we'll get lucky and they'll kill each other."

"I'd much prefer dozens of innocent women and girls don't get caught in the middle."

"I agree. That's why we're going to step up surveillance efforts. He'll slip up eventually."

Tyler's whirlwind visit left Sloane unsettled. *Maybe we'll get lucky and they'll kill each other.* Sloane closed her eyes and took a long, steadying breath. She wouldn't let that happen. She couldn't let that happen. Whatever there was or was not between her and Marisol, Sloane would not let The Bishop hurt her.

Sloane would get him first.

She opened her eyes and looked around the empty dining room. It felt cavernous now. Huge and silent as a tomb. She wished Tyler would come back in. Not to dump more bad news, but just to sit and keep her company. She didn't want to feel the empty chill on her bare shoulders. Sloane shivered, wrapping her arms around her middle.

When had she become so uncomfortable being alone? She'd always reveled in her solitude. Craved it even. She had never been able to make a relationship work for that very reason.

The women in her life always complained she was pushing them away. Most likely because she was. Being single had never bothered her before.

Since she'd returned from South America, just the thought of retiring to her opulent suite in the Governor's Mansion filled her with dread. She slept little, and that was all to the good considering her troubled dreams, but it wasn't the sleeping that made her stay in her office late and arrive early. She hated the loneliness of that bedroom.

Sloane grabbed the picture of Marisol kissing the missing woman and brought it close. Was it wishful thinking that made her notice that Marisol's hands weren't on the woman's body? Isabella clung to her, but Marisol seemed far less enthusiastic about the embrace. She shook her head and turned away. It was ridiculous to think she could deduce that from a still photograph taken from across the street at night. Her loneliness and her regret made her wish it.

"Finished, madam?"

Sloane jumped at the unexpected voice, flipping over the photograph guiltily. "Yes. Thank you. Please tell the chef it was excellent. Exactly what I wanted."

The waiter cleared her half-full plate and silverware, leaving a mug of milky Earl Gray tea in its place. Once she was alone again, Sloane turned over the photograph and looked at it one more time. She traced the curve of Marisol's jaw with one finger, then ripped the picture down the center. She'd intended to separate the two bodies, but the paper tore crookedly, straight through Marisol. She tore it again and again, letting the pieces fall to the table.

Sloane stood, her chair screeching as it scraped along the hardwood, and took her tea to her bedroom. She left behind a pile of scraps, the intact logo from Marisol's leather jacket sitting on top.

CHAPTER FOURTEEN

The sun was setting, casting distracting shadows through the slats of the blinds in Sloane's office and shining directly into her left eye. She growled about the inconvenience for the third time in ten minutes but continued scrolling down the document on her computer screen rather than getting up to close the blinds. If she could focus for another half hour, she could get out of here on time for the first time all week.

A soft tap on her office door announced the arrival of yet another distraction, and this time Sloane clucked her tongue and slapped her palm on her desk. She did not stand to open the door or even call out for her visitor to come in. She didn't want them to come in. She wanted them to leave. Especially if it was Tyler.

Sloane had managed an entire week without a single visit from the agent and her manila folders. Not a single photograph of a missing girl, and, even better, no more pictures of Marisol kissing someone else. For an entire week, Sloane was able to just be Governor of Illinois, with the extraordinarily long work hours and the massive responsibility. She could forget for five whole days that she didn't also have the title of Crusader Against Human Trafficking to live up to. It was a lovely feeling. She wanted it to last.

When the door creaked open, Sloane sighed and finally peeled her eyes away from her monitor. She registered delight at first. It wasn't Tyler. The delight was quickly replaced by dread. Her office door closed with an authoritative snap, but instead of approaching Sloane's desk, Lily went to the line of windows along the far wall. A sharp clap of wood slapping wood accompanied each deft flick of her wrist and the blinding light of the setting sun finally stopped tormenting Sloane.

"How long have you been squinting at that screen?"

Sloane dropped her eyes to her desk. "A while."

"And how long would you have continued squinting if I hadn't arrived?" Lily asked, shifting a thick binder from under her arm.

"A while."

"Indeed," Lily grumbled as she approached the desk. "Per your request, I've compiled your prosecutorial records."

Sloane accepted the proffered binder. It was heavier than she'd expected. "Thank you."

"As I was unaware of what you were looking for." Lily sniffed and cut her eyes back at Sloane. "They might not be complete."

If there was one thing she could count on Lily to do, it was dig for more withheld information. She'd learned long ago not to fall for the trick. "I'll let you know."

"No doubt you will."

Rather than leaving, Lily stood with her hands clasped in front of her. Sloane's shoulders slumped and she braced for the lecture. Her secretary wasn't one to be deflected from a mission.

"Do you intend to have dinner this evening?"

Sloane scribbled a quick note on the crammed legal pad beside her keyboard. "Don't nag, Lily. I've just had lunch."

"It's seven o'clock and I never nag."

"It is not…" Sloane focused her stinging eyes on the large wall clock over the door. It was, in fact, quarter after seven. Had she really been here working without recognizing the passage of time for over six hours? "Perhaps a break would be a good idea."

"I'm certain that was either a joke or a turn of phrase peculiar to your little lakeside city," Lily said, sitting down on the very edge of a chair and crossing her ankles. "But your scheduled break was several hours ago. You have only missed the end of your office hours by ninety minutes, but your workday should nonetheless be ended. Shall I type your notes?"

Sloane was going to snap back with a sarcastic remark, but the curl of Lily's eyebrow made her bite her tongue. She gave a brief shake of her head and started closing documents on her computer.

"Ever since you returned from that hastily planned trip to South America"—Lily looked away for a moment, then a hint of mischief enlivened her voice—"I've noticed a lot more late nights."

Sloane grunted in response. This had been their game for months now. Lily was furious to have been left out of the planning and shrewd enough to know there was more to the South America story. When Sloane had returned to Illinois, several pounds lighter and with obvious bags under her eyes, Lily had said nothing. She was far more sly than that. Still, prescription sleeping pills had made their way into Sloane's private apartment and Lily made sure she rarely missed a meal.

"And now you're spending those late nights with your new bodyguard," Lily said, drawing out the last syllable in an invitation.

This was a new element to the fruitless interrogations. There was a sparkle in Lily's eye that belied her genteel propriety. She was, of course, aware of Sloane's sexuality and her lack of a steady romantic partner. Even the casual visits of which Lily had given her winking approval had ceased since her return. Apparently, she thought Tyler was the reason.

"Special Agent Graham is not a bodyguard," Sloane said, injecting as much professionalism as she could without discussing her love life. Lily was not only her secretary, but she was Sloane's mother's age. "But she's not…that either. She is a liaison from the National Security Agency."

"You should certainly make that arrangement clearer to Hawkins and Clarke. They scowl at her dreadfully when you're not looking. They think she's trying to take their jobs. Too bad about the other, though. She's quite good-looking."

"She's not my type."

"Do you have a type? You don't seem to see anyone recently."

"Yes, I have a type." Images draped in sultry moonlight flashed through her mind and she couldn't stop her blush. Squirming in her chair, she continued, "I've been busy."

Lily stood and circled her chair. "Well, be careful you don't die busy and alone. Perhaps you could flirt with Hawkins and Clarke if you don't have something going with Special Agent Graham. You know, just to settle the hurt feelings."

Sloane's jaw nearly hit the desk. "I am not going to flirt with my security detail!"

"All I'm saying is it would help."

"That is sexist and demeaning and…What a ridiculous idea! Surely they know I'm gay?"

Lily scoffed and headed for the door. "Like that's ever stopped a man from believing a woman's interested in him. Have it your way. I doubt you even remember how to flirt anyway. Goodnight, Madam Governor. Eat some dinner before bed."

She was out the door and gone, leaving Sloane to blink in confusion after her.

"That is the most unprofessional thing you've ever said," she shouted at the closed door. She leapt from her chair and ran as quickly as her stiletto heels would allow, ripping the door open and yelling at Lily's empty desk, "I remember how to flirt and I'm damn good at it, thank you very much!"

The desk, of course, did not defend itself. Clarke, stationed as usual in the hall outside the outer office opened the door and looked around in confusion. "Ma'am? Everything okay?"

"Yes, fine. Thank you, Officer Clarke."

He nodded and asked, "Anything you need, ma'am?"

For a heartbeat she considered proving Lily wrong with a strategically lifted eyebrow or a well-placed compliment, but she shook herself and said, "No, thank you."

Clearly, she was overtired. She had never, even in her confused youth, flirted with a man and she wasn't about to start because her meddling secretary teased her about her dry streak. After all, it wasn't nearly as long as Lily thought it had been. Before more images of her night with Marisol could flood in, she turned to retreat into her office.

"Ma'am," Clarke said. "Ms. Holmes said you'd be heading to dinner?"

"Mrs. Holmes," she corrected automatically. It did seem a waste to go back into her office now that she was out here, which obviously had been Lily's intention. "Damn that meddling woman."

"Ma'am?"

"Nothing, Clarke. Yes. I'll go to dinner now."

Sloane ended up taking her dinner to her apartment with her. Or rather a server and Officer Clarke carried her food on a silver tray into her sitting room while she huffed about how she was perfectly capable of carrying a plate of eggplant parmesan across a building on her own. For the most powerful woman in the state of Illinois, very few of her support staff listened to her or did as she asked. She didn't even decide her own menu—Lily and the chef conspired on that. She forgave them their meddling with every bite of the perfectly fried eggplant and slightly burnt cheese.

She slipped into bed thinking, as she did every night, that the bed was too big, the mattress too stiff, and the sheets too cold. She fell asleep quickly, which was a blessing since she did not sleep for long. Nightmares of bloody knives, a sparking cattle prod, and looming, evil eyes. Eyes that did not widen in surprise when Sloane leveled a gun at them. There was no gun. There was no rescue. There were only those evil eyes. Just like always, it took Sloane ages to realize the screams which had woken her were her own.

When she made her way down to her office early the next morning, showered and dressed in a crisp black suit, Tyler was waiting outside her office door, holding a manila folder.

CHAPTER FIFTEEN

The fist came out of nowhere, only appearing in Marisol's peripheral vision at the last moment. She had just enough time to tilt her head and duck the quarter inch necessary to avoid the blow. The wind of its passing washed across her face as she spun, whipping out her arm to lash her assailant with the side of her clenched fist. His arm shot up and her attack bounced off his beefy forearm. Still, it was a sharp enough sting to make him hiss through clenched teeth.

"Nice one, boss."

Gray retreated two steps, bouncing on the balls of his feet over the springy canvas. When he stalked forward again, Marisol dropped her arms, shook them out, and brought them back up into guard position.

"Not a bad attempt, Gray," she said as she sent a lazy jab close to his chin. "You're getting quicker."

He feinted right, hopped left, and threw out a quick jab Marisol easily dodged. "Maybe you're just getting slower."

She dropped to the mat and rolled beneath his next parry, jumping up behind him and landing a light hook to his side.

"Maybe not," she said. Then she added a wink to twist the knife.

He growled and unleashed a flurry of blows. She let each of them come within a breath of landing before she dodged. With each miss, Gray's annoyance etched deeper into his face. His footwork got sloppier so she bounded away, dropping one hand as she skipped backward around the ring. Gray stalked after her.

The move had been poorly calculated. As she moved, she watched the frustration wash out of him. The technique used to work on him, but he knew her too well. Gray had always been a fast learner. It was also why she kept secrets from him.

It wasn't that she thought he'd object to what she was doing for the NSA. Technically speaking, she wasn't an agent, just a resource. That's how Dominique and Washington referred to her. A resource to be used, and not always for the right reasons. Gray respected women and children to the point of mania, so he wouldn't object to the nature of her work. He would object to the level of danger and the pay—which was nothing. He was as pragmatic as she was passionate, so it was best to keep her secrets for as long as she could. She had no illusions she could keep them forever.

"You never were a very good dancer, boss," he said as he descended.

Without realizing it, Marisol had pranced directly into a corner. She'd been distracted by her thoughts and he'd taken advantage. She dodged his punch, but his body blocked her escape.

"There is a brain in that thick skull of yours after all," she teased.

Flexing and drawing back a knockout blow he said, "The brain's just another muscle, and I love to work out."

Dropping to her knees, Marisol launched herself into the air just ahead of his right hook. It slammed hard into her thigh, but she was already jackknifing in midair. As she fell behind him, she wrapped an elbow around his tree trunk of a neck, pulling him backward as she fell. He stumbled, trying to catch himself, but her momentum was too much to overcome. She landed hard and he came crashing down with her. Grabbing the arm wrapped around his neck with her other hand, she pulled him into a chokehold. He slapped her bicep hard, grunting as she released the grip.

Marisol jumped to her feet and strutted, fighting to ignore the myriad of new bruises that little maneuver cost her. Every eye in the gym had been trained on their match, and the roar of applause had her bowing. Her smirk hid her pain.

"That's cheating," Gray said, still on the mat and gripping his lower back.

"That's creativity," she replied, crouching in front of him and tapping a finger to his forehead. "And the brain's not a muscle. It's an organ comprised of mostly gray matter, though, so you've at least got a leg up on the rest of us."

He groaned and pushed up onto his feet, transferring his grip to the base of his neck. "You read too much."

"The better to exercise my brain muscles."

He swiped a massive paw at her, but she was already scampering across the ring. Sliding between the ropes, she noticed that most of the gym's patrons were still watching her. That was good. Sparring matches like these, when she whipped poor Gray who was twice her size, helped her image. There were more than a few intelligent, scheming faces in the crowd, and they would think twice before coming after her now. She had enough enemies. She didn't need her own people turning on her to get a piece of what she had.

Once she reached the women's locker room, the looks changed dramatically. There were still a few hungry stares, but most weren't after a piece of her territory. Most were just after a piece of her. Women who'd been turning backs and swapping bras under their shirts a moment before suddenly abandoned discretion at the sight of Marisol. She let her gaze linger over exposed breasts, careful not to let her disinterest touch her eyes.

Now that she'd held the woman of her dreams in her arms again, she compared every woman she saw to Brin. Their too-thin bodies and sharp curves proved easy to ignore. Luckily, none of them followed her into the shower. Rejecting them took so much energy these days and she'd spent the night before in dirty alleys rather than her bed.

Her shower was quick and her exit from the gym quicker. She made sure to walk past the construction site near Justino's bodega. The latter was in much the same state she'd last left it, but the construction was certainly making progress. The skeleton of a building was growing out of the vacant block. Walls were up, and some were even getting the first layers of facing. Men in harnesses crawled across crossbeams, laying the foundations for floors above. Stacks of brick, metal, and wood dotted the scene, neatly tucked behind chain-link fence.

As Marisol surveyed the scene, the door of a construction trailer burst open, the metal door whacking against the wall beside it. A man who looked only slightly less dirty than the rest came scuttling toward her, the tail of his denim button-up shirt flapping behind him.

"Ms. Soltero," he said when he arrived in front of her, the fence between them. He snatched off his hard hat and twirled it between his hands. "Good to see you here."

Marisol took in his weathered face. A strip of pale skin marked the spot where his hard hat normally sat, the skin beneath tanned at least two shades darker. He had a two-day growth of beard and his fingernails were chipped, but his eyes were soft and sincere.

"Is there a problem, ma'am?" he asked, his throat quivering and his eyes scuttling away from hers.

"Put your hard hat back on," she growled.

He practically threw it onto his head, shoving his now empty hands deep into his pockets. "Of course. Just didn't want to…"

"Has everyone on site been following safety protocols?"

"Yes, ma'am. We're being very careful. There won't be any trouble."

She squinted at him, letting her eyes remind him that he shouldn't have removed the hard hat. He touched the molded plastic with shaking fingers.

"There won't be any injuries," he assured her. "Nothing will delay the project."

Marisol watched two men climb a ladder to a platform on the skeletal second floor. They unhooked their harnesses from the ladder and immediately hooked into the second-floor safety rope. Both of their hard hats were secure and looked new. The men who hoisted a stack of lumber up to them wore gloves.

Marisol nodded and turned away. "See that it doesn't."

When she passed the construction site again near midnight, the workers were long gone, but Justino's bodega teemed with life. She kept to the shadows across the street and kept moving, away from the laughter and muffled music. Two blocks away, she glimpsed a familiar pair of taillights. She sprinted down the alley and caught sight of the black Suburban, its ChromaFlair paint job more obvious at this distance.

The stop signs at each cross street worked in her favor and Marisol was able to keep pace with it for several blocks. A well-lit taqueria drew the driver's attention and made Marisol's stomach roar with hunger. She was able to get the rest of the plate number while an indistinct shape in a hoodie hopped out of the passenger side and disappeared inside long enough to collect a fistful of foil-wrapped packages.

Two blocks later the Suburban picked up speed and she lost it as it rumbled south out of Humboldt Park. She retraced her steps and grabbed a pair of fish tacos. The cashier couldn't give her any more description of the Suburban's passenger than she'd gotten herself, but the cod was perfectly seasoned and the slaw had the right bite of citrus to keep her awake for her trip back to Alhambra. Too many consecutive nights stalking the streets had taken a toll, so Marisol didn't even check in with Gray before heading up to her apartment on the top floor.

CHAPTER SIXTEEN

"What am I looking at?" Sloane asked, sliding her rarely used reading glasses onto her nose to keep from squinting at the photograph.

"It's an industrial district on the West Side. Just south of Humboldt Park."

"What's the street?"

Tyler consulted her notes. "Kilbourn Avenue."

"K-Town."

"The neighborhood is called North Lawndale."

"Trust me," Sloane chuckled. "I was a prosecutor in Chicago for a long time. I'm very familiar with K-Town."

"Why's it called K-Town?"

"Because it's eleven miles from the border with Indiana." Sloane adjusted the photograph as she spoke, lining the satellite image of streets with the woodgrain in the table beneath it. "Easiest way to assign street names is alphabetically. So the eleventh mile uses the eleventh letter of the alphabet, and the street names begin with K."

Tyler pulled a folded map toward her and scanned the layout. "Huh. Clever."

Sloane slid the glasses off and rested her chin on her palm, looking across the desk at Tyler. The agent was wearing another in an endless line of well-fitting men's suits, this time in navy. She sat back, crossing one ankle over her knee, a hint of maroon sock showing above her shining oxford shoes. Her body language was relaxed even if her face was set.

"The area is about three blocks and consists mostly of warehouses and trucking companies. Some auto shops. The target is definitely one of those warehouses."

"How do you know?"

"Following the car. Chevy Suburban. Black paint job that turns purple in the right light. Windows tinted way past the legal limit. Illinois plates turned out to be stolen."

"How'd you get the plate number?" Sloane asked, not really wanting to hear the answer. She had a feeling it wasn't going to be a good one.

"Headquarters."

"How'd they get it?"

"There are some questions it's better not to ask. But maybe we aren't the only ones working on this." Tyler gave the ghost of a wink. "Once we knew the plate to look for, it was easy to check security camera footage in the area."

Sloane's face went numb as her world spun. She focused every ounce of energy on not letting her emotions show. Her worst nightmare was coming true and she had to act like everything was fine in front of Tyler. If they weren't the only ones spying, there was only one other person who could be involved. Marisol was after The Bishop. She had to be the one who reported the plate number to Washington. She was playing right into his hands and she had no idea.

"And how exactly did you gain access to so many private security systems without alerting The Bishop he's being watched?"

Tyler scowled and responded, "I still think it could be Soltero."

"We've been over this and you know it doesn't make sense for her to be involved. She wouldn't break trust with her own people." Tyler opened her mouth to argue, but Sloane held up a hand and said, "You didn't answer my question. How'd you get access?"

"Most security systems are wireless these days. Internet-based."

"And?"

"And the NSA does more than just investigate human trafficking."

Sloane planted her elbows on her desk and glared. "You mean domestic spying."

"I mean a way to end Soltero…or The Bishop," she added when Sloane bristled. "Aren't you willing to utilize every resource to do that?"

Sloane thought of the trap being laid for Marisol and what would happen if she couldn't avoid it in time. "Yes. I am."

"It'll all be admissible in court." When Sloane looked skeptical, she grinned. "I promise."

Unwilling to argue the point, Sloane looked back at the photograph. It was clearer now that it lay on her desk, farther away from her eyes. She stood, hovering over the image.

"Half these places look abandoned," she mused.

Tyler appeared at her side, standing close and looking over her shoulder. The warmth of her struck Sloane like a physical blow. She had a presence that was undeniable and she smelled good. Really good. Like sandalwood and the hint of leather polish.

"Half of them are. It's gonna make scouting the place a bitch, but we'll figure out something."

Sloane turned her head to look at Tyler. Seeing her there made her body feel even closer. How long had it been since she was this close to another person? Parts of her that had been cold for months started to thaw.

"You want us to scout the location in person?"

"No," Tyler said, backing away and circling the desk. Sloane immediately missed the warmth of her presence, but Tyler's next words swept a chill back through the room. "*I* want to scout the location in person. There's no way to know which of the buildings are being used unless I can get in there myself."

"We're a team on this, Special Agent Graham."

"No, we aren't, *Governor Sloane*." Tyler's face was as hard as Sloane had ever seen it. There was no negotiation in her tone when she continued, "I am a liaison to your government, but that's it. I keep you abreast of *my* investigation, but this is an NSA matter. Civilians are not a part of that investigation."

"I'm hardly a civilian. I'm the…"

"I'm well aware of your title, but you're not federal law enforcement." Sloane crossed her arms and Tyler sighed, slumping against the back of the chair in front of her. "Perhaps I've not made the nature of our relationship clear. Allow me to do so now. I am here to advise you on human trafficking policy. My investigation is separate from that and I have kept you updated as a courtesy. Perhaps that was a mistake I should remedy now. We aren't partners."

The determination in Tyler's glare made the whole thing so much more fun for Sloane. The involuntary grin that spread across her face made Tyler scowl even harder.

"And I suppose you have a plan for getting in to look around?"

"I need to scout the area first. Then I can formulate a plan."

Sloane sat down behind her desk, crossing her legs and leaning back into the deep leather chair. This was going to be even easier than she thought. "And how do you plan on that?"

"What do you mean? I go down there and take a look."

"Tyler," Sloane said, aware of how condescending she sounded. "It's rather fortunate you have me to advise you on the area and the people. Otherwise you'd be lost."

Tyler stood taller and crossed her arms. "I'm listening."

"This industrial park." She swallowed hard and adopted her prosecutor's tone. "I'm not familiar with the complex but I'm extremely familiar with K-Town. The chances of you getting into that area to look around without being spotted, even at night, are zero."

"Why's that?"

"You're a white, well-dressed outsider. And honestly, you look like a cop. It'll get you killed. If not by one of Marisol's people, then by a Lawndale gang. There are quite a few of them."

"And you think you can go down there without being noticed?"

"Of course not." When Tyler just stared, she continued, "I'm *supposed* to be spotted. Especially when I go on official state business. My security detail will also be spotted, but they'll be expected to check out the area for anything threatening."

Tyler dropped her arms, the hint of a smile reaching into her eyes. "Including the warehouses, both occupied and abandoned."

"Precisely."

Sloane reveled in her victory for a few long moments, but then Tyler's face fell.

"It won't work."

"Why not? It's a great plan."

"You have no reason to be there. If you just show up out of the blue, it'll look suspicious. We need to lay a groundwork. Bring in the local government. Set the expectation that a visit would be a reasonable next step. We don't have that kind of time. Women are going missing every day."

Even while Tyler spoke, Sloane rummaged among the papers stacked neatly on her desk. She found the folder she wanted in the third drawer, waiting for a revision to her reply. That revision would be much more extensive now.

"That industrial park is part of the Roosevelt-Cicero Industrial District." She flipped open the folder and spun it toward Tyler. "It's been designated a growth zone by the city under a Tax Increment Financing program."

"What does that mean?" Tyler asked, squinting at the memo the mayor of Chicago had sent her weeks ago.

"It's a program that helps redevelop abandoned properties and reinvigorate struggling businesses." She reached over and flipped a page since it was clear Tyler had no idea what she was looking at. "New infrastructure, roadway improvements, utility upgrades."

"Sounds like a great idea. Will it work?"

"Progress has been slow," Sloane admitted. "The region was designated for investment in 1998, but you can see there are still areas that need a lot of work."

"Sounds like old news," Tyler said, looking up from the file. "How can this get us in?"

"The program is set to expire next year. The mayor wants state aid to extend it since his City Council isn't sold on the idea."

"But you're a popular Governor who could help him gain public support."

Sloane leaned back and steepled her fingers in front of her. "Exactly. A tour of the area would be a logical first step."

Tyler's grin was half-impressed, half-predatory. "Not bad, Governor. I suppose I need you after all."

"Yes, Agent, you certainly do."

CHAPTER SEVENTEEN

When Marisol spotted Lips, she knew it would be the night she caught up with the Suburban. Lips was a hustler. A low-level nobody from West Humboldt Park who'd tried to get in with Marisol for years but didn't really have the clout or brains to offer anything Marisol wanted. Until tonight.

Lips had a bike. Not just any bike. A sleek, flashy red crotch-rocket that looked nothing like Marisol's Ducati. A bike she could use to tail the Suburban and keep her nose clean.

Marisol slid down from the Throne Room and pushed aside Lips's small fan club. She bought them a bottle to share. She smiled and winked and it was all completely unnecessary. All Marisol had to do in the end was give Lips a free night in one of the exclusive boxes across the bar from her own and open up the tab. She didn't even have to hotwire the bike. Lips handed her the keys and grabbed three men by the wrist, dragging them toward her borrowed celebrity.

Gray was waiting for her behind the dumpster at the mouth of the alley. She slipped into the shadows and he kept his eyes on the street.

"Mel and Alejandro have joined the others. No sightings of the Suburban yet, but they're watching a couple of women who are likely to be grabbed."

"Make sure they intervene before anyone else is taken. Text me an address if they spot him." Before she slipped into the night, she added, "No one takes my people again, Gray. No one."

If he responded, she didn't hear it.

Fifteen minutes later, her helmet's mirrored black visor rendered her anonymous as she idled the bike on the corner of West Ohio and North Kilbourn. The chain-link fence surrounding a trucking-company parking lot concealed her, but the sound of breaking bottles and the occasional shout filtered through her helmet just above the purring engine. The mingled smells of exhaust from Lips's bike and piss from the parking lot made her edgy. She'd been waiting here too long.

Just when she'd decided to try her luck on another corner, Marisol spotted the Suburban roll through the stop sign and turn onto Kilbourn. The sweep of bright halogen headlights skimmed the cracked concrete inches from her front tire but didn't reach her. She let the Suburban drive for a half block before she pulled out, heading in the opposite direction.

Marisol drove slowly, counting to fifteen in a low rumble before spotting an alley and whipping the bike around. She roared south, chewing up pavement as she caught back up to the Suburban. If they suspected she was following, nothing in their driving indicated their concern as she settled into traffic behind them. She kept a respectful distance as they drove, allowing a car between them when one was available.

Her eyes were feeling the strain of focusing on a black car on a black night when the Suburban finally slowed and then turned onto a side street. There were no streetlights here. Whether it was the Humboldt Park section or the Lawndale section of K-Town, the city didn't waste electricity illuminating garbage.

Marisol continued until a parking lot yawned to her left in the darkness. She killed the engine and the lights, waiting for her eyes to adjust to the darkness.

Losing the Suburban was inevitable, but it didn't matter. Marisol was all too familiar with this part of town. She peered into the close alleys and poorly lit streets. Buildings were dark and ominous, uninhabited at night, but the couple that still did semi-legitimate business were lit up like a Las Vegas casino. Even without the lights, the whole complex was being watched. She could feel eyes in the night. Marisol could never enter without being seen.

She didn't need to. This place was a dump. Half the buildings were abandoned, the rest were inhabited by rats of both the rodent and human variety. Within a few days, Marisol could own one of them. Tomorrow night she could skip the pursuit and come straight here.

Turning back into the shadows, she made her way onto the roof of a shuttered convenience store. She spent an hour watching, but no one emerged. When the sun rose over the distant lake, she climbed down using a drainpipe and a strategically placed dumpster. It wouldn't do for her to be seen skulking around on a roof.

She dropped off Lips's bike outside her building and walked the rest of the way in the center of the sidewalk. She adopted the self-important strut that typified her existence and casually wiped at her shirt and pants, checking for any evidence of her nighttime activities. When she turned down an abandoned alley, she snuck out a palm-sized bottle of cheap tequila from her jacket pocket and splashed it on her neck and stomach. Mixed with her dried sweat and the swagger, anyone would guess her night had been spent in a very different way.

She turned a corner in time to see Justino huffing and puffing as he pulled up the metal shutters that covered his bodega overnight. Marisol moved silently, but he smelled her coming, his rabbit-like nose wrinkling until he turned to see her at his side.

"Señora Marisol," he said, his big cheeks wobbling as he nodded. "Looking for some café?"

"I'd kill for it," she said, her lips curling up to show her bright white teeth.

Alarm settled onto his features for a moment and Marisol forced herself not to laugh. It wouldn't do for her image if she took pleasure from hurting a good man. Still, if anyone would spread the story of her night of conquests, it was Justino. The only thing this man loved more than Puerto Rican coffee was a good story.

"Fortunately for me, I already made a pot," he said, a nervous chuckle tacked onto the end of the words.

She slapped his back and followed him into the bodega. Once inside, she scanned the street one last time. Finding it empty, she relaxed and leaned against the counter, allowing Justino to pepper her with a mix of questions over whose bed she'd occupied the night before and tall tales about his youth in San Juan.

Despite two cups of coffee, her eyes were all but shut as she arrived at her apartment door. She hadn't needed sight to get home once she hit Club Alhambra's back door. A private staircase led from the main floor and connected to her Throne Room, her office, and finally to her apartment. Only three people had keys to the stairwell and only two to her apartment door, but she checked her security cameras before entering. Marisol didn't like surprises.

The cameras showed an empty apartment, but she still slipped her pistol from the shoulder holster as she let herself in. She did a full sweep of her living quarters before allowing herself to sleep. She stripped naked and dropped on top of the covers, falling asleep the moment her head hit the pillow. For perhaps the first time in six months, she did not dream.

Marisol was wide awake the moment her eyelids opened. She lay perfectly still, her face pressed into the soft warmth of her pillow, the chill of conditioned air pimpling the skin on her bare back. She hadn't woken from a nightmare, but she had woken to the knowledge that there was someone else in her house.

Keeping her eyes slitted, she let her body relax so she could take in her surroundings. There was a light from the living room, but it wasn't daylight. Her aching limbs told her she'd slept well and long, and the light had the warm, orange glow of an incandescent bulb. There was a rustle and then the rich, dull scent of a very familiar perfume.

"Good evening, Marisol," Dominique cooed from the couch. "Please don't shoot me."

Marisol groaned as she turned over, feeling the ache of forty-one years of hard life in her bones. "They'd hear a gunshot down in Alhambra. I'd have stabbed you."

"You've got a gun and a knife under that pillow?"

"The knives are between the mattress and box spring."

"That sounds safer."

Marisol spent a moment or two wondering how many weapons were hidden in Dominique's bed. A gun was inevitable. Even after all these years, she wasn't sure if Dominique would be willing to slit someone's throat with her own hands.

The cumulative effects of so many long nights slowed her movements as she crawled from bed, but her muscles loosened during a quick shower. When she emerged into the living room, Dominique flipped her hardback novel shut on a linen bookmark. She was curled against the far end of the couch, her feet tucked beneath her, and a thick folder rested on the couch cushion beside her.

"What's that?" Marisol asked as she crossed to the kitchen.

"A gift from Washington."

Marisol grabbed a bottle of coconut water and an energy drink from the fridge. "I've never been a fan of their gifts." She smiled as she handed Dominique the coconut water. "Except for you."

Dominique laughed and Marisol took a full breath for the first time in three days. "Likewise, darling." She leaned forward and ran a thumb under Marisol's eye. "But this one might help with these bags. Washington used the license plate you sent to track the Suburban. They have security camera footage of it going to some warehouses in Lawndale."

Marisol pressed her lips into Dominique's palm and placed it gently over the folder. "They're a bit late. Found the place myself last night."

Dominique's pout held a hint of contrition that was mirrored in her voice as she said, "I'm sorry. I should've brought this to you yesterday so you could've slept last night."

"I slept today." Marisol half-emptied her energy drink in one gulp. "Did you have a date with Maddy last night?"

Dominique reached over and snatched the energy drink from Marisol's hand, replacing it with the coconut water. "Don't drink that trash. You need to fuel your body, not poison it. And for the last time, I will not date a costar." After a long moment in which Marisol grudgingly drank the water, Dominique asked, "What's your plan?"

Marisol nodded to the corner, where a backpack slumped against the wall. It had been packed for days, staring at her accusingly every morning she returned without a destination. Tonight, she could finally put it to use. "Surveillance."

"You won't make any drastic moves, will you?"

"When have I ever done that?"

"Let's see," Dominique answered, ticking off the responses on her delicate fingers. "Ensenada. Champaign. That little trip back to Detroit. Akron Eddie."

"Enough." Marisol took a deep breath and said, "This is just surveillance. I don't even know what building they're in yet. I'm going to hunker down and watch for a couple days. That's all."

"A couple days? What've you got in that bag?"

"A bottle of tequila and a titty magazine. What else would I need on a stake out?"

"Marisol…"

"I'm literally just watching a bunch of abandoned buildings and trying not to fall through rotten floors."

"That doesn't mean you don't have to be careful."

Marisol lifted Dominique's hand to her lips, brushing them against two knuckles before she hopped off the couch and headed for the door. "I always am."

CHAPTER EIGHTEEN

Sloane perched on the sofa, folders surrounding her on the stiff cushions. She'd never found the Residential Suite of the Governor's Mansion particularly comfortable, but tonight it was even more forbidding. The dark wood paneling spoke of excess and the Regency furniture was far from inviting. In the low light of evening, the walls closed in on her.

At least her pajamas were comfortable. The soft cotton was crisply ironed and the shirt's pearl buttons glowed in the lamplight. She tucked her bare feet beneath her thighs and reached for the binder Lily had compiled the previous week. Sloane hadn't touched it since. She knew time was running out. The article would appear soon. It was, in fact, a miracle it hadn't already dropped. But Nia's accusations of bias rankled and Sloane had not found herself in the frame of mind to tackle her past objectively. The folders on the other side were from Tyler. Sloane was even less prepared to open them in her current state of mind.

Flipping open the binder, Sloane took a deep breath and let her eyes settle. Lily had included a table of contents, neatly organized and indexed. Sloane shook her head and an indulgent smile touched her lips.

The binder was two inches thick and, as was indicated by Lily's table of contents, each page was a summary of one case. The rare case took up two or three pages, but only if Sloane was involved in the appeal. Many of the defendants' names stood out to her. She could remember the arguments she'd used to send many of them to prison. Even picture a few of their faces.

The first name on the list brought a very different face to her mind. She didn't think about the trial, but rather the weekend before the preliminary hearing. The weekend that started in a cheesy wine bar and continued in a hotel room with a gorgeous stranger.

Sloane let her head fall back and her eyes close. She and Marisol hadn't exchanged names in the bar. There had only been lingering looks as they inched closer together on their bar stools. Sloane had been the one to issue the invitation. It wasn't outside her normal practice to take a casual sexual partner, but it was unusual for her to spend an entire weekend with them. Marisol had whispered her name into Sloane's ear while they tangled sheets on Saturday. Or maybe it had been Sunday. All she could remember was the thrill that coursed through her, carried along by those enticing syllables.

On Monday morning they'd had to both hurry home to prepare for work. Sloane's shock at seeing Marisol at the courthouse so shortly after leaving her in bed had been pleasant. The shock she'd felt when informed of Marisol's infamous criminal network had been decidedly less so. The betrayal, not only from Marisol, but also her own traitorous body, had taken a decade to overcome.

Truthfully, she hadn't overcome it until Marisol had appeared outside her condo nearly seven months ago. She'd been moments from death—literally staring down the barrel of a gun—when Marisol had swooped in and scooped her up. She'd thought it was her mind and body betraying her again, replaying the most pleasurable moments of her life before she died. Then more assailants appeared and pitched her headfirst into hell.

Sloane shook herself before the memories of Colombia started. She didn't want to go back there again. She couldn't. Not when she was so close to catching The Bishop and ending the nightmare. If she was patient, she could have everything she ever wanted. If she wasn't, the woman she loved would die.

Turning back to the binder in her lap, she scanned the trial summary. The particulars of the case came back slowly. Apart from Marisol's presence, the pretrial hearing went well. McLean, a Chicago gang leader, had little with which to defend himself against a mountain of evidence. At the time she'd wondered how so much had fallen neatly into place. Blinking, she fit pieces together.

She'd thought Marisol had been in court that day because she'd been McLean's friend. They'd been competitors, but their territories hadn't crossed. That often led to a camaraderie in criminal circles. But now Sloane knew Marisol was not that type of criminal. She'd be hard pressed to believe Marisol was a criminal at all.

"All that helpful evidence," Sloane murmured to the empty room. "Do I have you to thank, Marisol?"

She'd have to ask sometime. Fanning through the pages, words flipped past too fast for Sloane to read. How many of these cases hinged on evidence anonymously supplied by the woman she loved? How many criminals were behind bars because of their joint efforts? Sloane had wasted so much time trying to lock Marisol away, now all she wanted was to know the truth. All the truth. Every little secret Marisol hid from the world. All the little bits that made her a hero, though no one would ever know.

"You just have to keep her alive until then," Sloane said. "And maybe stop talking to yourself."

A knock at the door interrupted Sloane's whirling soliloquy. She called out an invitation for her guest to enter while checking to ensure her pajamas were tightly closed. It was an automatic gesture, but an unnecessary one. She'd not had the privacy to be indecent since she moved into the Mansion.

Tyler snapped the door closed behind her and marched across to echoing hardwood floors. Halfway through her journey she looked up, a crease forming between her eyebrows.

"You okay, Sabrina?"

"Of course." Sloane touched her hair and face, wondering if she'd mussed her makeup while changing. "Why?"

Tyler dropped onto the sofa beside her, moving a pair of folders aside so she could scoot closer. "I don't know. You look… sad?"

Sloane gave a wry laugh and flipped the binder in her lap shut. "There's very little to be happy about these days."

It was a calculated dismissal, intended to sweep aside Tyler's concerns with the vagueness of her day-to-day obligations. She should have known it wouldn't work. Tyler was the sort of woman who trusted her gut, and if her gut told her Sloane was unhappy, she would work to find out why.

Tyler slid her hand onto Sloane's knee, propped so close to her own, and gave it a brief squeeze. Sloane could feel the warmth and weight of the touch through her thin pajama pants and found unexpected tears prickle the back of her eyes. How long had it been since a friend had offered her such a gentle reassurance? How long had it been since anyone had touched her? It was quite possible Marisol was the last person. Very few people dared reach out to such an important government official.

"I know you have a lot going on right now." Tyler's eyes caught her and held. "It's a tough situation and it's scary. If you need to talk about it…"

"I don't."

"I'd like you to think of me as a friend, Sabrina."

Sloane bit back another refusal. It was so easy to get lost in this office. To let Governor Sloane take over all the parts of her that used to be Sabrina. *Or Brin*. What she wouldn't give to hear Marisol call her that again. The nickname no one else had ever used. The person she could be if everything went right and

The Bishop ended up behind bars. Even when that happened, a friend would be nice to have. She didn't have many anymore.

"Thank you." Sloane smiled and patted her hand. "I do think of you as a friend, Tyler. And I appreciate that you care."

"I do," Tyler said, her voice low and kind. A smile split her face and she continued in a lighter tone, "And I have something that will make you happy."

"No more folders?"

Tyler's chuckle rumbled through her body and into Sloane through their joined hands. "No folders. Things were quiet last night. Hopefully the trend continues."

"That is good news."

"And the happy news is that the mayor seems to actually work for a living. Your plan to scope out the warehouse worked. He agreed to a press conference, so we can get down there legitimately and check it all out. It's set for Thursday."

"That was quick. Can we be ready in two days?"

"One day." Tyler removed her hand and leaned back against the arm of the sofa. "I'm heading to the site tomorrow."

"How close can we get to the area?"

"We'll be right in the heart of it. The Roosevelt-Cicero Industrial Zone is pretty big, but I had Lily convince the mayor's office that Kilbourn is a key spot for us. They agreed the abandoned buildings would make a good backdrop for the cameras."

"Of course." Sloane rolled her eyes. "The optics are the point for him."

"I don't much care about his motives. They work in our favor."

Since she understood politics, Sloane did care about his motives. And how much this favor would cost her. No doubt she'd find out when he was ready to announce his reelection campaign.

"Don't think I haven't noticed you charming my secretary. Be careful or she'll take you under her wing."

"Is that a bad thing?"

"She may look like a doting grandmother, but she's sly. No one has more power in Springfield than Lily Holmes."

Tyler laughed and leaned back into the sofa. "Not even you?

Sloane hugged her knees to her chest. "I don't have power, Tyler. I have an office."

A moment of quiet passed, long enough for Sloane to look up at Tyler. She looked inquisitive again. And kind. "There you are looking sad again."

"I'm…just tired."

"You might consider staying in Chicago for the weekend." When Sloane didn't respond, Tyler continued, "You need a break, Sabrina."

If only she knew.

"I'll think about it."

CHAPTER NINETEEN

From the top-floor offices of an abandoned machinist shop three buildings away Marisol watched the news cameras descend. It had taken her two nights of surveillance to determine which building The Bishop was using. She'd spent the previous two days sleeping on this garbage-strewn, dirty floor with the rats. Today she'd woken up to the sound of her plans shattering around her ears.

It had been a good plan. A simple plan. When the Suburban had pulled into the warehouse's bay doors in the early hours of the morning, Marisol had checked her supplies. They were the bare necessities. Her Colt, three spare clips, and a boot knife. She'd never needed more than that. Most jobs required far less. When she was sure she had everything within arm's reach, she'd curled her knees to her chest and closed her eyes. She'd planned to rise with the moon and bury The Bishop with the dawn.

Then Brin had arrived with her puppy.

Her town car arrived around noon, an hour after the news crews and two hours after her security detail. Marisol recognized the two state cops. She'd spent a good amount of time confirming their loyalty when they were assigned to Brin's protection. Her research had told her they were innocent idiots. The woman with them was the new addition.

She had the unmistakable look of one who bought her suits on a government salary. Dominique could confirm that Brin had replaced Marisol with a woman who fit better with the Girl Scout image. A woman who could do everything Marisol did, but in the light of day, openly and legitimately. She was too afraid of the answer to ask the obvious question.

Marisol watched her move from building to building, surveying the area. Little did the agent know Brin's biggest threat was only a few feet away, skulking in his dirty hole the same way Marisol skulked in hers. When the woman approached the warehouse in question, Marisol's whole body tensed. The Bishop wouldn't be stupid enough to attack Brin's security detail in broad daylight, but it seemed as if he hadn't snagged a new victim in a week. Maybe he was desperate. It occurred to Marisol for the first time that this may have been his plan all along. Lure Brin back within his grasp.

If it was a trap, Marisol had to stay. She had to break in. She had to end him once and for all. Brin would never be safe until she did.

Risking the noise and the ping on the closest cell tower, Marisol put a call through to Dominique. It rang once before picking up and Dominique didn't bother with a greeting.

"What do you think brings our governor here?"

"I thought you'd be able to tell me that."

The probing statement had the effect she'd expected. Dominique hesitated for a few seconds and then said, "Sabrina's on the same track we are."

"Not just her," Marisol said, watching the woman in the cheap suit.

"There may be another party involved," Dominique hedged.

"How involved?" Marisol asked through gritted teeth as Brin stepped out of a limo and the woman leaned in close to her ear, a hand going to the small of her back.

"Marisol…"

"Get her and her cop out of here."

"I can't."

"Our friend in Washington can."

"Our friend has neither the ability nor the interest to intervene."

Marisol swore. She stopped just short of throwing the phone into the wall. Her eyes inevitably travelled back to Brin. She wore a pale blue sleeveless dress and sensible, if stylish, heels. The day was warm and she carried her black blazer over her arm. The dress would've fit well last time Marisol had seen her, but Brin had lost a few pounds since Colombia. She tortured herself by wondering if Brin was staying up late at night, riddled with the same nightmares as Marisol.

"Stay out of their way, Marisol." Dom's voice was quiet and kind, flooding Marisol with regret for her anger. "Do what you need to do without getting in their way and I'm sure they'll do the same."

Marisol hung up without another word. Brin and this woman were a *they*. Of course. Brin was a crusader. The woman with the scar was obviously one, too. They were a matched pair, but they were no match for The Bishop. Unless she acted quickly, she'd be saving Brin again. Not that a quick strike was an option now. This circus meant she'd have to wait.

Marisol had always hated waiting.

Brin slid on her blazer and stepped in front of the cameras while the woman in the suit melted back into the crowd, leaving the two men to flank the governor. Marisol watched the cop scanning the buildings, her eyes constantly returning to His warehouse. She was smarter than Marisol thought if she'd found him already.

Marisol scanned the surrounding buildings herself. She shouldn't sleep here when she came back. If anyone saw her leave they would expect her to come back and this spot didn't have the vantage point she needed for an effective strike. It only took her a moment to find the best option. Fortunately, it seemed the auto shop on the other end of the alley didn't have an occupant. She'd make sure it stayed that way.

Melting back into the shadows, Marisol left her hiding place without making a sound. All eyes were on Brin, delivering her speech.

Soon, Marisol was back in the familiar streets of Humboldt. She relaxed after a few well-trodden blocks, but it didn't last. Images of Brin flooded back. The woman with the scar putting her hand on Brin's back and leaning in close. So close her face nearly brushed against Brin's neck.

"Morning, boss."

Mel had gotten a new tattoo. A clockwork crescent moon beneath her right ear, a chain of stars travelling down her neck. She fell into step beside Marisol, the tattoo shining with ointment in the sun.

"It's three o'clock."

Mel yawned, her eyes flicking lazily across their surroundings. "So early."

Marisol chuckled and shoved her hands into her back pockets. "Late night?"

She knew the answer, but she wanted to see what Mel would say. She didn't even look embarrassed. "I was trying to get picked up."

"Which I've told you not to do."

"How are we gonna catch these assholes if we can't get someone inside?"

Marisol stopped in her tracks, the laughter in Mel's voice made her fist her hands until her knuckles cracked. "You think this is a fucking joke?"

Mel smiled until she saw Marisol's face, then she stopped walking and looked scared. "It could work. I could help. And I can take care of myself with any thug in this town."

"Thug?" Marisol stepped into Mel's space, her snarling lips inches from her lieutenant's. "These aren't thugs, Mel. They are pure evil on a level you've never seen before."

A pained looked crossed her face. "Isabella and Analise are my friends."

"Isabella and Analise are gone," Marisol said, guilt wiping any kindness from her voice. "They aren't some princesses waiting in a castle for you to save them like a fucking video game. These guys are human traffickers. Do you know what that means?"

Mel didn't answer, but she was regaining her nerve, which was at least a good sign.

"It means that, if Isabella and Analise are still alive, they're going to wish they weren't. The people who bought them are worse even worse scum than the men who took them."

"I know that," Mel said, her eyes filling with angry tears. "And I want to make them pay for it."

"That's my job. The women they took are my people and it's my responsibility to avenge them."

"They're my people, too."

Marisol laughed and put an arm around Mel's shoulders. She looked so young and Marisol felt the weight of her responsibility to this neighborhood like an anchor around her neck. It would take her down, but she would gladly do so for these people.

Her people.

"No, Mel, they're mine. And so are you. Get your ass home and stay there tonight." Just to make sure the request stuck, she hardened her features and said, "That's an order."

Mel sighed like a moody teenager, but she nodded and peeled off in the direction of the apartment she shared with her girlfriend. She'd stay in tonight, but if Marisol waited much longer, her anger and fear would break down her loyalty. Brin or no Brin, Marisol needed to hit the warehouse soon.

CHAPTER TWENTY

When Sloane found her, Tyler was peering into the cracked windows of a warehouse around the corner from the microphones and cameras. She'd left the mayor to field the reporters' questions and he was clearly annoyed at being abandoned. Considering he was perfectly useless to everyone in the city who hadn't grown up with a trust fund, Sloane didn't feel the least bit bad about forcing him to do some heavy lifting.

"Anything interesting?" Sloane asked as she came to a stop next to Tyler.

She answered, jerking her chin toward the warehouse in front of them. "This is the one."

Sloane's eyebrows shot up. She squinted at the windows, trying to see through the cloudy muck. "How do you know?"

"New tire tracks in the dirt around the rear entrance," she replied, moving along the wall and casually glancing toward the roof. "Padlock on the front door is old, but it's not corroded. Scratches around the doorknob from a key."

"Not conclusive," Sloane replied, keeping pace.

"Enough," Tyler said confidently. "I've got a camera on the rear entrance and another covering this alley. We'll know in a day or two if I'm right."

Sloane shook her head, noting Tyler's smirk. She was convinced, but she'd pretend to keep an open mind until she was proven right. It was Tyler's style and Sloane had to admit her instincts had so far been flawless.

Sloane played nice with the press for another hour, then with the mayor for another three. He wasn't one to work late and announced his satisfaction earlier than she would have liked. Sloane declined his dinner invitation and asked her driver to take her home. It felt strange to refer to her penthouse condo as home when she hadn't seen it in seven months, but she supposed it was, strictly speaking.

Tyler joined Hawkins and Clarke in escorting her to her front door. The moment she stepped into the elevator, her stomach knotted. She waited for a malevolent face to appear as the doors slid shut, but the ride was uneventful. The doors opened onto a hallway that would always remind her of the carnage that had taken place there. Three officers had died defending her here, their blood seeping into this blue carpet. From the moment the elevator door opened until she unlocked her front door, Sloane held her breath.

"Will you be okay?" Tyler asked, concerned. "I can check the place again."

"It's fine," Sloane answered, her voice shaky. "You've checked it twice today. Besides, the hallway's the scary place."

"Clarke is ready to take your dinner order whenever you're ready and we'll all be downstairs if you need us. You know the number."

"I do." Sloane made eye contact with all three of them, hoping they took the hint to be quick as they left. She didn't want anyone else to die in this hallway. "Thank you all."

"Ma'am," Hawkins and Clarke said in unison.

She breathed more easily when her front door closed and her security team was heading downstairs. To her surprise, the rooms she hadn't occupied in months still felt like hers. She kicked off her shoes and dropped onto the couch, letting the cushions envelop her. Hopefully she'd get to spend a few nights here before heading back to Springfield. She had the feeling that she might sleep better in Chicago than she had been in the Governor's Mansion.

Before her thoughts strayed to Humboldt and Marisol, she jumped up and headed into her bathroom. An oval tub, deep and welcoming, sat on a platform in front of the wall of windows, the lake shimmering in the setting sun beyond them. Sloane briefly considered taking a long soak in the tub, but the glass shower with its waterfall showerhead offered a quicker and equally soothing option.

CHAPTER TWENTY-ONE

As Marisol climbed the stairs to her office a notification she hadn't seen in a long time flashed onto her phone. She stood frozen in place, her heavy boot halfway to the next step, staring at the screen until it went dark. She slowly slid the phone into her back pocket and kept climbing.

Once she was settled into her office chair, she entered a series of passwords on her computer to access a live feed of a very familiar hallway. Brin entered the shot a moment later, her security team following behind. The men were wary, constantly checking over their shoulders. The woman with the scar kept her eyes on Brin's rigid shoulders.

Marisol switched to a different camera with the tap of a few keys. She could see the scarred woman's face now. Her eyes roamed over Brin and Marisol's teeth ground against each other. There was a confidence in this woman's stride that Marisol recognized. She walked that way, too. Brin had mentioned it during their first, flirtatious conversation a decade ago. Brin had said that's what had drawn her eye to Marisol. She liked the power and grace in her movements. Marisol had spent the rest of the weekend demonstrating her power and grace in a hotel room.

Brin stopped in her doorway and turned to speak to the woman. She didn't invite her inside, but that was cold comfort. They stood close to each other as they spoke. The camera feeds had no sound, but their body language spoke of lowered voices. Secrets they were keeping from the State Police officers hovering in the background. How would their body language change if those men weren't there? Marisol closed her eyes and forced the thought away.

When she opened her eyes again, she set the jealousy aside and turned a more critical eye to Brin's companion. She studied the woman's frame for anything remarkable. There wasn't much. The cheap suit and nondescript haircut were almost too obvious. Even from here Marisol could detect the strings attached to her back. The strings that tied them both to a man in Washington DC.

"Only she's standing at Brin's door," Marisol grumbled. "And I'm not."

That was something new for Anderson. As far as Marisol knew, he'd never operated in the open before. His affiliation was legitimate, but his agents didn't have badges. Marisol bashed a key and the camera feed blinked out. She closed her eyes again, allowed exactly one heart-wrenching, face-twisting moment of pain, then shook herself.

Opening another, even more heavily encrypted file, she scoured its contents. She'd been reviewing subfolders and notes for ten minutes when Gray entered without knocking. He stood in front of her desk until she acknowledged him. She made him wait ninety seconds as punishment for the intrusion. Just long enough to make him shift his weight from one foot to the other.

"Perfect timing," she said, gesturing for him to sit. "We need a favor. I'm looking for a debt to call due. Thoughts?"

The chair creaked under his bulk. "What kind of favor?"

"We need to buy a building." Gray's forehead wrinkled and Marisol continued, "Quietly."

Marisol watched him form the request for more information and then dismiss it. The whole battle flashed through his eyes. He'd never been good at hiding his emotions.

He finally asked, "Is the building actually for sale or do we need to do some convincing?"

"It's for sale and the seller is eager. Word is a cash offer will mean keys in hand within a week."

"When people find out, will it ruin the buyer's reputation?"

"Unlikely." Marisol churned over possible outcomes. "At worst, it'll look like a shady investment. Most people will see it as a cynical cash grab given the state government's development plan announced today. If the owner is smart, they'll spin it as community investment."

Gray tapped a fingernail on his chair's armrest. "The mayor's press conference."

Marisol nodded but let him continue to put the pieces together. He was smart. Hopefully not too smart. It was good, at least, that he saw it as the mayor's doing, not Brin's.

"You just spent two days there with no issues. Why buy?"

"Spent too much time looking over my shoulder." She thought for a moment, examining the decision from many angles. "In fact, let's buy the block. Make it less suspicious. The other buildings will take time, but this one needs to happen now. We need it to be in someone else's name. If it's traced back to me, he'll know I've made him."

Gray nodded as she spoke, then replied, "Someone whose reputation is wobbly, but untarnished. That rules out the Boy Scouts and do-gooders."

"Exactly what I was thinking." Marisol pointed at her screen. "Alderman Coats?"

"Too wobbly, I think. Everyone knows he takes bribes. Pretty sure the *Tribune* is working on a piece."

"What about the real estate investor? He seems like a logical choice."

"He's one of the people dropping off envelopes at Coats's office."

Marisol scrolled farther down the page and noted a familiar date on a file. She clicked it open to see pictures of a twenty-something idiot passed out with his face in a line of coke. "Judge Marshall?"

Gray crossed his ankle over his knee and rubbed his chin. There was more stubble than usual on his weathered cheek. "Not a bad thought. He's had to cash in a lot of investments recently."

"His son still getting into trouble?" When Gray nodded, she continued, "Then he'd probably be willing to buy a chop shop and a few crumbling warehouses to keep those pictures of Junior we took in the club off the Internet."

Gray made some comment about logistics of the deal, but a new series of notifications flashed on Marisol's screen. The last one made her fingertips tingle. She didn't hear Gray's final comment. He left her office, shutting the door behind him, giving Marisol a chance to let out the lungful of air she'd been holding.

She'd installed motion detectors in every room of Brin's condo but had stopped short of installing a camera in the bathroom. Now she congratulated herself on the decision. The urge to watch Brin bathe would have been unbearable, no matter how inappropriate.

Pacing to the window, Marisol's phone vibrated in her hand. This time the notification was for a picture text from Dominique. It showed a nearly bare chessboard, Dominique's painted fingernail resting against the white queen. In the background stood the black king—Marisol's king—backed into a corner.

The word "Checkmate" popped up beneath the photograph. It was a demand and an invitation, as Dominique's messages always were. Marisol grabbed her leather jacket from the back of her chair and replied.

Time to start a new game.

CHAPTER TWENTY-TWO

Steam filled the bathroom and the water pounded onto her shoulders as Sloane felt the worries of the last few months melt away. This comfort was exactly why she'd avoided Chicago for so long. She didn't want to feel this until she could stay. Now that her determination had put The Bishop in her sights, she could let herself be in Chicago. It was almost over.

She changed into pajamas and, after a moment's hesitation, sent a text to a number she hadn't contacted in too long. To her surprise, it was well received and so she ordered dinner for two. Allison arrived just before the food and they lounged together on the couch, Allison just as comfortable as Sloane in joggers and a long sleeve T-shirt.

They had plenty to catch up on and they made their way through their pasta primaveras and a bottle of rosé. Night fell and the almost full moon shimmered across the mirror-smooth surface of the lake. They opened a second bottle and took it with them onto the balcony that faced the city skyline. Allison stretched her legs out on the cushioned lounger and wiggled her toes. A stiff wind, bordering on brisk at their height thirty floors up, whipped loose strands of her bangs around her forehead.

"So who is she?"

Allison's knowing smile set off warning bells in Sloane's brain. The wine had dulled them just enough to make her voice falter as she asked, "What do you mean?"

"Come on, Sloane," Allison teased, turning on her lounger and draping an arm over the side. "You know I'm fine being just friends and having no benefits, but a year ago you'd have had me on my back by now. Some woman's gotten a hold of you. Is it that sexy new bodyguard you've got? The scar is enough to soak my panties."

"Tyler and I are not…" Sloane felt herself blush, wondering how she'd managed to be so transparent. "There isn't anyone. I've just…been busy."

"Okay," Allison purred. "Keep your secret."

"There's no secret, honestly." Then, because she'd been feeling guilty about it all night, she said, "I didn't mean to give you the wrong idea about this invitation. I've enjoyed our arrangement, but I'm just not in the mood."

Allison laughed and for a moment Sloane remembered how fun it had been when they dated and then how much more fun it had been when they had broken up and just been an occasional, casual hookup for each other. There'd been no drama. No emotion. Nothing but good sex with no strings.

"It's fine, babe. In fact, I was gonna have to turn you down. I've gone and fallen in love. Can you believe it?"

"Not a word of it," Sloane responded, drinking deeply from her wineglass. "Did she put a spell on you or something?"

"Something like that." Allison's phone rattled against the glass-topped table while a ring-tone of a canned laugh track broke the peaceful night air. "Speak of the devil. Mind if I…"

Allison snatched up the phone and sprinted for the balcony door. The door clicked back into place, shutting out the contented murmur of Allison's voice, leaving Sloane alone on the shadowy balcony. She let out a long breath and laid back, staring at the stars.

"Are you gonna fuck her?"

Sloane flew out of her chair, her wineglass shattering on the stone at her feet.

"Marisol?" She stared into the shadows, seeking out the voice. Nothing moved, but she could feel her presence. "Marisol? Is that you?"

"What's the matter, Brin?" The darkest corner of the balcony shifted and formed into the vision she dreamt of every night. "Don't even remember what I sound like anymore?"

Sloane shot a look across at the door, watching Allison pace across the living room, her phone stuck to her ear. She hurried across the balcony, her voice coming out as a hiss. "You can't be here. You have to go."

"Sure," Marisol said, pushing off the wall and emerging into the faint glow from the living room. "I'll go. I'll go and never come back. That's what you want, isn't it? That's what you did."

"Marisol, please." A burst of laughter muffled by distance had Sloane whipping around again. As she looked toward her friend inside, she noticed lights come on in a condo across the street. Movement on another balcony caught her eye. Suddenly the night was full of prying eyes, closing in on Sloane. Closing in on Marisol. "It isn't safe for you to be here."

"Not safe? You think your bodyguard could hurt me? I'd give her a matching scar if she tried. Or is it that *you* don't feel safe around *me*?"

Marisol stepped out of the shadow, but Sloane grabbed her wrist and dragged her to the far corner of the balcony. She couldn't see Allison anymore or the light from the living room. Her eyes adjusted slowly, but her body didn't follow suit. Every muscle was tense and her shoulders ached with the strain.

"If anyone sees you…"

Marisol leaned in, her hands locked on the railings either side of Sloane's hips, pinning her in place. "Worried your constituents will find out you're rutting around in the gutter?"

"That's not…"

"Then why?" Marisol growled. Her teeth shone, wet and sharp in the moonlight. "Why don't you want me anymore?"

Marisol's words dripped hatred, but Sloane could hear the pain in them as well. Her breath caught in her throat, settling in next to her fear to make her head spin.

"I do."

Marisol stared at her silently, a hard stare turning her perfect face to stone.

"I do want you," repeated Sloane. Her eyes fixed on Marisol's lips and the rigid set of her jaw, but her body trembled. It took all of her might not to reach up and trace Marisol's bottom lip with her fingertip. "But I can't."

Marisol's eyes fluttered shut then snapped open. She leaned in closer, bringing the mingled scents of leather and skin. Her lips brushed against Sloane's cheek on the way to settle next to her earlobe.

"Brin…"

Her whisper was heavy with longing and Sloane's body reacted in kind. Her hands slid up and over Marisol's shoulders, settling onto her neck and the burrowing into her hair. She felt Marisol drag in a sharp breath before pulling her tight. Their bodies met, pressing the chill from Sloane's skin for the first time in months.

"Marisol…"

She was barely able to utter the word. Sloane had avoided saying her name aloud over the last months. She hadn't trusted herself to put the syllables on her tongue. It had been hard enough to hear Tyler speak them.

Sloane hadn't registered how Marisol's cheek was sliding against hers until she tasted Marisol's breath. Their lips brushed, released, and then settled against each other. Marisol was always tender on the first press of a kiss, and this was no exception. When Sloane parted her lips, Marisol's composure broke. She surged forward with hips and chest and tongue. Sloane groaned into her mouth, losing herself in the friction of Marisol's body against hers. Marisol's mouth against hers. Marisol's tongue against hers.

Sloane lost herself in the kiss. She let the world fall away. The wind whipped her hair but she was only conscious of

Marisol's heart pounding against her chest. She floated in the feeling, until the rasp of a calloused palm against her bare side broke the spell.

"Marisol!" She broke the kiss with a gasp, forcing her body back with difficulty.

Marisol let her go, releasing her lips and hands as though she'd known all along that this kiss would lead nowhere. That this meeting would lead nowhere. Sloane's head whipped around, trying to see the balcony door first, then others within view. The one that had been lit moments ago was shrouded in darkness again. When she peered into the gloom, Sloane thought she could see someone stalking along the railing down there, but it was too far away to be sure.

She was more sure of the suctioned pop and smooth glide of the balcony door as it opened. Blood roared in her ears and she fought for breath to speak.

"You have to go," Sloane hissed, pushing past Marisol to peer around the corner. "It's not safe."

There was no response from the railing, so she spun on her heel. Wind whistled through the gaps, but there was no one there. She jerked around, but there was not so much as a rustle of fabric to show where Marisol had disappeared. She'd left so silently, she may never have been there. Sloane screwed her eyes shut, willing herself not to look over the railing. Marisol was angry, not foolish enough to leap off a thirty-story balcony.

"Sloane?" Allison's voice was light and inquisitive as she stepped out onto the balcony. "What happened? Is everything okay?"

"I…" Sloane's eyes couldn't focus. Her mind couldn't settle. Had Allison seen Marisol? Had someone else? Who were those neighbors with such unobstructed views of her condo? Had the State Police or Tyler investigated them?

"What happened to your glass?"

"My glass?" Sloane turned again to see Allison indicate the pile of shattered glass and spilled wine. "Oh. I…um…dropped it."

"Are you okay?"

"Yes. I'm…Let's go inside. It's cold."

"Are you sure you're okay?" Allison's hand on her shoulder stopped Sloane's sprint to the living room. She swept a lock of hair off Sloane's forehead and said, "You look like you've seen a ghost."

Sloane's fingers slid up to touch her lips. A ghost. Had Marisol really been there or had she been a ghost? A dream? A fantasy to fill the yawning emptiness that had settled into Sloane's life since she pushed Marisol out of it. If it weren't for the tingle of blood returning to her lips or the lingering reaction the kiss had left in her body, Sloane might believe she'd dreamed the whole thing.

"I'm fine. Let's go inside."

They spent the rest of the night laughing about how Allison had somehow fallen for a twice-divorced comedian with a pocket dog and the most intoxicating smile she'd ever seen. They had met after a show at The Laugh Factory and, in true lesbian fashion, had moved in together a month later. Fighting through the pangs of jealousy, Sloane managed to be happy for her friend. But if Allison of all people could settle down and be monogamous, Sloane's life had well and truly changed.

CHAPTER TWENTY-THREE

Marisol's boots hit pavement before she really became aware of her body. She had stumbled more than once on her trip down from Brin's balcony to the street. All she could remember were Brin's lips.

Her lips and her insistence that Marisol leave.

She still couldn't decide if it was fear or disgust she'd seen in Brin's angelic face. Neither explained her absence over the last months. Both explained the way she'd kissed Marisol like it was the last time they'd ever meet.

She'd gone to talk. She kept telling herself that and believed it less every time she repeated it. She'd seen the notification that Brin was home and she just…couldn't stay away. Just like she had the night she'd saved Brin's life seven months ago, she'd snuck in through the building's maintenance corridors and avoided detection thanks to her access to the security cameras. The security detail remained oblivious outside Brin's building. She'd climbed up the drainpipe from the vacant condo one floor below to Brin's balcony, but Brin's guest had arrived before Marisol could go inside.

Marisol knew the woman's name. She also knew the nature of her relationship with Brin. So she'd stayed and listened and watched. Her broken heart had brought her to the balcony and it wouldn't let her leave until they'd spoken. If only she'd skulked away before they'd shared that kiss.

At the last moment, Marisol stopped her forward momentum and that saved her from slamming into Brin's scarred bodyguard. She hadn't realized how close she'd been to the mouth of the alley. Fortunately, the bodyguard was jogging with headphones in, so she didn't hear the slap of Marisol's boots as they ground into the concrete. She jogged past, heading toward the lake and checking traffic both ways before crossing the street.

Once she was out of sight behind a neighboring skyscraper, Marisol emerged onto the street. There was a thin crowd dotting the sidewalk, and she followed a small group to the next corner and through the crosswalk. She left them behind and ducked into the alley where she'd parked her bike. As the engine roared into life, she gave one last look up toward Brin's balcony. She couldn't see it through the dark and distance, but she knew it was there. She knew Brin was there. It wasn't much to hold onto, but it was more than she'd had for half a year.

The drive back to Humboldt was a blur. She didn't realize until she arrived at her borders that she'd been so distracted. Her normal caution—complete with backtracking and checking for tails—had been given over to memories of Brin in her arms. Of the ferocity of her kisses. Climbing off the saddle across the street from Alhambra, the consequences of Marisol's distraction collided with the side of her head.

Marisol's motorcycle helmet absorbed most of the blow. It also absorbed the impact of her head hitting the broken blacktop. Her head rattled in the padded confines of the helmet for a heartbeat before they were on her. The number of fists raining down on her body had to belong to more than one person, but she couldn't tell how many. She curled into a ball, tucking her arms and legs around the soft parts of her body.

Underneath the tinted visor, Marisol's teeth showed in a wide grin. This was easier than talking to Brin. Easier than stalking the night looking for The Bishop. This was something she understood. She'd been jumped so many times as a kid on the street that it felt more normal than the relative safety of shelters. It hadn't taken long for her to expect the beatings. Expectation led to acceptance. Once she accepted it as a part of life, she figured out how to use it to her advantage.

Marisol waited out the beating until her attackers started with the jeers and insults. That was the sign they thought they had her, but no one ever had The Queen of Humboldt. The cadence of blows slowed, with the inevitable pauses that came with gloating, and Marisol struck. Her right foot shot out and landed squarely on target. One of her attackers crumpled, groaning and clutching his groin, but Marisol had already whipped around. This time her heel cracked into another's ankle and the cry of pain was sharp and short. Shooting to her feet, she shut the man up entirely with an uppercut to his jaw.

This was the most dangerous moment. On her feet, with new bruises forming and no curled limbs to protect her, Marisol was vulnerable to a serious attack. But this was also the moment when she shone. She was most dangerous when she was backed into a corner and had to fight her way out.

With the helmet muffling her senses Marisol didn't hear the movement behind her, but her attacker was stupid enough to grab her rather than lash out. Beefy biceps pinned her arms to her side, but she threw her head back and rattled her brain again as the helmet struck home on her attacker's face. It took three blows, but he eventually released her and a solid hook to his jaw finished the job. When he hit the deck, he didn't get back up.

Whipping the helmet off, Marisol clutched it hard in her fist as she spun. The helmet spared her a bruise to her knuckles and took the next attacker out with a single blow. The last man standing yanked a folding knife out of his pocket and slowly stalked toward her.

"I'll do you a favor," Marisol said, bending over to set the helmet on the ground. "I'll let you live if you drop the knife and run like hell right now."

"Fuck you, bitch," he spat back, still holding his battered balls. "I'm gonna slice you to pieces."

"Sure you are."

Marisol straightened, her boot knife gripped loosely in her right hand. She considered throwing it into his left eye and calling it a night, but she had some pent-up energy to expend. A knife fight would be the perfect way to push through it.

"Come one then," she said, bouncing on the balls of her feet and flipping the knife around so the spine lay against her forearm. The steel was cold against her overheated skin. "Let's go."

The fight wasn't nearly enough to satisfy her. He lunged and she hopped back, curious to see how he'd respond. He bared his teeth and lunged again, this time even sloppier than the first. She gave him an experimental cut across the arm. It was deep enough to scar, but not enough to make him bleed out. He tried for a back cut as he charged past her, roaring in pain, but a casual flick of her blade blocked the strike. Before he could turn to face her, she plunged her knife deep into his shoulder blade, careful not to go so deep she lost her grip or got stuck in bone. She had a backup in her other boot, but this was her favorite knife and she didn't want to lose it.

"I'm going to kill you for that," he growled, pawing at the puncture on his back.

"I doubt it, but you can try."

She knocked the blade out of his hand on his next attack and slashed his left forearm to match his right. The man with the broken ankle was crawling toward them, so Marisol decided to end the game. Grabbing her opponent by his mop of curly hair, she stuck her knee in his back and the tip of her blade against his throat. Broken Ankle stopped moving and stared, his hands held open, palms out, at his side.

"Good boy," Marisol said. He clearly chafed at the suppliant stance, but not as much as the man with Marisol's knife to his throat. "Now tell me who sent you or I'll splatter your face with his blood."

Broken Ankle didn't even look at his friend. He kept his eyes squarely on Marisol and his lips shut.

"Oh, so you want him dead. How interesting."

The man squirmed in Marisol's grip, so she dug the point of her knife into his neck until a stream of blood trickled onto her hand.

"It's him, isn't it?"

Broken Ankle didn't speak, but his growing smile answered the question.

"I'd tell you to send him a message," she said, sliding the knife across her captive's throat. "But I think this will send one clear enough."

She released the curly hair and the man dropped with barely a twitch. His blood had sprayed across Broken Ankle's face, but it hadn't altered his smile. His smile still didn't falter when she threw her blade, burying it deep in his chest. When he fell, she let herself slump back to her knees.

As running footsteps shattered the calm, the pain of every punch and kick she'd taken slowly settled into her bones. Initially she worried it was one of her assailants getting away, but she recognized Gray's weighty footfall. She didn't have the strength to stand and greet him. It was just as well he hadn't brought anyone else with him. It wouldn't do for anyone in her gang to see how heavily she leaned on him as they walked together up to her apartment.

CHAPTER TWENTY-FOUR

Sloane awoke screaming. She lay still and tried to control her breathing. Long, deep breaths brought her heart rate down to normal. She clutched the sheets and stared at the ceiling while she reminded herself that dreams couldn't hurt her. That dreams couldn't hurt Marisol.

At some point Sloane must have dozed off again. She turned onto her side and the glow of weak sunlight lit her curtains. She showered and dressed for her day, taking coffee to the dining table strewn with papers. She should have secured all of it before Allison arrived, but she couldn't muster the energy then. Instead of cleaning them up now, Sloane flipped through a few pages of notes on her upcoming meeting with the mayor.

As she tossed aside an updated utilities map, she spotted a familiar binder. She hadn't looked at her prosecutorial record since Lily had delivered it, but now seemed an appropriate time. Perhaps it would take her mind off Marisol's visit—both to her balcony and to her dream. After a few pages, she retrieved a legal pad from her desk to take notes.

Three hours later, when Tyler knocked on her front door, she'd filled two legal pads and only churned through half the binder. The results were not what she had expected.

"Whatever it is, can it wait an hour?" Tyler's eyebrow shot up and she softened her tone to explain, "I'm in the middle of something."

Once Tyler had left, she flipped through her notes. She didn't like what she was seeing. Nia had implied her record showed bias, but she hadn't truly believed it. She'd been certain of both her objective commitment to upholding the laws of Illinois and her fairness in sentencing recommendations. It was hard to miss, however, that the people of color she'd prosecuted received much heftier sentences than the white defendants. The disparity with Black defendants was particularly egregious.

How had this happened? She hadn't meant to pursue them more aggressively, but when she looked at plea deals she'd negotiated it made her sick to her stomach. Things had only worsened when she'd been elected State's Attorney. It was a nightmare scenario. Hundreds of potential lawsuits. Convictions could be thrown out, regardless of the defendants' guilt. But worse, Sloane would never really know how many lives she'd ruined with harsh penalties.

Sloane slapped the binder closed and pushed it aside, dropping the legal pads on top. Whatever mistakes she'd made in the past, she couldn't let them distract her from her work now. She needed to focus on the good she could do here and now or else the pain she'd seen in Marisol's eyes last night would be the last look she ever got.

On the drive from Springfield, Tyler had given her an updated file of everything she'd uncovered in their investigation into The Bishop so far. She'd wanted Sloane to review it before the press conference, but there hadn't been time. Sloane set aside Lily's binder, reaching for Tyler's folder.

She jumped at a knock at the door. The file tumbled to the floor, photographs and maps slipping across the hardwood. She scrambled to collect everything as she called out for her guest to enter.

"Everything okay?" Tyler asked, striding into the room, her stance wary.

"Fine," Sloane grumbled, bending to retrieve the scattered file.

Tyler knelt to help, but Sloane waved her off. When she stood again, Sloane noticed she carried another new file.

"Something new?"

"Possibly."

Sloane slapped the last of the papers on the table and turned to face Tyler. "Go on."

"Something happened in Humboldt Park last night."

Sloane's stomach clenched, waiting for news of another missing woman.

Tyler flipped open the new folder and held it out. The contents were very different from the others she'd shared. Typed reports and a stack of photographs. Not the grainy security footage she was used to but crisp shots in full color.

"Three bodies. All male, mid-twenties. No ID."

The photographs transported Sloane back to her days in the State's Attorney's office. A body, eyes glazed over and a pool of blackening blood under his cheek, an evidence marker positioned near his scraped knuckles.

"Gang related?"

"Probably." Tyler fell silent until Sloane looked up to meet her eye. "They were found in an alley across the street from Club Alhambra."

Tyler said more, but Sloane's ears were ringing and the sound of her heart slamming against her ribs drowned out the words. She flipped through the next few photos, not really seeing them, until she got to one showing a cracked and bloody motorcycle helmet. She knew that helmet. How many times had she seen in it surveillance photos of Marisol? Described in reports she'd requested back when she was State's Attorney. Sure, there was a chance Marisol had switched to a new style in the intervening years, but the location was as good as confirmation.

"Are you listening?"

"What?" Sloane said, dragging her eyes away from the picture.

"The knife?" When Sloane shook her head, Tyler continued, "The knife removed from the second victim. That and the helmet didn't make it back to the station with the rest of the evidence."

"What?"

Tyler huffed, both hands going to her waist. "Disappeared in transit. And the detective who questioned Soltero lost his interview notes. He was also resistant to bringing her in for an official interview. Said he was convinced of her innocence."

Sloane couldn't stop the skeptical snort. "You're kidding?"

"Nope. He's been put on leave, but it doesn't matter. Without physical evidence, there's nothing to link Soltero to the murders."

Sloane indicated a close up of one victim's knuckles. "Murder is a strong word. These aren't the hands of a victim."

"Come on, Sabrina."

"Gang fights always end like this. I'm more interested in missing women than a couple of guys who picked a fight they couldn't win."

"They could be connected. Somebody could be after Soltero for that," said Tyler, pointing at The Bishop's file on Sloane's table.

They are. Sloane swallowed the words and her fear. Marisol was jumped by at least three men outside her club. While she was on her bike, coming back from her visit to Sloane's balcony. Sloane had been in Chicago for less than a day and Marisol had been attacked. What would happen if she stayed any longer?

"We're leaving."

Tyler took a step back. "What? Why?"

"I need to get back to Springfield." She slapped the folder closed and held it out to Tyler. Her hand shook, making the pages inside rattle. "Today."

"What about the warehouse? We're so close."

Tyler took the folder and Sloane whipped around, resting her fingertips on the tabletop to keep them still. "We can monitor the camera feeds from there. I have work to do. I want to leave within the hour."

"And this incident in Humboldt?"

"Has nothing to do with us."

Sloane squeezed her eyes shut, pushing down the nausea her lie caused.

"Sabrina, I..."

"Within the hour, Tyler."

There was a long moment of silence, but she finally replied with a curt, "Fine."

Sloane barely made it until the door shut behind Tyler, then she lowered herself to the ground, her body shaking with silent sobs.

CHAPTER TWENTY-FIVE

Brin left Chicago just as quickly as she'd come. Marisol disabled the camera notifications immediately after the attack in the alley. The more she thought of the incident, the more she realized how careless she'd been. She'd been so desperate to see Brin—to talk to her and understand why she'd been gone for so long—that she'd let her guard down. It had been years since anyone had attempted to jump her in Humboldt, but she'd removed herself from the safety of her lair and paid the price.

In the end, she found out from the news about Brin's departure. It was for the best. As it was all she could think about was the kiss. If Marisol saw Brin again, something she'd been holding onto tightly for the last seven months would crack and she wouldn't be able to put it back together again. Too many people counted on her being whole, so she needed to give her broken ribs and bruised ego a chance to heal.

Instead of returning to K-Town and the warehouses, she sat on the red leather couch in her Throne Room at Alhambra and guzzled tequila. Her head spun pleasantly and women draped their warm bodies across hers. She couldn't find the energy to push them away early in the night, and by the time to tequila took hold of her she didn't want to push them away. She stopped short of inviting any upstairs, but only just.

After two endless nights and days, the ghost of Brin's kiss had left her but Marisol couldn't risk going back to K-Town. There was still too much focus on the area after the mayor's announcement, but at least that was keeping the Suburban off the streets. She decided to wait another few days for the press to die down before she went back in. It wouldn't hurt to have the building purchases in the works before she went back either. The most important set of keys had already been delivered, but the other sales would take eyes off her hiding place.

Fortunately, she had other things to distract her. While she'd been squatting in K-Town, the exterior walls had been completed on the new community center across from Justino's bodega. They were still weeks away from opening, but close enough that a new stage of planning had begun. The nonprofit group that would run the center was holding a donation drive before the grand opening. Marisol sent Gray and Mel out to load a box truck full of books, sports equipment, art supplies, and anything else they could think of. Two hours later they returned, giddy and sweating, to collect Marisol and a few others to help unload.

The parking lot glistened with fresh pavement. Mud caked high in the medians, unprotected grass seed poking out in clumps. Gray had pulled the box truck alongside a pair of rickety folding tables with plastic tablecloths and handwritten signs. A dozen residents stood around the parking lot, carrying tattered boxes with even more tattered donations inside. Most of them smiled or at least nodded acknowledgement of Marisol.

"Where should we put all this?" Marisol asked, throwing the truck's rear door open with a flourish. Sun shone off plastic wrapping and shiny finishes.

"I don't know," replied a young woman with her hair pulled back tightly and the early afternoon sun making the smooth curves of her red-brown skin glow. "Where do you keep all your stolen goods? Take it there, we don't want it here."

Her statement ended with a curled lip, and she turned her back. Marisol felt the rebuke like a slap across the face. Her eyes narrowed and she pushed her shoulder off the truck, circling the table to catch the woman's eye.

"It's not stolen. It's a donation. You wanna see the receipts?"

"I want," the woman said slowly, leaning forward and planting her fists on the table. "For you to take your people and go away. You aren't welcome here."

The world around Marisol went eerily quiet. The crowd froze. Marisol counted to ten in her head, letting the discomfort stretch and keeping a tight hold on her anger. An adhesive nametag sat crookedly on the woman's chest, proclaiming her name to be Clarita. It curled up on one corner.

Marisol leaned over the table, mimicking Clarita's stance, and lowered her voice. "There's no need to be rude. I came to make a donation. I care about this community. Who do you think paid for this center to be built?"

"That doesn't mean you own it or me. Why do you think we needed this center in the first place? Take your thugs and your drug money and get the hell out."

Marisol couldn't keep the growl out of her voice as she spat out, "I don't sell drugs."

"So there's one law you don't break, do you want a medal?"

"I want," Marisol's heart was thudding in her ears and her vision was narrowing so all she could see was this smug woman and her curling name tag. "To make Humboldt a better place. Take the fucking Monopoly boards and say thank you like a good girl."

It was a tactical error. Clarita's smug smile twitched higher. "The only thing you could do to make Humboldt a better place would be to leave it."

Clarita turned and walked away, passing behind the stunned volunteers and the terrified eyes of the gathered crowd. When she finished her journey, all those eyes turned on Marisol. Each of them was washed in naked fear.

"Boss." Gray's hand landed on her shoulder. His voice rumbled like the quiet start of an earthquake. "Let's go."

Marisol unclenched her teeth and straightened to her full height. It wasn't quite as impressive as Gray's, but she felt more like herself. Gray hopped up onto the tailgate to pull down the truck door and Mel dropped down out of the cargo area, her eyes blazing and fixed on Clarita. She tried to push past Marisol, who grabbed a fistful of her jacket and pulled her back. A collective murmur escaped the crowd. Marisol could feel them preparing to bolt.

"Leave it," Marisol told Mel through clenched teeth.

"She disrespected you, Boss. I'm gonna teach her…"

"You're gonna get back in the fucking truck," Marisol said, raising her voice. "This center is under my protection. It's off-limits."

The crowd let out a collective breath, but they were still on edge. Mel was a lit cannon, begging to be pointed toward something to destroy.

"That's bullshit. She…"

"She is under my protection. Off-limits."

The argument still raged in Mel's eyes, but she wrenched herself free of Marisol's grip and climbed into the truck cab. Marisol turned to see how Clarita responded, but she was busy at the far end of the tables, her eyes never lifting to acknowledge the scene. Marisol watched her as the truck turned and they lumbered out of the new parking lot. Clarita went back to accepting donations. She didn't look toward the truck.

CHAPTER TWENTY-SIX

Sloane hadn't wanted to go back to Springfield, but she found staying in Chicago too hard. She didn't dare go back to K-Town, hoping The Bishop would do something stupid because he thought she wasn't paying attention. She didn't dare go to Humboldt because she knew *she* would do something stupid if she wasn't paying attention.

In the end, going back to the Governor's Mansion wasn't much better. She arrived Saturday afternoon to Lily waiting for her in the driveway. She held a glossy magazine curled in her fist.

"Shouldn't you be at home, enjoying your weekend?" Sloane asked as she stepped out of the town car.

"You need all hands on deck to deal with this."

Sloane swapped her briefcase for the magazine. Lily had helpfully marked the first page of the article. She looked at her own face on the cover as they entered the Executive Wing of the mansion. The image was several years old and Sloane's decidedly smug grin flashed from behind a bank of microphones. The banner asked, "Governor for *all* the people? Sabrina Sloane's prosecutorial record raises questions of racism."

"Subtle," Tyler quipped from over her shoulder.

Sloane didn't respond, but she felt Lily's glare. She flipped open the magazine and scanned it as she marched through the familiar halls. Flashy graphics complete with pie charts squeezed the copy down to a thin bar through the middle of the page. The format allowed the article to take up several more pages than were strictly necessary.

"Clearly she isn't interested in keeping access to the Governor's office," Lily sniffed. "And no courtesy call announcing publication. Is there no decency left in journalism anymore?"

As she skimmed, Sloane recognized some of the cases she'd written on legal pads. The article was well researched.

"Has it hit the news yet?"

"Of course," Lily sneered. She held open Sloane's office door, even allowing Tyler to enter uninvited. "The phone's been ringing off the hook. The weekend operator is practically in tears."

"Is Bill here yet?" Sloane's Director of Communications was usually under her feet when she didn't want anything to do with him and nowhere to be found during a crisis.

"On his way back from fishing at Williams Bay."

"Figures," Sloane mumbled as she dropped into her office chair. "Well, let's get everyone else together to talk."

"The team is waiting in the main conference room."

"Great." Pressure built behind Sloane's eyes, throbbing quickly into a headache she doubted would ease anytime soon. "Give me thirty minutes to read this first."

Lily spun on her sensible heels and marched to the door. She held it open and turned back. "Special Agent Graham."

Tyler leaned over the desk and asked, "Do you need me to stay?"

"That's kind, but I don't think your expertise is suited to this issue."

"Understood." She dropped her voice and continued, "Don't worry about the other thing. I'll keep an eye out."

Before she could leave, Sloane said, "This will not distract me, Tyler. Don't make any moves without discussing them with me."

Tyler scowled, but nodded and followed Lily out of the room, leaving Sloane alone with her headache and the article.

CHAPTER TWENTY-SEVEN

"Interesting that you've opened twice now with Two Knights' Tango."

Marisol leaned back from the board, her knight wobbling on its felt pad as she released it. "With what?"

Dominique's eyes remained fixed on Marisol, even as she slid a pawn up to rest next to the first one she'd moved. They hadn't started a game on the last visit. There'd been too much to discuss. Then she'd made that monumental mistake of driving a block from Dominique's to Brin's and that trip had resulted in a week of missed meetings to heal broken ribs. Today Dominique forced Marisol to sit at the table because the pacing was making her nervous.

"Your opening moves," Dominique replied. "Bringing out both your knights for the attack rather than sacrificing your pawns. It's a chess opening known as Two Knights' Tango."

Marisol's left shoulder twitched before she could stop it. Mel hadn't reported in the previous night. Gray was out poking around, but Marisol had a sneaking suspicion the girl had grown tired of waiting for Marisol to make a move and had taken matters into her own hands.

"They're more effective."

"Sure." Dominique lifted her teacup to her lips but didn't drink. "It's an aggressive stance. Two powerful players, going straight for the kill."

Marisol froze in her study of the board. "Why so interested in my chess strategy all of a sudden?"

"Is it a strategy?"

"You know more about chess than I do, Dominique. If it's a stupid move, just say so."

"It isn't. Two knights can be an effective weapon. They move together but never meet. Working toward the same goal."

Warning bells sounded in the depths of Marisol's mind. Dominique's unflinching stare was as empty as a cloudless sky.

"It's a dangerous strategy, too," Dominique continued. "What if your knights get in each other's way?"

Marisol remained silent, waiting for Dominique to say more. She didn't speak, but finally returned her gaze to the game. Her delicate fingers moved to her own knight, twisting it to face the backs of a row of pawns. Marisol was hypnotized by the movement of her hand. Though she spoke, the words faded out to a pleasant, almost musical hum. Her fingertip slid across the wooden horse's mane and then hopped to the polished ball atop her bishop. She twirled the piece then immediately released it in favor of the queen at his side. Her fingernail ticked against the wooden crown, a low drumbeat to join the cadence of her speech.

"Do you sacrifice one knight to save the other? Or maybe let them both go down to save the game?"

Marisol's voice was hoarse with strain when she asked, "Which option is better?"

Dominique's eyes locked on her again as she said, "I'm not the one moving the pieces."

The statement was true enough, but, then again, neither was Marisol. The man in Washington was making the moves. He always did. He always would. Even when Marisol controlled her own fate, Anderson was manipulating her.

She thought about Dominique's words all the way back to Humboldt Park and the familiar confines of her Throne Room. The club filled around her as the hours ticked by. The hum of the crowd was far less pleasant than the melody of Dominique's voice and the noise settled under her skin, irritating her.

Gray arrived with a small army of scantily clad women. Marisol sent them to her personal bar and dragged him aside.

"Mel?"

"No sign of her."

"What does that mean?" Marisol growled. "She didn't just vanish into nowhere."

"Of course she didn't," he said, holding out a crystal tumbler full of her special tequila. "We both know what's happened to her."

Marisol threw the tequila down her throat and the glass onto the floor at his feet. It shattered in a particularly satisfying explosion. The women gasped, then giggled and went back to their drinks. Gray looked less amused.

"Stupid fucking girl," Marisol growled, her chest heaving and her head aching.

A red-eyed waitress arrived with a broom and dustpan, keeping her eyes down while she swept up the mountain of broken glass.

"It wasn't the wisest decision, but Mel was trying to help," Gray said, his voice low and steady. Marisol wanted to rip his throat out for being so calm.

"I specifically told her not to put herself at risk. I told her, but she didn't listen." Marisol paced the room, her boots banging against the bamboo floor. The waitress swept and sniffled. "She had no business going out there."

"She was getting impatient," Gray replied. He swept a hand through his tightly cropped hair. "She's lost friends. She wanted to help bring them home."

The girl's sweeping ended in a wail and she sprinted from the balcony, tears sending rivers of mascara down her cheeks. Gray and Marisol watched her go, not speaking until they heard the bathroom door slam.

"Helena," Gray said, rubbing his chin. "Why's she so upset?"

The name rang a bell, and Marisol allowed herself a moment of silence until the pieces clicked into place. "Mel's girlfriend. Shit. I forgot."

Gray looked after her. "I didn't know."

"I should've remembered." Grief, guilt and anger coated Marisol's tongue and throat. "We shouldn't have talked about Mel in front of her."

"I didn't know," Gray repeated.

Marisol stared at his back. His thick neck and wide shoulders. There was no judgement in his words, but Marisol swam in guilt nonetheless. She should have gone back to K-Town. She should've kept to her plan and let Brin do whatever she wanted, up to and including going straight to hell. She didn't owe Brin space. She didn't owe her anything. She owed her people something though, and she'd let herself get distracted. She had let Mel down.

Movement over Gray's shoulder caught her eye. The old theatre she had converted into her nightclub didn't just house the box she used as her Throne Room. All the boxes had been converted into luxury private areas where wealthy patrons could see and be seen.

The largest and most expensive box was directly across from hers and currently occupied by half a dozen men in custom suits, each with a bottle of vodka in hand. The only thing louder than their suits were their voices, shouting and laughing over the music below. Peppered throughout the box, each looking more uncomfortable than the last were a handful of women. They had bunched together where they could, though they didn't appear to be friends. Most of them looked like they were chosen at random from the dance floor downstairs or the sidewalk outside. Two waitresses, looking more annoyed but no more comfortable than the other women, moved between tables, cleaning up used glasses and empty plates.

As Marisol watched, one of her waitresses bent over to collect a bottle and the closest man reached under her skirt. The waitress sprang up and slapped his hand away and the man laughed even louder, reaching for her again.

"Marisol…"

Gray's warning echoed in her ears as she marched out of her box to circle the balcony. Each box went silent as she passed. Within moments she was standing in the arched entry to the men's box. They didn't notice her arrival, but the waitresses did. Marisol glanced at the women huddled against the back wall and the waitresses sprang into action. Within moments they had herded the women out and the men finally noticed they were alone.

"Yo, what the fuck?"

The man's roar of indignation was echoed by his buddies. One by one they stood and looked around the room, their mouths hanging open so their unshaven chins wobbled.

"Who sent the bitches away?" the man who'd reached under the waitress's skirt whined. His suit was silk, the shimmering blue darkening at the armpits where sweat soaked through his shirt. He finally noticed Marisol and pointed at her. "What the hell?"

Marisol stood, her boots planted shoulder-width apart and her leather-clad arms crossed over her chest. The longer she stared at them, the more they gawped.

"What's the matter?" A man in a green suit laughed, slapping his buddy's shoulder. "You want us all to yourself?"

They hadn't noticed how quiet and still the club had gone. The music still played, but there was no movement from the dance floor. Marisol tracked the men's faces as they looked at each other and her.

"Sorry, babe." Blue Suit smirked. "You ain't our type. And we don't speak Spanish."

He laughed, but the others were starting to look nervous.

Marisol took a long step into the room and said, "I didn't learn to speak Spanish until I was a teenager. Why would you think you need to speak Spanish to me?"

Blue Suit's grin faded, but Green Suit jumped in to defend him. "Look, we just figured. No offense. We're cool, right?"

Marisol shook her head.

A man in a gray suit spoke up. "Look, we just wanna have a good time. We don't want any trouble."

"You are trouble, though," Marisol said. "And I like trouble."

"Look." Blue Suit looked furious now. Marisol's insides purred happily. "We paid for this box for the night. Paid a fuck ton for it. We can do whatever we want, okay?"

"You didn't pay for them," Marisol said, pointing toward the far door the waitress had closed on her way out. "And in my place, you don't get to treat women like that."

"You better fucking believe we paid for them," Blue Suit said, getting into her face. He smelled like sweat, vodka, and too much cologne. "Women always have a price. I'm pretty sure you already know that."

He was at least six inches taller than her, but he never saw Marisol's fist coming. When it smashed into his nose, several bones crunched and his eyes rolled up. She heard Gray behind her, warning her not to make a scene, but the minute Blue Suit hit the carpet she was moving. The next two men didn't even have time to throw their arms up in defense before Marisol's fists connected with their bellies and then their jaws.

The next one covered his face, so she smashed the toe of her boot into his crotch. The whimper when he crumpled made her giggle. Blood from the next man's nose splattered her lip. Those still standing decided to fight back and things started to get fun. Only one landed a punch. The silk suits should have clued her in, but she'd expected more of a fight.

Looking over her shoulder, she saw Blue Suit trying to get to his feet. She was on him in a heartbeat. She dug her knee into his stomach while she yanked his face up by his silk tie.

"You're not from around here, are you?"

He whimpered a little and shook his head.

"Then you don't know." She pulled him closer and whispered, "There's only one rule in Humboldt."

"What's that?"

"Don't fuck with Marisol."

The first time her fist smacked into his cheek, his already bloody nose started gushing. After a few punches, his cheek opened up. She switched her target to his jaw and then his temple until her fist was slipping off his bloody skin in every spot she could see. Only then did she release his tie and push to her feet, her knuckles dripping blood that might've included some of hers.

Marisol panted, trying to catch her breath, and her eyes fell on Helena, crying onto a bartender's shoulder down on the main floor. The bartender stare was unreadable. Helena shook in his arms.

It wasn't only the bartender. All of Club Alhambra was silent and staring. Every eye was on her as she stood, enraged. Gray reached for her shoulder and she shook him off.

"I'm the fucking Queen of Humboldt!" she roared to the crowd. "This is my place! ¡Yo hago las reglas!"

"Boss." Gray touched her shoulder and she spun on him.

"¡Te chingaré!" Her fist was in the air, but she didn't swing. Her vision blurred and the anger drained out of her. "I make the rules."

"I know."

"This is what happens when they aren't obeyed."

"I know."

One of the men nearby groaned. She slammed her boot into his gut and stormed out of the box, nearly colliding with the two waitresses waiting outside. Pushing past them, she turned a corner and pushed aside a panel in the wall. It slid back just enough for her to squeeze through and swung back into place when she released it. Music roared through speakers over, under, and beside her as she sprinted along the catwalk hidden in the ceiling. A panel identical to the other deposited her into a stairwell leading up to her office and the apartment above it.

She didn't stop to check the cameras. She didn't search the apartment when she entered. She tore open the door to her walk-in closet and retrieved the same bag she'd packed a week ago. Marisol pushed the straps onto her shoulders as she marched back into the living room.

She saw the package on the dining room table. It sat beside two large bottles of her favorite water. The gun was in her hand before she thought to pull it from the holster, but her feet never stopped their journey across the room. She holstered the pistol again when she saw the white knight. It sat on top of a thin piece of paper.

Be careful. I can't lose you.
-D

After a moment's deliberation, she tucked the knight into her pocket. The bottles went into her bag and she unwrapped the package. Inside was a tactical vest of overlapping plates the size of silver dollars. It looked like it weighed a ton, but it was surprisingly light compared to other bulletproof vests she'd worn. With her jacket zipped, the vest was invisible.

Gray was on the other side of the door when she opened it. "Mel wouldn't want you to get yourself killed."

"I don't intend to," Marisol replied.

She wasn't Mel. She wasn't some wide-eyed kid with more guts than good sense. One night looking around and another day to make her final plans, then she would go in. She would get Mel and anyone else who was lucky enough to still be there.

"Keep an eye on the neighborhood," she said at the kitchen sink as she washed the assholes' blood off her hands. "Send the boys back out to keep an eye. Not the women. I don't want to lose anyone else."

She took the stairs two at a time as she descended one floor to her office.

"Where are we going?" Gray asked, his voice still cold and calm.

"We aren't going anywhere," Marisol replied as she snatched the keys to the recently purchased auto shop from the top desk drawer. She turned her back to Gray so he wouldn't see the vest as she secured the pistol into her shoulder holster. The weight of it pressed against her ribcage made her feel better. "I'm going alone."

"Bad call, boss. You aren't thinking straight."

She shot him a look that was a warning. "I always think straight."

"Then you aren't doing this because of Mel?"

"I'm doing this for a lot of people. A lot of *my* people. I'm going to get them back."

"Then you need my help."

"Nope." Marisol grabbed a fistful of ammunition clips and stuffed them in her bag next to the food and water. "I need you here."

"Boss…"

She was in front of him in a flash, a wad of his shirt held tight in her fist. There wasn't time for this. "I gave you an order, Gray. Don't make me regret trusting you to take care of what matters to me most."

His jaw flexed a few times, seemingly biting back words he didn't have the courage to toss at her when she was in a mood like this. He lost the staring contest. He always did. That's why Marisol trusted him. In the end, he always knew she was right.

"Fine."

Without another look Gray left the room. She hated to leave him angry, but he was sensible. Much more sensible than she was. His anger would burn out and he would know how important he was to her.

"That's enough," she whispered to herself, knowing that it wasn't.

CHAPTER TWENTY-EIGHT

"It's very kind of you to meet with me on such short notice."

"I always give those I interview a chance to respond," Nia said, her smile thin but surprisingly genuine.

Sloane returned the smile, choosing not to point out that it would've been kinder to let her respond before the article was published. But that wouldn't have been Nia's style. Before scheduling this meeting, Sloane had finally done her research on Nia Hamilton. What she'd found had impressed her. Nia had put in her time, and every article was well-researched and fair. Just like the one Nia had written about her. She turned her gaze to the stack of legal pads and the binder of Lily's research. She tapped her fingernail against the stack and forced down her annoyance.

"I wanted to thank you."

Nia's eyebrows slid up her forehead. "For what?"

"For bringing my attention to the mistakes I've made in the past." She sighed and met Nia's eyes. They were so close to the color of Marisol's. "I hadn't taken the time to examine my record. Hadn't looked at it through a different lens."

"And now you have?"

"I have. And I don't like what I see." Sloane pulled the top legal pad from the stack and flipped several pages deep. She let herself feel the shame she'd felt when she first made these notes. "I've spent my whole career…my whole *life* so sure of everything that I've done. So sure I was making my city and my state a better place. I still believe in that work, but I know I've gone about it in the wrong way. I've spent too much time repeating the mistakes of the past. Listening to my teachers and my mentors and never thinking critically about what they said. I should have thought for myself, but I didn't."

"It's easy to make the mistakes we're taught to make," Nia said. Her eyes flicked to the legal pad in Sloane's hands and the others stacked nearby.

"It's not an excuse," Sloane said, straightening her back. "It's an explanation. And one I hope to never have to use again. I am committing to doing better."

Nia nodded and her smile was much warmer. "How?"

"What do you mean?"

"How will you do better?"

"I'm committing to being genuinely antiracist. I won't let ignorance be an excuse any longer."

"That's an excellent step. You should know better than anyone, that in America, ignorance is not innocence."

How often Sloane had heard those words in the context of the law. When she prosecuted people for possession of stolen goods or drugs found in their cars that they swore a passenger had left, she'd always used that ideal as her strongest argument. She just hadn't heard it in the context of racism.

"What else? Saying that you'll be antiracist is not a concrete action. It doesn't shorten the prison terms of the people you sentenced. It doesn't change the mindset of the current prosecutors' office you helped shape."

Sloane leaned forward in her chair, a smile pulling at the corners of her lips. "If you were sitting at this desk, what would you do?"

"I'm not sitting at that desk."

"You could be. Probably sooner than you'd think." When Nia's eyebrow shot up, Sloane continued, "Tell me what you would do if you could make real change."

"Start with mandating implicit bias training in the State's Attorney's office. And a bias-based review of sentencing recommendations. Create a framework to review cases under appeal to determine if bias played a role in original sentencing decisions."

While Nia spoke, Sloane's office door eased open and Tyler slid into the room. She held up a folder, raising an eyebrow at Sloane.

"There are a whole host of changes you could make right now that would turn your words into action."

Sloane's fear and doubt were split evenly between the folder in Tyler's hand and the woman sitting in front of her. Exhaustion washed over her as she thought of implementing the ideas Nia proposed. She sighed and said, "I agree. There is more I can do. But I have too much on my plate at the moment to add more."

Perhaps it was a mark of Nia's respect for her, how disappointed she looked as she stood. "Then this is just a cop out. Speaking to me off the record means nothing."

Sloane stood and leaned on her desk. "This is so much more. I should have been clearer. I have too much on *my* plate at the moment, but government does not only function at this desk. I have legions of staff members who do the real work of government."

"Then get them working."

"I already have. I'm forming a taskforce." Sloane circled the desk and stood toe to toe with Nia. "They need a leader."

"And?"

"And I like having people on my staff who aren't afraid to challenge the status quo." She held out her hand. "Who aren't afraid to challenge me."

Nia's eyes flicked down to her outstretched hand, then back up to Sloane's face and narrowed. "If you think I'll be a rubber stamp for pretty words and empty promises…"

"That's not what I want."

"Good." Nia took her hand and squeezed it hard. "Because if you think that article was harsh, you don't want to see what I'll write if you try to use me."

Sloane smiled at the twinkle in Nia's eye. It reminded her of Marisol and made her heart ache. "I'd expect nothing less."

Nia turned and walked toward the door. Tyler gave her a hard look, but the protectiveness made Sloane squirm. She stood and called after Nia, "I have a major policy announcement coming in the next few days that will take all my focus, but I assure you I'm not dodging this. When this is over, we're going to do good work together."

Nia replied with, "Damn right we will."

Nia left, closing the door sharply behind her. Tyler's only response was the slight lifting of her left eyebrow. Sloane turned her back, crossing to the sideboard and a pot of stale coffee. It smelled like death, but Sloane had the feeling she'd need a very strong drink to deal with Tyler's newest manila folder. Too bad whiskey wasn't appropriate so early.

Tyler spoke from just over Sloane's shoulder. "I thought we talked about holding off on the announcement."

"We did," Sloane replied, turning around slowly. The steely determination in the set of Tyler's shoulders and jaw left her speechless for a long moment. *This really is it. After all this time.* "But this Anti Human Trafficking Initiative is a first of its kind in the US, and it will be my legacy. I want to get it going."

"You're a little young to worry about your legacy, aren't you, Sabrina?"

Sloane forced herself to walk away, to go back to her desk and the evidence of her past neglect and prejudice. She could still feel Tyler behind her, but she didn't think she could maintain eye contact right now. "It's never too early to think about doing the right thing. I'm guessing I already know the contents of your folder?"

Sloane held out her hand, but Tyler picked at the corner of the folder rather passing it over. "If this Bishop guy has any hint of your interest before I strike, it could spook him. I don't want him running."

"He won't run," Sloane said. She stepped forward and slipped the folder out of her hand. "He hasn't gotten what he came for."

The way Tyler's eyebrows knitted together, Sloane knew she'd said too much. Tyler's eyes hardened. "What aren't you telling me, Sabrina?"

She didn't answer. What could she say that wouldn't ruin all her carefully laid plans? Render her sacrifice of not being with Marisol meaningless. She flipped open the folder and looked at a page of thumbnail stills from surveillance cameras. The Suburban leaving the warehouse she'd seen Tyler examining the other day. Shots of it returning and leaving again in an endless procession. The time stamp at the bottom of each photo indicated the passage of hours rather than days. The next page was a similar collage, but this time with another vehicle, one she hadn't seen before.

"What's this?"

When Tyler didn't answer right away, Sloane looked up at her and watched the battle raging across her normally placid features. The way she tightened her jaw stretched the scar on her cheek and chin. Finally, she settled and answered in a level voice, "Increased activity. Something big is going down, and it'll happen soon."

"You think they'll move their captives?"

"I think they've already moved some. What I'm worried about is what he's doing with the newest ones."

"And what do you suspect?"

"That he's pulling up stakes. He can only prey on one community for so long."

"Understood. How did you get SWAT approval? I didn't get the impression the Chicago PD wanted to help."

Tyler was silent and she wouldn't meet Sloane's eye. Her face was rigid when she answered, "They don't want to help."

"Then what are you…"

"I don't have time to play politics on this one, Sabrina. He's leaving and there isn't time to get a team together."

"So you're going in alone? Your superiors approved that?"

"Not…exactly."

"Tyler?"

"Like I said, there's no time for politics." Tyler pointed an accusing finger at the folder. "I've wasted too much time already following the proper channels. A big raid will make too much noise and he'll bolt. Better to go in quietly and catch him by surprise."

"You know that's insane." Even as Sloane said it, her hope soared. Quiet was exactly what she wanted. What she didn't want was Tyler's death on her conscience. "Can you really pull this off alone?"

"This isn't my first day on the job," she bit back.

They stared at each other, a pair of wolves trying to assert their dominance. All of Sloane's instincts told her to do what she'd always done—to fight until her last breath. Her opponent always backed down. Always. But Tyler wasn't her opponent. They were on the same side and, more importantly, Sloane needed Tyler. She needed her for her insight and her expertise. If Sloane ever wanted to stop The Bishop, she needed help and the only person she trusted was Tyler. She let her shoulders slump.

"Of course it isn't. I'd never question your instincts. Let me help. What do you need from me?"

"Nothing," Tyler responded, though her mood and tone had softened noticeably. "Just making you aware that I'll be gone for a few days and, when I get back, it'll all be over."

Not that she was surprised in the least, but Sloane noted how certain Tyler was that she would be handling the raid on the warehouse without her help. That was not an option, and Tyler knew there would be a fight. Sloane watched her subtly shift her body in anticipation. Her shoulders pulled tightly together, her hands balled into fists and her knees slightly bent. She knew what was coming.

"That's obviously unacceptable," Sloane said, handing the folder back to her.

Tyler dropped it onto the table and crossed her arms firmly over her chest. The movement made the seams of her jacket pull taut. "We're not having this discussion, Sabrina. I allowed you to be part of the reconnaissance and that was obviously a mistake. You have to know I cannot take the Governor of Illinois into a late-night raid on a human trafficker's headquarters. If something happened to you…"

"Nothing will happen to me."

"If something happened to you," Tyler plowed ahead as though Sloane hadn't spoken. "It would be impossible to explain. The scandal would undermine everything that we've worked on together. I would just be the first person to lose my job, but, worse than that, people would die. It's out of the question."

"I appreciate that I'm putting you in a difficult position. Perhaps that's evidence enough of how important this is to me."

"I don't care. It's not happening."

"Yes, it is."

"There is literally nothing you could say that would convince…"

"He kidnapped me." Sloane's words made Tyler swallow hers. The shock on her face was evidence enough that only the truth would work to convince her. At least part of the truth. "My security detail didn't die protecting my empty apartment. They died trying to protect me, but The Bishop got me anyway. He flew me to Colombia in his private jet. There was…a great deal of violence involved." Sloane shook her head to banish the memory, squeezing her hands into tight fists. "Torture. Killing. I didn't make a surprise tour of South America. I was taken there against my will, and when I escaped and turned up at the Embassy, it was determined that the truth would spark an international incident. And drive The Bishop further underground. The tour was my idea. Cover for my presence there."

"How did you escape?"

"That's a story for another time," Sloane replied, flicking her bangs and holding her chin high.

She doubted she would ever tell Tyler the full truth. She certainly had no intention of blowing Marisol's cover, despite the unsettled nature of their relationship. None of it would matter if she didn't bring The Bishop down, and she had to bring The Bishop down. Now.

"So this is about revenge for you?" Tyler asked. The way she looked at Sloane changed subtly. There was something that may have been respect there now. Or fear.

"This is about ending the reign of terror of an international criminal, nothing more."

"With all due respect, Sabrina, that's bullshit." Tyler turned her back, walking toward the door. "And it's more proof that you can't be there. I'll call you the moment he's in custody."

Sloane's jaw dropped open. It hadn't worked. The only card she had left in her hand and the one that should have convinced anyone hadn't worked. She took an uncertain step forward, then stopped. She half-expected Tyler to relent, to turn around and say she'd changed her mind. But she didn't. She opened the door. She took a step through it and she was taking with her everything Sloane had sacrificed. Everything she'd worked for.

Anderson had been very clear. The Bishop would never leave Marisol or Sloane alone as long as he lived. Arresting him wasn't enough. He had friends, and those friends would spring into action if he ended up in handcuffs. If The Bishop didn't die, Marisol would, and Sloane wouldn't let that happen. But Tyler wouldn't kill him. She was a Girl Scout if ever there was one. She would arrest him and that would be the same as letting him walk free. Sloane had to be there to make sure the man died. She'd spent the last seven months preparing herself for the inevitability of another death on her hands. She was ready, but Tyler was taking that away.

In that moment, the truth descended on Sloane like a shroud. It hadn't been worth it. It had been a waste. The pain and the longing and the loneliness. Living her nightmare again and again day after day had been nothing more than an exercise in futility. It wasn't just her pain. It was the pain she'd caused. That hurt more than anything. She had convinced herself that, once it was all over, Marisol would forgive her. Would still want her. Would still love her. But now she wouldn't. Sloane had nothing to offer. No olive branch. No gift that would explain why she had forsaken Marisol. Tyler was walking out the door and taking it all with her.

"If you don't take me, I'll go on my own."

The words hung in the air. Something in that truth must have shone through because Tyler stopped and whipped around, her face twisted in a rage made more terrible by the scar that split her smooth cheek.

"The hell you will," she shouted. "You want to get us both killed?"

Sloane walked forward numbly. "I will gladly die to bring him down. You have no idea what he's done."

"I know exactly what he's done and what he will do." Tyler's eyes were haunted and Sloane wondered for the hundredth time how she got that scar. If perhaps they were chasing the same monster. "You think you understand what he's capable of? You think that visiting a few villages handpicked by government officials tells you what those women go through?"

They could argue all night, but Sloane had made up her mind and Tyler would just have to put up with it. She could get on board or get out of her way. Sloane marched toward the door, heading right for Tyler.

"I'm going to change and pack a bag. I'll be downstairs in ten minutes." At the last moment, Tyler slipped aside, out of her way. "Whether or not you're waiting for me, I'm going back to Chicago tonight."

CHAPTER TWENTY-NINE

The Suburban left a few minutes after nightfall. The other vehicle—a similar chunky black SUV—pulled out of the warehouse on its heels. That one must have started its rounds while Marisol was brooding and beating up assholes in her club. No matter. With them both gone, it was time for Marisol to act.

The cash contract on the chop shop had gone through in record time so she now officially owned this dump. It hadn't been used in years. Where she'd squatted before had fewer rats and less trash, but this one had a better view of The Bishop's warehouse. The trash wasn't a big deal, but she really didn't like rats. She'd had to sleep on top of a rusted old desk to avoid them. Now she used it to lay out her tools. Selecting a few essential items, she packed them back into her messenger bag and strapped it diagonally across her chest. It was smaller than her backpack, but she jumped around a few times and was pleased that nothing banged together. Even the slightest noise would be a disaster tonight.

Marisol slipped through the shop's roof-access door and bent low, crab-walking across the roof to avoid detection. She made it across the warped surface without incident and scanned the area for movement. Her luck held out—the neighborhood remained quiet. It was an easy scamper across the rooftops separating her from her goal. Two nights ago, she'd noticed the warehouse's camera pointing at the front door and rear garage exit, so her entrance would be undetected from above. Whether the cameras were courtesy of Brin's agent lapdog or The Bishop himself, someone was keeping an eye on this building. Fortunately for Marisol, her days of kicking in the front door and entering guns blazing were long over. She'd become more subtle in her old age.

When she dropped onto her target's roof the first item came out of her pack. No doubt to keep the place looking abandoned, The Bishop had made few improvements since setting up his operation. The hinges on this roof door were caked in rust. Marisol applied a liberal coating of automotive grease to each and worked it in with a rag before applying a second coat and finally testing the door. She moved it achingly slowly, but her patience was rewarded with silence.

Once inside, Marisol found herself on a dark landing overlooking a dark stairwell. She waited, letting her eyes adjust. After a few moments, she could make out the stairs and started a quiet descent.

Like the building where she'd been squatting, the top floor of this one was offices. Marisol inspected each room as she passed, but most were strewn with trash and caked with dust. Only one appeared to have been recently occupied.

Scrabbling noises made Marisol freeze in her tracks, listening hard. It sounded like rats, but she waited for another sound to be sure. After seven or eight shallow breaths, the noise came again. It was a much larger animal. Besides, the accompanying sneeze and whimpering were definitively human.

Marisol moved silently across the hall and pressed an ear to the closed door. It could be the women she'd been looking for, or it could be The Bishop's men. Marisol had to take a chance.

Tonight was going to end in blood sooner or later. Might as well set the bullets flying now. She eased her Colt from the shoulder holster and attached the silencer. There was no way to know how many of the enemy lurked in this warehouse, and it would be wise to alert as few as possible.

Feet braced, Marisol slowly twisted the doorknob. Once the lock was free, she banged her hip hard against the door to send it flying and charged into the room, pistol first.

Cages. Lining the room were dog crates meant for the sort of massive animals that would make the neighbors cringe. There had to be a dozen of them and each one had a pair of lantern-bright eyes peering warily out. They were not canine eyes. Marisol knew all too well the look of fear in a caged woman's eyes.

Scanning the room and finding it free of guards, she closed the door gently and shoved some discarded blankets under the crack at the bottom of the door. Once it was sealed, she flipped the light switch and winced as the bare bulb threw harsh light onto the harsh scene.

Women, bent and twisted into spaces far too small for them. Each had a thin blanket either wrapped around or underneath them. Each was filthy and frightened. Hollow-cheeked as well as hollow-eyed. Bile rose in her throat to block out her scream of rage and disgust.

"Boss?" squeaked a voice from nearby.

A clockwork moon tattoo under greasy hair. She dropped to one knee to look through the crate's bars. "Mel? Are you okay?"

"As well as can be expected," she whispered hoarsely. Her face pinched in pain as she adjusted her position. "I wouldn't mind getting out of this cage, though."

Marisol shot her a grin as she dug in her pack. "Helena would kick my ass if I left you in here a minute longer."

Tears filled Mel's eyes so fast Marisol stopped moving and watched for signs of a breakdown. Mel was made of strong stuff. She smiled through her tears and asked, "She's okay then?"

"She's fine. Pissed at me for not protecting you," Marisol whispered, finally yanking her bolt cutters from the pack. "How 'bout I get you outta here so you can go find out how she is for yourself?"

"I'd like that."

Mel held the thick body of the lock against the bars while Marisol cut through its shackle. It still couldn't muffle the clink of snapping metal, but she didn't think the sound would make it far. Once free, Mel gritted her teeth while stretching limbs too long constrained. After a few minutes, she was able to help Marisol free the other women, some of them less subtle in their movements or sounds. All were crying by the time they were free.

Marisol had thought that all the kidnapped women were from Humboldt, but she recognized less than half of them. Turning to Mel, she whispered, "Where are the rest? Where's Analise and Isabella?"

Mel dropped her eyes and another woman, one of the strangers who had eyes more haunted than the rest explained in a low voice, "There's another room. The ones who've been here longest go there. There aren't cages in that room, only chains and…beds."

Marisol's jaw tightened. Her mind's eye flashed to the sanctuary she'd created for women like that. To The Hotel full of women with dead eyes. The thought of sweet Analise and silly, young Isabella in that place made her sick. She held out the bolt cutters to Mel, who took them unquestioningly.

"Find the room. Get them free. The roof access is at the far end of the hall. The fire escape is sound enough, but maybe go down one or two at a time to be safe. Can everyone walk?" Mel nodded, looking like the capable lieutenant she had always been. "Take them to the back entrance of Alhambra. Gray will keep you safe until I get back."

Mel put a hand on her arm. "You're going to kill him, aren't you?"

"Yes." Then she hardened her eyes and stared down Mel until she knew she wouldn't ask to come along. "Alone."

Marisol flipped off the lights and pulled aside the blankets under the door. This time she gave herself more time for her eyes to adjust. She listened and heard nothing. She looked under the gap and saw no feet. With a last nod to Mel, she eased the door open and checked that the hall was clear, then she took off toward the stairs presumably heading down to the main floor while Mel checked the last of the rooms.

Marisol's skin was prickling with mistrust at the emptiness when she finally spotted someone moving between the shadows. Ducking behind stacks of large wooden crates on the main floor, she waited for any sound of her movements to pass. This floor was poorly lit and dominated by long, wicked-looking shadows. The person she'd seen stepped out into the wide-open center of the room.

Marisol let out a breath and whispered to herself, "You've got to be fucking kidding me."

CHAPTER THIRTY

From the moment Sloane had stepped foot in the warehouse, she'd known it was a trap. It was too quiet. Too empty. Besides, it was The Bishop. How could it be anything else?

If she was honest with herself, Sloane had known all along that it was a trap. From the first time Tyler had shown up at her office door with a manila folder. Even before that. From the moment she'd told Marisol she'd see her in Chicago. She wouldn't see her. Not alive. Not whole. The Bishop had won and the proof was that Sloane was standing here now, in the center of an abandoned warehouse floor, in the middle of a pool of light surrounded by stacks of crates like the walls of a prison. Why had she been so stupid?

The drive from Springfield had been tense. Tyler had allowed her time to change, but what did a politician wear to storm an enemy stronghold? Tyler hadn't exactly looked on her black yoga pants and navy pullover with disdain, but it was close. At least she felt like she could move without making noise or being seen in a moonless night. When they entered the city limits, Tyler started lecturing her on what she could and could not do. The first point, of course, was that she couldn't go off on her own.

That rule was out the window the moment they pulled up and Tyler saw movement on the roof. Lots of movement. She tried to send Sloane back to the car but gave up quickly. Loitering outside the warehouse seemed equally dangerous, so she told Sloane to go inside and wait in the shadows, keeping communication open through their earpieces.

Instinct told Sloane that staying still was a great way to die, and she had no interest in dying today. As she slowly explored the main floor, she wished Tyler had consented to give her a weapon. Even the can of mace she used to carry in her purse would make her feel safer, but that was packed away somewhere in her suite at the Governor's Mansion.

Most of the floor had been in shadow, and she'd been drawn to the pool of light like any insect careless of its safety. Her tennis shoes squeaked on bare concrete. By the time a familiar voice spoke up behind her, Marisol was close enough to grab her.

"What the hell are you doing here?" Marisol growled.

Despite the anger lacing the words, Sloane's heart rate doubled at the sound of Marisol's voice. Her body tingled with the knowledge she was so close. Sloane turned, trying to move casually, but aware of every muscle and inch of skin. As soon as her eyes swept over Marisol, her throat went dry.

So little had changed since Colombia. All that Sloane couldn't see in the dark of her balcony was illuminated now. Marisol was motionless as a jaguar, her body tensed and ready to strike. Her eyes were still ice-cold, her jaw still chiseled, and her body still lean. She wore her signature leather pants and biker's boots. The part of Sloane that had been so achingly lonely for the last seven months wished Marisol had left her leather jacket unzipped so she could study all her delicious curves and sharp edges.

Reality returned to Sloane as soon as her inspection was done. The reminder of the earpiece she didn't know how to switch off. All that she had done to save Marisol from this and still she was here, her life balanced precariously. Fear and anger rippled through her in equal measure. They made her words come out with acidic sharpness. "I should've known you'd be here."

Marisol's expression had been carefully schooled as Sloane's words hadn't been. With her response, simmering rage bloomed across Marisol's face. She took a long stride forward, crowding Sloane's space. "You know nothing about me."

"Don't I?" Sloane asked with a squeak of uncertainty in her voice.

"If you did," Marisol continued. "Then you would know I would do anything to stop this. I would die for two things in this life and stopping this is one of them."

Before Sloane could ask what the other was, a crackle of static came through her earpiece. She could hear Tyler but couldn't make out the words. Marisol was close enough to hear the burst of sound. Shock cut across her face.

"You brought her?"

"I had to," Sloane said, trying to communicate a warning with her eyes. "She's…"

Bright lights popped on across the warehouse, travelling across the concrete floor and illuminating the catwalk that crisscrossed above them. Each new light showed another wicked face. Another muscle-bound man toting an automatic rifle. Another sneer. The last light to come on was directly in front of and above them and it showed the only person without a weapon.

The Bishop still wore a light linen suit better suited to his old base of operations than this far colder city. He still wore a dark shirt with a mandarin collar and the white fedora with a black ribbon shadowed his eyes though the rest of the warehouse now blazed with light. He still surrounded himself with others that would do his dirty work. Ten men flanked him, fanned out on either side along the catwalk.

"He does love to make an entrance," Marisol whispered as she moved to stand shoulder to shoulder with Sloane.

Between the snide comment and the fear pumping through her, Sloane had to fight hard not to laugh. The static in her ear cut off abruptly, and any thought of laughter died. What did Tyler's silence mean? Had they gotten her, too? Had she gone to get backup? Was the earpiece broken?

"How nice to see you both again."

The Bishop's voice was a rich, low baritone that carried easily across the massive room. There was a hint of an accent, but it wasn't the Colombian accent she had expected. It was the affected Transatlantic accent of old Hollywood movies, as though he had worked hard to cultivate a sense of class to which he may or may not be entitled. He crossed his hands behind his back as he spoke, a smile appearing on his thin lips.

"I wish I could return the sentiment," Sloane replied, hoping that verbal bravado was enough to dispel her fear and allow her to think.

A couple of The Bishop's men stiffened, squeezing their gun grips and glowering down at her.

Marisol took a step forward, subtly placing her body between Sloane and The Bishop. "Quite the reception you have for us. You been waiting like this every night for the last seven months? Sounds boring."

"Certainly not," he shouted down at her, making Sloane question the wisdom of Marisol antagonizing him. "You think I didn't notice you prowling around? Spending night after night in that rat-infested hovel next door. I suppose you were comfortable there, among your own kind?"

"There was a lot of shit and garbage in there, too. You would've been comfortable yourself."

"Marisol…" Sloane whispered, reaching out to squeeze her arm as The Bishop stepped forward and gripped the railing, his teeth bared.

Marisol didn't say anything in response, but she did reach behind her. Sloane expected she was trying to shake Sloane loose, but instead she lifted the back of her jacket an inch, revealing the shimmering grip of a handgun. Not wanting to draw attention to it, Sloane looked away, but she tucked her hand into the waistband of Marisol's pants, close to the gun. Marisol's head bobbed almost imperceptibly.

"Considering your current position, it might be wise to show me a little more respect," The Bishop said.

"Lo tendré in mente, mamahuevo."

The goons were restless now. Sloane could hear them shuffling their feet and adjusting their weapons. She could hear them panting, too. Like they were anxious for the chance to kill the intruders. But as The Bishop and Marisol continued to jaw at each other, Sloane realized she still heard the panting. It took her an embarrassingly long time to realize the sound was coming through her earpiece. Tyler must be running. Praying that she was running toward them to bring help, Sloane focused back in on the conversation.

"Enough!" The Bishop shouted. "You know what I want, Soltero. Give it to me or I will make you wish you had."

The Hotel. This was about The Hotel again. That meant that this had been a trap for Marisol, not her. It made sense. He said he'd seen Marisol prowling around the warehouse, but she and Tyler had only been here once. All their other surveillance had been electronic. So he had anticipated Marisol's presence, but he might not have accounted for her *and* Tyler. There had to be an advantage to that if she could only leverage it. She moved her hand closer to the pistol and Marisol twitched her chin just enough to make her stop.

"You should know by now that you won't get anything from me."

"No? I suppose not. Though I think perhaps I tortured the wrong woman last time. Perhaps you can be persuaded if I hurt your lovely governor."

He twitched a finger at one of his goons and the man moved immediately, hurrying along the catwalk toward the stairs. Marisol lurched forward, nearly pulling out of Sloane's grasp. Sensing the recklessness of Marisol's anger, Sloane shouted, "You can threaten me all you want, but you know the shitstorm that'll come down on you if you touch me."

"Almost there," Tyler whispered in her ear. Sloane prayed she wasn't exaggerating because the steps pounding down the metal staircase were getting closer.

The Bishop laughed. It was maniacal, like a man who had long since lost his grip on reality. While his laughter filled the room, Marisol said in a rush, "When I say, take out the one coming for us and then give me the gun."

Before she could acknowledge she'd heard, The Bishop's laughter cut off and he shouted, "You're quite wrong, Governor. I can do whatever I want."

"Why do you say that?"

"The rules the rest of the world has to follow no longer apply to me."

Marisol's body tensed as the goon's boots hit the floor. He walked toward them, the barrel of his rifle pointing harmlessly down. She shouted back, "Oh yeah? Why's that?"

Sloane had expected more posturing, but instead he went thoughtfully silent. A smile grew slowly and he licked his lips with almost indecent slowness. "Wouldn't you like to know?"

Marisol paused, looking up at him with her eyebrows creased as the goon got closer and closer. Just when Sloane was about to explode with anticipation, Marisol stiffened and said, "Now!"

The next few moments happened in slow motion. Sliding her hand across the warm skin of Marisol's back, she grabbed the pistol. It slid from the waistband easily when Marisol dropped to one knee. Sloane had it up and pointed at the man in seconds, her forearms resting on Marisol's shoulder. She'd only fired a gun once in her life, and her target had been much closer then. She told herself that this was the same thing and squeezed the trigger.

She missed with the first shot, but the second came right on top of the first and it hit him in the shoulder. The third made his chest burst open and sent his body flying. The gun had been so loud, and the pounding of her blood in her ears even louder, that she heard the shouting from above her as though she were underwater. She couldn't seem to move her arms or her legs, but she felt Marisol move out from underneath her and a moment later the gun was wrenched from her hands.

"Get down!" Marisol roared in her ear as the first shots slammed into the concrete in front of them.

Sloane moved, but not fast enough. Marisol's palm slammed into her back and she flew the last few steps, stumbling to her knees behind a stack of wooden crates. She expected Marisol to slide behind the crates with her, but, spinning around, Sloane saw her crouched behind cover on the other side of the gap. Despite the solid barrier between her and the armed men, Sloane felt exposed and alone. She wanted to be at Marisol's side, but the gulf between them was pockmarked with bullet holes.

Marisol leaned out, her arm whipping up and the pistol spitting fire. A heartbeat later an unnatural scream filled the room and Marisol ducked back behind the crates. A burst of splinters erupted from the crate. Bullets chewed through the wood while Marisol waited. Sloane wondered how long the crates would last under such a barrage.

Marisol slipped out of safety seconds after the last bullet hit. This time she aimed at two different spots before pressing her back to the crate again. A sickening thud sounded behind her and Sloane cringed at the sound of a body dropping onto concrete. She didn't dare peek around the crate to see how many gunmen were left. The catwalk was vibrating as the men shouted and scrambled around overhead. Eventually they would find a way to circle around until Marisol was in their sights.

An empty clip flew from the butt of Marisol's pistol and she replaced it with a fresh one from her jacket pocket. How many of those clips could she have? Enough to last against this army? How long before all those goons tightened the noose around them? And where the hell was Tyler?

As though speaking her prayer into existence, Sloane heard a new series of shouts and gunshots. Marisol took advantage of Tyler's diversion to fire off a series of shots without interruption. The tide suddenly seemed to turn. Screams of pain filled the air. Had Marisol and Tyler killed them all? Sloane shot to her feet.

Still hidden, she tried looking around to check on Tyler. That's when she saw her mistake.

The central spot on the catwalk where The Bishop had stood was now occupied by Tyler, blazing away with her service weapon. Following her gaze down the length of the catwalk, she spotted The Bishop, well behind his two remaining men and out of Tyler's range.

But The Bishop also saw Sloane. He bared his teeth and reached down to the body at his feet, ripping the pistol from the dead man's waist. At his new position, The Bishop had a clear shot at her and there was nowhere she could go.

He lifted the gun and Sloane stared down the barrel. Oddly, now that she was so close to death, she did not feel the fear that had paralyzed her earlier. Marisol was safe and Tyler would get The Bishop soon enough. Her work here was done. She had given her life for the greater good. Wasn't that what she'd always been willing to do?

Sloane closed her eyes, waiting for the bullets.

CHAPTER THIRTY-ONE

Marisol was slamming her last clip into the Colt when Brin looked up and froze. Whipping around, Marisol saw The Bishop lift a pistol, levelling it at Brin. She moved without thinking, propelled by instinct. She was a step away when she heard the pistol's first report. Leaping forward, she slammed her shoulder into Brin's chest, sending her sprawling. Her momentum spun her around, so she took the first bullet full in the chest. The second and third slammed into her body just below her shoulder on the right side and left.

All the air left her body and she staggered backward, dropping to a knee and gasping for breath. She heard Brin scream. Heard shouting and more gunfire from above, but none of it came her way. No matter how hard she struggled, Marisol couldn't make her lungs expand. Her mouth hung open but no air trickled down her throat. Her body begged for oxygen as pain tore through her. Her eyes filled with tears and she waited for her vision to dim.

When Brin's hand slid over her shoulder, her lungs finally remembered how to work. She sucked in breath after deep, life-giving breath. Brin's other hand snaked around her side, trying to pull her onto her back. Marisol straightened, focusing on the catwalk above her. The Bishop and his two henchmen were running away, guns still in hand and Brin's bodyguard hot on their heels. She tried to stand, tried to run after them, but Brin held her back.

"Don't move," she croaked, her voice full of tears. "I've got you. We'll get help. Tyler! Call an ambulance!"

"Don't need," Marisol groaned, pushing the words out almost as painful as the shots themselves. "Not hit."

"Shhh," Brin said over the crackle coming from her earpiece. "Don't talk."

Marisol couldn't force herself to utter another word anyway. The pain was lessening with each breath, but the ache across her chest was excruciating. Leaning into Brin's body—being cradled in those arms—was all the anesthetic she needed. With trembling fingers, Brin reached for the zipper on her jacket. She pulled it down slowly, as though she would rather not see what was underneath. For her part, Marisol mourned the loss of her jacket, the lining burst through three massive bullet holes.

When she saw the vest, Brin let out a sigh of relief and let her forehead fall against Marisol's. She breathed, "Thank god."

Another crackle in the damned earpiece, followed by Brin responding in a wavering voice, "It's okay, but we still need an ambulance."

"Like hell we do," Marisol growled, forcing her face away from Brin's.

"Stop being…"

Marisol cut her off by forcing herself to her feet. "Where'd he go?"

"I don't know."

"Damnit, Brin! Didn't your lapdog go after him?"

"She stopped to call for backup. You need an ambulance."

"Fucking hell! You let him get away?"

Brin jumped to her feet, staring Marisol down with a fury that almost matched her own. "Are you seriously going to attack me for putting your life ahead of him?"

"Hell, yes I am!" Rage flooded Marisol. "You will never be safe until he's dead! No one will be safe! Do you know how many women I found upstairs? Do you know what he did to them? And you just let him get away?"

Brin opened her mouth to respond and, based on the fire in her eyes, she was prepared to tear into Marisol. She didn't have the chance though. Sirens wailed in the distance and a door nearby slammed open. Marisol whipped around, holding her Colt level despite the blinding pain radiating through her chest. The figure that emerged from the darkness also had its gun raised. An anonymous Glock like a thousand others Marisol had seen held by cops around the country. This was the angle at which she usually saw them—pointed directly at her.

"Drop the gun, Soltero."

"Not a chance, cop," she responded, shifting her body ever so slightly to block Brin in case there was an exchange of gunfire.

"Tyler! Marisol! Stop!"

Both of them shot a glance over at Brin, but their eyes were back on each other a moment later.

"Sabrina, we need to…"

"Sabrina?" Marisol growled. "On a first name basis with your lapdog then?"

"Lapdog? Listen, Soltero…"

"I said stop it!" Brin roared. She took a long, deep breath and then put a hand on Marisol's arm, applying light pressure in a clear request that she stand down. "We're all on the same side here."

"I am *not* on her side," Marisol growled, refusing to drop her weapon.

"I'm definitely not on this killer's side."

"She saved my life, Tyler. Surely that's enough to make you listen to me for a moment."

The agent sighed and looked away, but she wasn't going to give up that easily. "I'll drop mine if she drops hers and not a minute before."

"Oh no." Marisol's wicked grin challenged Tyler as much as her words. "After you."

"Marisol, please." Brin's touch softened and she moved forward enough to catch Marisol's eye. There was a gentleness in her look that was hard to ignore. "Please."

The second "please" was enough. With a final frustrated grunt, Marisol slipped her gun back into her waistband, this time in front for an easier reach. In truth, she could barely stand to keep her arms raised another moment. Tyler dropped her weapon reluctantly a full minute after Marisol, slipping it into a shoulder holster.

Examining this woman up close, Marisol could see a lot of herself there. Determined and stubborn. No matter how much she wanted to ignore it, Brin had spent the last seven months with this woman rather than her, a woman who had put her life on the line to protect Brin. If she weren't so jealous, she might have appreciated that she'd done what Marisol couldn't.

"What now?" Marisol asked, unable to keep the bitterness from her voice. "We gonna sing 'Kumbaya'?"

Brin turned an angry look on her, but before she could speak they were all distracted by the screeching of tires and wailing of sirens outside. Brin and Tyler turned to the open door, watching the red lights flashing through the portal. Marisol gave them several moments of distraction, waiting for Brin to take a step forward before she took one back.

By the time the first cops burst through the open door, Marisol had already slipped through the alley behind the next building over. She'd be back at Alhambra before anyone knew she was gone.

CHAPTER THIRTY-TWO

Marisol uncrossed her legs, the leather of her pants creaking on the couch as she crossed them again. The movement shifted her arms, which were stretched across the back. The leather of her new jacket creaked against the couch the same as her pants had. Her chest ached from the previous night and she had to drop her arms to save herself unnecessary pain. She growled in discomfort and frustration.

Gray took a step away from her, lowering himself to the middle stair on the flight that led to her perch above Alhambra. His discomfort added to her own and she clenched her jaw. She'd been doing it so much recently that she felt newly toned muscles bunch under her cheeks. A headache bloomed in her temple.

Anger and resentment burned in her gut. She was uncomfortable because of the new jacket, the leather a poorer quality than her old one. Gray had tried unsuccessfully to replace the original. It wouldn't have been ruined in the first place if Brin had just stayed down behind that crate like she'd asked. But no, she had to be a curious little kitty. Had she put a little more effort into obeying a simple fucking request, Marisol wouldn't be sitting here itching on her throne.

Then worse, she'd wanted to take Marisol to a hospital in an ambulance surrounded by Chicago PD and that scarred bodyguard of hers. As though anyone would let her walk away. She'd had to slink off into the night and fall to the tender mercies of Gray. He'd asked where she got the bruises and, of far more interest to him, the bulletproof vest. She'd shaken her head and that was the end of it, but when the report of major police activity at a warehouse in K-Town came on the news, he gave her a hard look.

She'd had to sit there, ice packs balanced on the new bruises over her chest and watch that asshole give an interview. At least she knew who the bitch was now. Special Agent Tyler Graham of the NSA, assigned to the Human Trafficking Task Force. At least that explained why Marisol felt that they were so similar. Two sides of the same coin, only Tyler would always be heads, and Marisol would always be tails.

Brin hadn't featured in the report. No mention of her presence or any special protection visible to the cameras. It was like neither of them had even been there. Tyler got all the credit and Marisol got all the bruises. The world certainly still spun in the normal direction. She'd have to have a little conversation with Dominique about this one. Surely she'd known the bodyguard had been one of them? Washington wouldn't keep something like that a secret from her. Why had she kept it a secret from Marisol? Another person she'd trusted who had done her wrong, though she deserved none of it.

Marisol slid deeper into her couch, her rage simmering as she stared over the balcony of her club. Waitresses and bartenders were flitting around, getting ready for opening. Hustling through the back door and ripping off her purse in favor of an apron, Helena looked apologetically to her coworkers before looking up at the Throne Room. Her eyes filled with tears as she caught sight of Marisol and she clutched the apron to her chest, mouthing, "Thank you" and even dropping into a little bow. When she straightened, Marisol flicked one finger an inch off the back of the couch and slightly inclined her head. Helena beamed and Marisol favored her with the barest upturn of her lips before turning away and letting the darkness envelop her.

So, Mel had been allowed to return home. Last Marisol had heard she and the other women had been taken to a local hospital and treated before being questioned. Gray had sent someone over to check everything out. Analise hadn't been in the group. Neither had Isabella. She'd expected neighborhood anger over their loss, but this morning three mothers and a brother had shown up at Alhambra, begging to see Marisol. Gray had received their hugs and thanks since Marisol wasn't up to the show, but he'd told them all to come back tonight and she would move mountains to make sure they were acknowledged. After all this time hiding parts of her life, it was strange to be loved rather than feared.

Gray's phone buzzed and Marisol winced. The low rumble of his voice grated her nerves and she bit back an insult. She needed him to command authority with her people, which meant she couldn't humiliate him in public, no matter how much she wanted to.

"What the hell are you talking about?" Gray said into the phone, his voice rising in surprise.

He turned to look at Marisol. She kept her eyes purposefully averted. She didn't want conversation. Instead, she fixed her eyes on the staff below. They moved languidly, laughing and talking as they restocked glasses and bottles. They were relaxed. At ease. Their happiness made Marisol want to scream. It took all her energy to keep it contained.

When Marisol ignored his attempts to catch her eye, Gray gave up and came back into the Throne Room, standing close to Marisol with the phone still in his meaty hand. He didn't speak, just waited to be acknowledged like she'd taught him. His meekness pissed her off.

"What do you want?" she growled at him.

"Visitors at the back entrance."

When he didn't explain further, she spat her response. "Tell them to fuck off or kill them if they don't have any right to be here. Is this your first day on the job? Why are you bothering me with this, Gray?"

"I'm pretty sure you don't want to kill 'em," he said, twisting his neck with a look of annoyance. "It's Governor Sloane and an NSA agent."

Brin and Special Agent Graham, showing up at her place in broad daylight? She recalled Graham's arrogant smirk from the night before. Possibly the last person in the world she wanted to see right now. Except of course the woman who ensured Marisol couldn't even see her staff joke with each other without wanting to cry with loneliness.

"What do they want?" she asked through gritted teeth.

He blinked at her, staring blankly. Her friend and most trusted lieutenant rarely looked so stupid, even when sparring and she'd hit him a little too hard on the chin. Marisol almost laughed, despite her mood. Almost. Perhaps it was an unfair question. She'd never asked him to explain a visitor's reason for appearing at her door, preferring to get that information from the source.

"Uh...I'm not sure." He brandished the phone. "I can ask."

Marisol put her fingertips to the bridge of her nose and squeezed, trying to massage away the headache. "No, don't bother. Just get them in the building quickly before someone else sees them. And Gray? Keep an eye on the agent. That gun comes out of her holster you take it, but don't kill either of them. We don't need that kind of heat."

Rather than relaying the instructions through his phone, Gray gratefully descended the stairs at a gallop. It seemed he had finally read the room and wanted to avoid her tossing him off the balcony. His obvious discomfort made Marisol try to get a hold of herself. It wasn't Gray's fault she was in a sour mood, nor was it Special Agent Graham's, and it would be a catastrophically bad idea to lash out at the city's new hero because she was cranky. Satisfying, yes, but still a bad idea.

What about Brin though? Wasn't she entitled to lash out at the woman who had brought her so much ecstasy wrapped in so much misery? Not here. Not with Gray and Agent Graham and a half dozen busy employees who would wonder why Marisol was shouting at the Governor of Illinois, a woman they likely presumed she'd never met.

Her headache roared anew with thoughts of Brin. Marisol hadn't slept well. Between the bruised chest and the nightmares, she had barely closed her eyes before she was on her feet again, running from shadows. The shadows tortured her, as always.

In the last seven months Brin had tortured her far more. Last night—showing up when Marisol was set to revenge them both—that was the worst blow. She had been forced, yet again, to save Brin's life at the expense of what she wanted. Before Brin, Marisol would never have taken bullets for a woman who would not even look her in the eye.

Brin was her torturer and she would use this opportunity to rid herself of that pain once and for all.

CHAPTER THIRTY-THREE

The man who showed them up the dark, winding staircase was approximately the size and solidity of a brick row house. Sloane watched how he bounced on every stair and marveled at how quickly a man that size could move. There was something in his eyes that made Sloane trust him instantly. It was so like the way Marisol's eyes held vast anger close to the surface yet vast kindness hidden below. Sloane wondered if Marisol and this man had found both the anger and the kindness together.

At the first landing, the mountain of muscles turned on Tyler, crowding her to show off his advantage of height and size. He glowered down and said, "My boss said not to kill you unless you cause trouble. So please," he growled. "Cause as much trouble as you like."

Tyler laughed, but it didn't take the air out of the man. "My boss," she said, hooking a thumb at Sloane. "Told me not to cause trouble unless you do. I don't usually dance with men, but I'll make an exception for you if you push me."

They glared at each other for an uncomfortably long moment, but Sloane noticed both relax a fraction at the warning. These were people used to confrontation, Sloane reminded herself as the man finally turned back to the stairs. They liked being challenged.

"I'm asking you again," Tyler whispered in her ear as they climbed. "Reconsider this. It's stupid and foolhardy. Walking into Soltero's den is asking to be killed."

Sloane smiled, looking forward to the day when Tyler and Marisol would trust and maybe even like each other. She doubted it would be today, but it was a start.

"She won't hurt me."

Tyler shook her head rather than responding verbally. They'd had the argument so many times it was impossible to do it again. More to the point, they didn't have the time. Arriving at an ornate door, the man checked in with a pair of guards waiting outside. Sloane's jaw clenched as she saw their assault weapons. They were illegal in Chicago and yet Marisol's people carried them openly, even when the Governor of Illinois was in the building. Obviously, she was challenging Sloane with this blatant transgression, but honestly Sloane didn't care. After last night thinking she'd held Marisol's corpse, she would let this woman do anything as long as she stayed alive.

The door opened, but instead of ushering them through, the bodyguard turned and crowded Tyler's space again. "Your gun stays in the holster or we dance, cop. Got it?"

"That's agent."

"A cop's a cop, don't matter how fancy the suit."

Tyler smoothed her lapel and gave him another long look. Clearly his suit was fancier than hers, but she filled hers better. "And you're a poet, too," she said disdainfully.

He took another step into her space, one hand curling into a fist. Sloane prepared for the fight, but a shout from the room beyond stopped him like a brick wall. "Let our guests in, Gray."

That voice. Liquid smooth and decadent as chocolate pie. The voice had Sloane's knees quivering. She didn't feel the floor beneath her spiked heels as they marched in. Her eyes swept the room, searching for the lips that formed those words.

With her back to the door, Marisol sat on a gaudy couch with leather the color of freshly spilled blood. All Sloane could see was the sweep of her hair, the short waves just brushing the back of the couch. From experience, Sloane knew there was a spray of close-cropped hair beneath the wave. The hairs had tickled her palms as she swept her hands through it seven months before. Her arms, straining at the sleeves of her leather jacket, spread casually wide, showing off her full wingspan. No doubt a T-shirt was pulled tightly across her chest.

They had to stand against the balcony railing because Marisol's couch was pushed so far forward. She had the perfect view down onto the dance floor where her adoring masses would soon gather. For now, she was draped across her couch, ever the warlord watching over her domain. Sloane wanted to roll her eyes, but they were too busy taking in every inch of this woman, from the scuffed toes of her motorcycle boots to the dark hair falling across one eye. Sloane let a smile creep across her lips as her eyes touched Marisol's.

Marisol looked away, making Sloane's stomach drop, and she turned her full attention to Tyler. "Congratulations on your single-handed victory last night, Special Agent Graham. I hear it was quite the shootout."

Tyler stiffened and her cheeks blazed red. "Is that why you let us in here? To gloat?"

Marisol smiled and something inside Sloane's chest exploded. "I let you in here because it would not benefit me to kill you." She flicked her eyes over at Gray, who flexed his biceps inside the already straining fabric of his blazer. "Yet."

"I'm not interested in your threats, Soltero."

It was time for Sloane to interject before these three started a pissing contest. "Tyler, please."

"And you, Governor…" The venom Marisol attached to her title made Sloane's jaw snap shut. "Is your visit here part of an ill-conceived reelection strategy or are you just stupid?"

Cover or not, Sloane was becoming seriously upset by how this conversation was going. "Marisol…"

Leaping to her feet, Marisol stood with feet shoulder-width apart and laughed. Her lungs seemed to be bursting with it. She threw her head back and roared her laughter to the ceiling. Sloane thought at first that the laughter was directed at her, that Marisol was reacting to the way Sloane gasped and lurched toward that lithe body, that she was laughing at the way Sloane's world crumbled at the thought Marisol may be rejecting her.

The laughter, she soon realized, was not directed at her. It was directed at Tyler, who had crouched when Marisol moved so unexpectedly. Her hand had flown toward her shoulder holster, but the bodyguard's hand flew faster, catching her wrist in midair and holding it there as though Tyler was not straining to release herself. Marisol laughed and he smiled and Tyler shouted insults.

"Calm down, Special Agent Graham," Marisol said, striding around the back of the couch toward the bar in the corner. "I just want a drink."

"Damnit, Soltero! Tell your goon to let me go!"

Marisol ignored her and popped the top on a twisted, globe-shaped bottle of amber liquid. She tossed the stopper to the floor as though she intended to drink the entire bottle. Then she poured herself far more than anyone should drink at once and tossed it down her throat. Sloane's eyebrow raised. She couldn't drink that much in an hour and stand upright, but Marisol was apparently sturdier than her. Marisol poured herself a far more reasonable serving and splashed a miniscule amount into another glass.

Bringing both glasses back to her couch, she looked at Gray, who released Tyler and stepped back. Marisol held out the smaller glass to Tyler, holding eye contact for long enough to enforce the challenge. Tyler gave in, abandoning their staring contest with a huff and snatching the glass. Marisol slid back onto the couch and crossed an ankle over her knee.

"Don't misunderstand this visit, Soltero," Tyler growled. "The only reason I let Sabrina come here is because you saved her life last night. But you're on a tight leash, understand?"

Marisol shook her head and smiled at her knee. "I'm no one's dog, Graham. Get that straight. But you saved my ass last night, which is why I let you walk in here. I'll even let you leave unscathed. This one time."

Marisol held out her glass in a toast for long enough that Sloane thought Tyler would ignore the olive branch. Eventually she lifted her own and took a long sip. Marisol followed suit, her self-satisfied smile disappearing behind the tumbler.

"Not bad, Soltero. Tastes like something I had in Puerto Vallarta once."

"You know your tequila," Marisol replied, clearly impressed. "I get it flown in on a special plane once a month. A nice little old lady named Lucia sets aside a few bottles from every batch just for me."

"Did you just admit to smuggling in front of me?" Sloane asked, incredulous.

The two of them turned to look at her, for all the world like they'd forgotten she was there. Tyler's cheeks flushed and she rubbed the back of her neck, hiding her empty glass behind her back. Marisol, on the other hand, showed no remorse. In fact, Sloane thought as the full weight of Marisol's penetrating stare landed on her, she looked very much like a woman who had found her groove again.

"To what do I owe the honor of your presence today, Governor Sloane?" Marisol said through a smile that showed every one of her gleaming teeth.

Sloane had recognized the predatory nature of her smile before, but she had never looked so much like a hungry wolf as she did in that moment. To the casual observer, she was being polite, even respectful. Sloane was not a casual observer. She saw the anger in that smile. Heard the warning in the way she spoke Sloane's title. Rage was emanating from her in waves.

Sloane allowed her eyes to flicker to Tyler and Gray before returning to Marisol. She took a step forward, hiding the wobble in her knees as best she could, and extended a hand. "On behalf of the people of Illinois, I'd like to thank you for your actions last night. You saved many lives. Even though your presence at the warehouse will not be acknowledged, I felt compelled to thank you for your bravery."

She didn't mention the fact that she too owed her life, yet again, to Marisol's bravery. She didn't think any other attentive ears needed to hear more. Marisol's life would be in danger if her people knew she was an undercover government agent.

After a long silence that was anything but respectful, Marisol tipped her glass back, swallowing its contents before turning her attention back to Sloane. "You and the people of Illinois can take your thanks and shove it up your pretty little ass." Tyler stiffened at the remark and Sloane felt heat on her own cheeks as Marisol continued, pacing, "No one in Springfield, or even the Mayor's Office for that matter, gives a shit about Humboldt. I didn't do anything for Illinois. I saved my own people because no one else was willing to."

"You forget we were there last night, too, Soltero," Tyler barked.

When it was clear Marisol had no intention of shaking her hand, Sloane dropped it without embarrassment and turned to Tyler. "May I speak with Marisol alone for a moment?"

Tyler's jaw dropped, but she clearly didn't choose to have an argument in front of the two criminals. "I would advise against that."

"I'm quite certain I'll be safe with her," Sloane replied, her impatience showing in her forced smile.

"It's not only her I'm worried about," Tyler replied, giving Gray an angry stare. He returned it in kind.

"Please, Tyler."

She grumbled, nodded and walked all of two feet away, standing on the top stair heading down into the club. When Gray didn't follow, Sloane gave him a radiant, if pointed smile. He glowered in return.

Marisol laughed and slapped him on the shoulder, making him wilt just a little. "It's okay, Gray. I think I can handle her alone." She jerked her chin in Tyler's direction. "Keep an eye on the riffraff, would you?"

He gave her a crisp, almost military nod and went to stand next to Tyler, positioning his massive body to block her view of the two women. They were well within earshot and Sloane wanted more privacy. She gave Marisol a significant look before crossing the room to stand by the bar. She thought Marisol had no intention of following her and she wasn't sure what she'd do to convince her. Eventually she heard Marisol's boots on the hardwood and breathed a sigh of relief.

Sloane took a deep breath, trying to calm herself before turning to face Marisol. She had hoped Marisol might soften without the presence of the others. She didn't know exactly what she had been expecting to see when she turned around. An acknowledgement of what they'd shared? A glimmer of affection? Perhaps even anger at the silence and separation of the last months. There was nothing. Marisol was stone. Sloane would have preferred the anger.

"I heard one of the women rescued last night worked for..."

Marisol's hand whipped out and closed like a vise around Sloane's upper arm, just below her armpit. Her arm screamed under Marisol's punishing grip. A gasp burst through her lips as Marisol yanked hard, pulling Sloane off balance until she crashed against Marisol's chest. On instinct she tried to pull away and right herself, but Marisol yanked again, harder this time as Sloane's body pressed against hers.

Shouting through gritted teeth, Marisol's words came out as a hiss. "What the fuck are you doing here? Are you trying to get me killed?"

Several things happened at once, but Sloane was aware of none of them. All she was aware of was Marisol's eyes and the fear filling them. The rest of it happened outside her world. In a world where sound was muffled and movements were slow. By the time the shout from across the balcony registered, it was already fading away. A flurry of movement in the corner of her eye eventually resolved itself into Tyler struggling against Gray's grip.

"Marisol." Sloane's voice sounded strangely weak in her own ears.

"Let her go!" Tyler shouted.

Looking over at Tyler, Sloane saw her reaching for her weapon. If she managed to draw it, nothing good would happen on this balcony.

"Marisol, please," Sloane said, injecting calm into her voice though her heart thundered. "You're hurting me."

The words seemed to snap Marisol out of the moment. Her grip instantly relaxed and her eyes slid back into focus. She blinked and looked around, noticing the nearby tussle. With a look from Marisol, Gray transferred his grip to Tyler's wrist, stopping its progression to her gun.

"Please, Tyler," Sloane said, her voice still steady. "Everything's fine."

"Everything is *not* fine, Sabrina."

Sloane turned her attention back to Marisol, who was staring at her own hand on Sloane's arm with something akin to horror. Sloane put a hand on her shoulder and Marisol looked into her eyes. Those eyes. The ones that had been so angry were now flooded with pain. With disgust. All that hurt Sloane had been certain Marisol would direct at her were now firmly focused inward.

"I appreciate your concern," Sloane replied, her eyes fixed on Marisol's. "Marisol, perhaps there is a private location where we can speak? Do you have an office or…?"

"Sabrina!" Tyler shouted, ripping her arm free of Gray and preparing to march them back to the street. She made it clear with one glance that she would not accept further discussion.

Marisol was chewing on her bottom lip like she didn't trust herself to speak. She made a sheepish gesture at a staircase discreetly located in the corner behind a wooden screen. While Sloane ascended the steps, Marisol gave a quick set of instructions to Gray, who waited outside the door with a stricken-looking Tyler. Marisol entered a code into the door and gestured for Sloane to enter first.

Crossing the room, Sloane noted the much more comfortable couch and the glass desktop. She expected Marisol to sit behind the desk or maybe to lounge on the couch with the same casual arrogance she'd displayed downstairs, but she did neither. She stood just inside the door, her hands shoved into the shallow pockets of her pants. Sloane wanted to be near her, so she crossed the room, but lost her nerve when Marisol looked at her with those wounded eyes again. She hovered anxiously near the corner of Marisol's desk, fiddling with a sticky note attached to the corner of her computer monitor.

"Why are you doing this to me, Brin?"

Tears welled Sloane's eyes. The name she hadn't heard outside her fantasies for so long brought back all the loneliness of the last months.

"No!" Marisol shouted so loudly it made Sloane jump. "No, *you* don't get to cry! *You* don't get to leave me alone, not knowing if you were alive or dead, not knowing what was happening for weeks, only to show up on the news like some goddamn celebrity on vacation. You don't get to stay away for months and then appear out of the blue and nearly die. And you sure as shit don't get to stroll in here like nothing fucking happened."

Tears fell even though Sloane wanted them to stop. They fell in buckets and rivers and oceans. "I…"

Marisol moved forward, her shoulders rounded forward and predatory again, her muscles rippling. "You told me you loved me. You promised to meet me here in Chicago. What happened? Get cold feet? Decided your precious reputation wasn't worth being thrown away on scum like me? What do you have to cry about?"

Sloane sobbed. Her shoulders shook. She had not allowed herself to cry since she arrived in the embassy back in Colombia. She had seen terrible things, been through so much, but she had held it all inside. Now it escaped her just when she was desperate to keep it in and she was powerless to stop it.

"I…"

"Fucking say something already!"

CHAPTER THIRTY-FOUR

"I've missed you so much it's felt like I'm dying every single day."

As far as opening lines went, it was a hell of a good one. The fight dropped out of Marisol's body, leaving her feeling light-headed. She let her shoulders slump and mumbled, "Then why didn't you come to me?"

"I couldn't," Brin said. Her tears had finally stopped, but they left her eyes shimmering. "I would've put you in danger."

"I'm in danger every day, Brin. The only thing you did by staying away was leave me to deal with it alone."

"That's not…" She stopped and shook her head. There was a note of determination in her voice when she said, "You came to me one night and look what happened. Those men tried to kill you."

"That didn't have anything to do with me coming to see you," Marisol replied, though without conviction. It was very possible the men who jumped her had followed her that night.

Brin's watery smile showed she was no more convinced than Marisol. She took a few cautious steps forward, closing the distance between them and making it harder for Marisol to breathe.

"Marisol," she whispered, lifting a hand to cup Marisol's cheek. "I would do anything to keep you safe."

She took a deep breath. It rattled in her throat and she closed her eyes, pressing her cheek into Brin's hand. "Then stay."

"Yes."

Marisol wrenched her eyes open. "Really?"

"Really." She reached up with the other hand, cradling Marisol's other cheek. "I'm not strong enough to stay away any longer."

"Even though he's still alive?"

"Even though he's still alive."

"Why now and not before?"

Brin pushed up onto her toes and brushed her lips against Marisol's. "Because the last seven months and eight days have taught me that the safest place for us is at each other's side. Don't you agree?"

She didn't give Marisol a chance to answer. Their lips brushed. The press of them against hers as Brin leaned in to deepen the kiss made her knees weak. Then Marisol's body moved on instinct, unconsciously. She pulled Brin's body against hers, their soft curves melting together. Brin's hands left her cheeks and raked through her hair. Marisol pulled her tighter, lifting Brin's feet off the floor.

"Couch?" Brin panted, wrapping her legs around Marisol's waist.

"Too far," Marisol growled.

Sweeping an arm across her desk, Marisol cleared enough space to set Brin down. The moment she was settled, Brin tore clothing from both of their bodies. Marisol's hands moved more methodically, pressing back the hem of Brin's skirt until it bunched around her hips.

"Marisol," she whimpered as she struggled to free the button of her tight leather pants. "Please. I need you."

"Not nearly as much as I need you."

Marisol leaned into Brin's neck, inhaling the scent of her perfume, her shampoo, and her skin. A pen cup tumbled off the desk, spilling onto the floor beside them. She slid her hands up Marisol's back, clawing at the bare skin under her shirt. It took everything in Marisol to pull away far enough to rejoin their frantic kiss. All the times she'd dreamed of having Brin in her arms again, it had never felt like this. Solid and warm in a world that had become empty since Colombia.

As their kisses became more frantic, Brin grabbed hold of Marisol's shoulders and pulled herself off the desk. Marisol slipped Brin's panties off, yanking them as far off as she could without freeing herself from the circle of Brin's arms and legs. She should have been gentler as she settled her back on the desk, but they were both well past caring. Brin gasped as her bare skin landed on the glass desktop, but she didn't let the cold slow her down. She snatched Marisol's hand from the desk and guided it between her legs.

Marisol's eyes fluttered shut as she settled into Brin's liquid heat. Her moans began the moment Marisol touched her. As Marisol moved at a punishing pace, Brin released her shoulders and leaned back, propping herself up on wrist and elbow. Her eyelids squeezed closed. She clutched at Marisol with her ankles.

As much as Marisol wanted to continue kissing her beloved, she was mesmerized by the sight of her ecstasy. Brin began to pant, the force of Marisol's lovemaking pushing her farther back onto the desk. She threw her arm back and Marisol's computer monitor smashed into the far corner of the desk, tumbling to the ground with a series of tremendous bangs.

Marisol was only vaguely aware of the destroyed monitor coming to a rest on the office floor. As it fell, Brin tipped her head back and screamed. While she'd always been vocal in their lovemaking, it had never been like this. Wild abandon and primal release. Her scream was half pleasure, half pain, but when Marisol would have stopped her movements, Brin reached down, holding her inside and active.

The scream died as the office door burst open. In her peripheral vision, she saw Tyler drop to one knee, her service weapon extended and a bright red blush creeping up her cheeks. Gray was just behind her, looking even more confused and equally lethal. Marisol ignored them both. A goddess was spread out before her, a slight sheen of sweat dotting the skin on her chest and neck. Marisol leaned down, kissing her throbbing pulse point, secure in Brin's blood pounding against her lips.

Brin's scream faded away in the stale air and Marisol looked up into the sparkling sapphire eyes in front of her. Over her shoulder, Marisol could just make out the remains of her computer monitor on the floor.

Brin raised a hand and traced the firm line of Marisol's jaw, letting one finger linger on her lips. "I love you, Marisol."

Marisol choked out a quiet sob and leaned forward, sure she might fall down. Brin caught her face and pressed their foreheads together, whispering words that made a smile like the sun breaking through the clouds split Marisol's face. All the words she'd wanted to hear floated between them in the air.

Once she'd looked her fill into Brin's eyes, Marisol turned her head to stare directly into Tyler's.

"Enjoy the show?" she sneered. "Gray would you get her the hell out of my office?"

CHAPTER THIRTY-FIVE

Sloane stood perfectly still under the shower, allowing the jet of hot water to sting her face and slide down her body. Tension released from her muscles and joints. The heat and dust of the day sloughed off her. A smile crept across her face, allowing a trickle of water past her lips. Thinking of the day made her think of Marisol and thinking of Marisol made her body dance with happiness.

She had wanted nothing more than to throw herself at Marisol's feet and be forgiven. Forgiven her weakness and her absence and her silence. She had never in a million years dreamt it would happen. Sloane had anticipated that Marisol's wounded pride would be difficult to overcome. Better her pride was wounded than her body, Sloane had convinced herself, but she knew it might spell the end of everything she wanted.

But she had been forgiven. Marisol had welcomed her back into her arms and her heart. Sloane wondered idly if she was dreaming. If she would open her eyes expecting to be pummeled by the dual showerheads in her Gold Coast penthouse only to wake up back in that ostentatious bed in the Governor's Mansion. Still alone. Danger still lurking. She dropped her head and opened her eyes.

Her wide feet with short, stubby toes stood on the familiar subway tile. Water swirled around the metal grate of the drain, making a hollow gurgle as it flowed through the pipes. She was really here. It had really happened.

Sloane shut off the water and toweled dry, grabbing fistfuls of her sodden hair in the sage-green towel. She used it to wipe fog from the mirror in one long, broad stripe. The face looking back at hers was almost a stranger's. She had avoided mirrors since South America. Even when doing her makeup she wouldn't look herself in the eye. If she looked too deeply into those eyes, she might see a traitor and a fool. A cruel, heartless being who had let a woman be tortured for her but couldn't pick up a phone and call. Couldn't share her plans. Couldn't treat her with the trust and respect she'd deserved.

And yet Marisol had not called her a traitor or a fool. She had wrapped Sloane in her arms and kissed her and told her that her heart and her body would be Sloane's until they were both dust. There were more words that needed to be said. More confessions and more apologies. But Sloane had no more power to resist Marisol's kiss than Marisol had to resist Sloane's body.

Slipping into her silk robe and still dabbing her wet hair, Sloane left the steamy confines of her bathroom for the welcome chill of her bedroom. Apart from the short stay here earlier this month, she had not spent much time in this apartment. That would change now. She would reclaim her home from the terrible memories of death outside the door and the forced absence of the last months. Thoughts of who would share this bed with her when she visited made her skin hum.

Grabbing the lotion from her bedside table, she noticed a notification on her phone. Two missed calls. Two voice mails. While she spread lotion on her skin, she listened to them. The first call had come in five minutes earlier. It was an unfamiliar number and the message consisted of two words. *I'm coming.* Growled in familiar tones that made Sloane shiver with anticipation. Marisol would be with her soon. She hurried to prepare and checked the other message. She groaned at the familiar number with the Washington DC area code.

"Sabrina." Tyler's voice echoed in the large room, sounding robotic as it barked through the speaker. "We need to talk. I'll be waiting downstairs for your call."

Tyler's anger was warranted—she understood its origins. Had their circumstance been reversed, Sloane would have been equally concerned. If she got this over with now, she would have all night with Marisol.

The speed with which Tyler arrived at her door made it clear she hadn't been waiting downstairs, but rather in the hallway. Tyler's scowl was so deep it seemed to resonate along the lines of her scar. She started speaking the moment the door closed, not waiting for Sloane to offer her a beverage or even a seat.

"I suppose I know now why you constantly deflected the investigation from Soltero."

Sloane couldn't help but laugh at the barely restrained resentment in Tyler's speech. "Marisol was innocent. Surely you can admit that now?"

"You've been lying to me from the moment I met you." Tyler caught herself and sighed, pushing her fists deep into her pockets and speaking to the floor. "I hope you understand I'm coming to you as a friend. I have your best interests at heart."

"I appreciate your friendship," Sloane replied. "I sincerely do, but your concern is unwarranted."

"You don't know what you're getting yourself into," Tyler said, taking a few hesitant steps into the room. "I know lots of people are attracted to the 'bad boy' type, and Marisol fits that mold. But the bad boy is always the one that hurts you. How well do you even know Marisol Soltero? If you knew some of the things she's done…"

Sloane smiled indulgently. Rather than be offended by the implication that she was naïve, she found it rather charming coming from this woman. "I know many of the things she's done. I'm not blind to the fact that her life has been…unconventional.

Outside the lines of the law to be sure. But then so has yours. How much of last night was sanctioned?"

"That's completely different."

"Is it?" Sloane held up a hand to stop Tyler's argument. "I'm only saying that sometimes we have to operate outside the lines so that the lines stay intact."

"Marisol's not an agent, she's a criminal." It took everything in Sloane not to laugh, she pressed her fingertips to her lips to hold it in, but Tyler clearly misunderstood the gesture. She stepped forward, hands outstretched with palms up. "I'm not saying she's all bad. Last night proved that she has good instincts deep down. *Very* deep down. But her life is, as you say, unconventional. You have a pure spirit, Sabrina. I'd hate to see you corrupted by that."

"I'm not a child, Tyler."

"Neither is she. She's done things. Things you don't want to know about."

A muzzle flashed in her memory and light that had been in her kidnapper's eyes went out. Sloane shook her head to clear the image. "Maybe *I've* done things *you* don't want to know about."

If Tyler knew that she'd killed an unarmed woman, would she feel the same way? Even if it was a bad person, Sloane had killed her.

"I flatter myself that I know Marisol very well." Tyler opened her mouth to respond, but Sloane stopped her with an upraised hand.

"You are standing right on a line. Have a care where you put your foot next. It may be over the line or even in your mouth."

The words stopped Tyler in her tracks. She dropped her hands and squinted at Sloane across the room. "What happened today, Sabrina?"

Even with Tyler's role in the agency, it wasn't Sloane's place to reveal Marisol's. "Surely you're old enough to know what you saw?" she teased, feeling the ghost of Marisol's touch on her and shivering with anticipation for it again.

"This is not the time for jokes, Sabrina. You owe me an explanation."

She wasn't wrong, but what could Sloane say? *Sorry I've lied to you about almost everything for the last few months, but I was just trying to win the girl. You get that, right?* Whether or not she did get it, Sloane owed her more. Fortunately, she was saved further explanation by a knock at the door.

Marisol didn't wait for an answer, opening the door and marching in, her eyes fixed on Sloane. She felt those eyes wrap around her. Engulf her. Pull her down and up at the same time. Sloane was powerless under that gaze. It reduced her to nothing and made her more than she was all at once.

Marisol had changed from the leather pants to a pair of skintight jeans riding low on her hips, and her T-shirt showed several inches of her midriff. A few lines of defined muscle bracketed her navel. Her jacket was not as bulky as her usual, but no doubt sported her gang logo on the back. Her eyes travelled appreciatively from Sloane's face down the length of her body, lingering on the small gaps in the silk dressing gown that hinted at how little was underneath.

Marisol pulled Sloane into the circle of her arms. Sloane melted willingly into that touch, allowing the length of her body to press against the steel wall of Marisol's form. Without hesitation, Marisol pulled her in for a kiss so hard it bent Sloane back. She returned the kiss with equal passion, forgetting their audience. When this woman held her, the rest of the world didn't matter.

Marisol's hand crept down the back of her robe toward the swell of her ass, but Sloane heard a sharp and impatient cough from over her shoulder. She pulled back from the kiss reluctantly, sucking gently on Marisol's tongue as she released her lips.

Marisol said over her shoulder, "Hello, Agent Graham. You certainly have a knack for being where you aren't wanted. Get out."

"Charming as always, Soltero."

"Don't be rude, Marisol," Sloane said, pressing her body harder against Marisol's, making sure that their hips rubbed together in a way sure to distract her lover. When Marisol's eyes slipped out of focus, Sloane looked past her and gave Tyler her most winning smile. "Do you think we could continue this conversation another time?"

"What?"

Marisol whipped her head around. "Leave. We have our own plans for this evening."

"How did you get past the State Police?"

Marisol laughed. "Wouldn't you like to know?"

Tyler looked past Marisol to make eye contact with Sloane. "If you need anything…"

"I'll give her everything she needs," Marisol spat back.

Sloane saw the color rising in Tyler's cheeks and didn't know if it was from anger or embarrassment, but it seemed a good time to step in. She pulled away from Marisol and put herself between them. "Please, Tyler, if you'll excuse us. Marisol and I have a lot to discuss and it's somewhat sensitive. I promise you and I will talk soon."

Whether or not she was appeased, Tyler seemed aware she was fighting a losing battle. She gave a little nod, slamming the front door on her way out. Marisol's hands snaked around Sloane's waist, pulling her back in.

"Are you really going to talk this time, or are you going to seduce me again?"

"I think you seduced me," Sloane said, wrapping her arms around Marisol's neck.

"Either way," Marisol said, letting her words fade away as her lips dropped to Sloane's collarbone.

Sloane's body ignited at the spot where Marisol's lips touched. They moved to her neck, trailing along her skin and leaving a wake of electricity. She pressed kisses up Sloane's neck slowly, first an inch above the slope of her shoulder, then just above the spot where her soft flesh fluttered as her jugular pounded beneath. The third kiss, just below the soft curve of her jaw, had Sloane gasping.

"You were very rude to Tyler," she said before words failed her.

"I don't care about that idiot cop."

"Should I be concerned about your ability to slip past my guards whenever you want?"

"Trust me," Marisol murmured against her skin. "You are going to very much appreciate my ability to slip in whenever you want me."

Marisol's lips danced across her cheek. Sloane's eyes fluttered shut and she smiled as she breathed, "Well, you did tell me once that you're a selfish, hedonistic criminal."

"You have no idea how hedonistic I can be," Marisol whispered into her ear as her teeth wrapped around Sabrina's earlobe and her hand slipped the tie of her robe free.

As she bit down, the fabric fell open, exposing Sloane's overheated body to the cool air. Gooseflesh erupted on her skin, both from the bite and the air-conditioning. She groaned, gripping fistfuls of Marisol's jacket as she clung to her shoulders.

"I suppose you'll have to show me then," Sloane whispered as Marisol reversed the line of kisses, trailing back down her neck.

Marisol grinned against the soft flesh of her neck, sliding the silk robe back to expose her shoulder. Sloane closed her eyes, trapping the sensations close, giving her something to hold on to while her body wanted to float away. She focused on the warm, wet press of Marisol's lips. On the smell of her like leather and sandalwood. On the sound of her own heartbeat, pounding in her ears.

"Brin!" Marisol shouted, ripping Sloane from her daze.

When she opened her eyes, it was to find Marisol staring in horror at her bicep, now exposed to the light of the setting sun after the robe fell away. Just below her armpit was a cluster of purple splotches. They were red and lavender, but by morning they would be as dark as Marisol's jacket.

"Your arm," Marisol said, her voice croaking and tears pooling in her eyes. "I didn't realize I grabbed you so hard. Brin, I'm so sorry. Please forgive me!"

The last came out almost as a shout. A begging, desperate sound. The distress in her voice and the tears in those eyes that had withstood torture without showing emotion shocked Sloane. She had noted the bruises before her shower, and she had intended mention them when they were alone, but the way Marisol looked at her and kissed her drove everything else from her mind. Marisol stared at the ugly bruising and Sloane stood still, letting her look her fill before responding.

"I will forgive you exactly one time," she said, keeping her voice steady and controlled. "There were…circumstances. Understand, Marisol, I will not forgive you if it ever happens again."

"It won't."

"If it does, I'll leave." She waited long enough for Marisol to look up at her, holding her eyes before saying, "No matter how much I love you, I will not allow you to hurt me."

"I swear on my life, I'll never hurt you again."

"I promise you the same thing. There are no marks on your skin, but I know I hurt you far more deeply. I made a mistake and it hurt you and I'm sorry." Sloane moved forward, slipping her arms around Marisol's neck and pulling her down into a kiss. It wasn't a chaste kiss or even a gentle one. She sucked Marisol's bottom lip into her mouth and gave it the lightest bite before fisting her hand in Marisol's hair and kissing her with every ounce of passion she'd stored for months on end. She pulled away slowly, her tongue flicking lightly at Marisol's teeth. "Now…I believe we started something in your office."

Marisol's eyes had slid out of focus, dancing over Sloane's body with a hunger that made her skin burn. Grabbing Marisol by the belt, she walked slowly backward, steering them toward the couch. Marisol allowed herself to be led, the wolf smile slowly curling on her lips.

Her eyes cleared just as Sloane's legs hit the couch. She started to lie down, intending to pull Marisol on top of her and not rise for at least a day, but Marisol stopped, drawing her back to her feet. When she spoke, there was regret in her voice, but also resolve. "As much as I want this, Brin, and I want it very, very badly…"

Her words trailed off as Sloane pressed her fingers up the hard plane of her abdomen, slipping underneath the fabric of her shirt. Marisol's eyes fluttered shut and her smile grew, but they shot back open almost immediately.

"Brin," she said, taking Sloane's hands in hers. "I think we should talk."

"We tried that in your office." Sloane grinned. "We didn't get very far."

Marisol moaned her assent and for a moment Sloane thought she might relent, but then her face fell and her eyes swam with all the confusion and pain that Sloane had seen in them last night.

"Please, Brin. I need to know what happened." She swallowed hard and looked at their clasped hands. "You promised you'd meet me here and then you ignore me like…Like I'm trash. I think I deserve an explanation."

It was the pain and sadness in that statement that finally made Sloane pull the ends of her robe together and sit down on the couch, Marisol beside her, and tell her story.

CHAPTER THIRTY-SIX

"You saw how much danger you put her in when she loved you from afar. Imagine how much that's compounded now this man knows you feel the same way."

Marisol's face went numb and her ears rang. "What?"

Brin swallowed hard and looked down at her lap. "That's what he said to me."

"Who?"

Her eyes shone when she looked up at Marisol. "The man at the Embassy."

Brin fell easily into the story, obviously she'd been anxious to tell it. Maybe she'd even practiced it once or twice. God knew Marisol had obsessed over what they'd say if they ever saw each other again. At least Brin seemed to have felt the same.

The story started off simply enough. Arriving at the US Embassy in Bogota. Telling the story of the attack and the kidnapping.

"That's when things got weird," Brin said, leaning back into the arm of the couch.

The hair on the back of Marisol's neck stood up. "What do you mean 'got weird'?"

"Ambassador Perry left suddenly and someone else came in," Brin explained. "It was a man I'd never seen before. He walked right in, locked the door behind him, and disabled some listening devices. Then he sat down on the edge of the desk like he owned the place."

It sounded all too familiar to Marisol. She closed her eyes and asked, "What did he look like?"

"African-American. Tall. Slim build. Perfectly tailored suit. Shaved head. Gray eyes. Thin beard with no mustache."

The facial hair was different and the man who'd walked into Marisol's prison cell sixteen years ago had hair, but it had been receding even then.

"Did he show you a badge?"

Brin nodded. "NSA. He introduced himself as Anderson, but he held the badge so his name was obscured. I didn't realize that until later."

"What else did he say?"

"He told me that we had a mutual friend who was in danger."

Of course. Brin wasn't the sort of woman who could be manipulated so easily. Not like Marisol had been back then. Just a kid in her twenties without anyone who had ever loved her. It took a little more persuading with the governor. A bittersweet smile crept onto Marisol's face as she pictured the scene Brin described. How she refused to roll over. If only she'd been strong enough to fight for herself like Brin. Then she wouldn't be stuck in this miserable double life.

Marisol's smile vanished when Brin told her about the video.

"He turned the computer monitor around to face us," Brin said. She frowned at the memory and pulled one knee up to her chest. "Then he started up the video from a flash drive he took from his pocket."

"What was on the video?"

The haunted look in Brin's eyes was enough to tell the story, but she explained anyway. Explaining how she'd had to watch Marisol's torture. Her hand was shaking on the back of the couch, and Marisol reached out, caressing Brin's palm with her thumb until it went still. "It's okay, Brin. I'm okay. I'm here."

She looked up at Marisol, her eyes sparkling with tears. "Say it again."

"Which part?"

"All of it."

Marisol scooted closer, covering Brin's hand with hers. She whispered, "It's okay, Brin. I'm okay. I'm here. I love you."

The sparkle stayed, but there was a different quality to it now. The shine of happiness. She leaned forward and cupped Marisol's face, pressing their foreheads together. Brin released the knee she'd been clutching and draped it across Marisol's lap. Marisol wondered if Brin had to watch herself kill their kidnapper.

Marisol remembered with intense clarity the first time she'd killed someone. She'd been thirteen and a man had thought she was nothing more than a little girl to do with as he pleased. He had discovered that he'd poked a sleeping tiger. Just like Brin, Marisol had killed out of self-defense, but that didn't change the fact that she'd killed.

That death had finally proven to Marisol that she was not helpless. She was not a perpetual victim. She had the strength and the will to defend herself when the world wouldn't take care of that for her. That was not how it would affect Brin. Was perhaps already affecting her. Brin had not known desperation all her life. Marisol would need to watch closely for the moment the break came in Brin. She would need someone who understood and Marisol may be the only person in her life who could.

But Marisol didn't press her. She simply shared the space and waited to see if Brin needed her. When it was clear she didn't, Marisol rubbed her thumb against Brin's knee in her lap and listened.

"After the video ended, he removed it from the computer, put it on the floor and dropped his heel on it until it cracked and sent little electronic bits flying. Then he took something from his pocket about the size of a bar of soap and ran it across the monitor and the computer. Both sparked and went dead.

"He told me that was the only copy of the video and now it doesn't exist. Nothing that happened in that shack exists."

"He got rid of everything?"

"That's what he said." Brin shrugged. "He said 'I watched this twice and you watched it once and now we share something.'"

Marisol's throat tightened. If that man had something over Brin—something with which to threaten her—Marisol didn't care that he was one of the good guys, she'd hunt him down and kill him. She soothed her anger by watching the path of her hand caressing Brin's thigh.

"That's when he said the thing. That it was my fault that you…I don't like threats," Brin said, her voice hardening like Marisol's body had. "I asked him what exactly we shared."

"What was his answer?"

It took Brin a long time to answer. So long that Marisol looked up to see Brin looking at her, trying to catch her eye. When they locked on her, Brin said, "He said I'm now one of three people in the world that know Marisol Soltero is a hero. I'm one of three people in the world who know she's rescuing women The Bishop is enslaving and he would do anything to kill her because of it."

The air around her rattled as Marisol took a low, long breath. Part of her had accepted that she was a marginally good person. Part of her had known for a while that she wasn't the piece of garbage she had once been. But to hear a woman like Sabrina Sloane call her a hero made something shift inside her soul. She knew that, from this moment on, she would do anything and everything she had to do to make Brin call her a hero again.

"He asked me if I was willing to do anything to keep you alive," Brin whispered. "And I told him I was. Anything. Everything. Even if it killed me."

They moved together with the simple need to touch. To kiss. Their bodies were magnets. Their lips met gently. Reverently. Marisol held Brin's face as their lips danced across each other without hunger. With purest, simplest love. Time stopped and sped up and ended as they explored each other's mouths. They parted by mutual, silent consent, both knowing that the story must be completed or there would never be understanding between them.

"He'd already set up the story about my being on a tour of South America," Brin continued as she eased back into the couch. Marisol resumed tracing the lines of her leg. "And he told me Tyler would be waiting for me when I returned."

Marisol growled at the name, but Brin only smiled indulgently at her and continued, "She thinks I found out about The Bishop during my tour and that I wanted to do something about it, so I contacted the NSA and she was assigned. She knows a little bit more now, but nothing about you. No one does."

"I could tell from the warm welcome she gave me," Marisol grumbled, spreading her palm on Brin's thigh to cool her anger. It worked remarkably well. "I think Gray knows something is up, and your little friend is too smart not to guess some of it. Especially after what she saw this evening."

"She thinks I'm into the 'bad girl' type. Hopefully that cover works for a while."

Marisol's heart pounded against her chest, the thought sending unexpected joy through her. "Are you? Into bad girls?"

Brin's smile was wicked enough to give Marisol's a run for its money. "At the moment I am reassessing what exactly my type is. It's become very specific recently."

"Has it?" Marisol leaned forward, her hand purposefully slipping higher up Brin's thigh. A barely audible catch of breath was her extremely welcome reward.

"If you keep doing that, I won't be able to talk."

"You better tell the rest of the story fast then," Marisol said as she slipped one of Brin's legs behind her, hooked over the back of the couch, and brought the other into her lap.

Brin groaned, but Marisol refused to move closer or touch her again. She struck a pose of intense focus and waited for Brin to continue her story.

"That was it really. I did the South American tour and met with Tyler. We've been working together on a new statewide initiative to combat human trafficking as well as tracking down The Bishop. Taking him down so he couldn't hurt you anymore."

Now it was Marisol's turn to groan, but for a very different reason. She thought of the warehouse and how close Brin had come to dying at that man's hands. "I'll stop short of calling your plan stupid because mine was pretty much the same, but it was too dangerous, Brin. Why didn't you just come to me?"

"I couldn't," she said, tears sparkling in her eyes. "There was a cost and I knew it from the start. I couldn't tell Tyler about you—our mutual friend Anderson made it clear your cover was the only thing keeping you safe from more people like The Bishop—and us working together would be impossible. Someone would find out and, again, you would be in so much danger."

"You could've at least come to Chicago," Marisol grumbled, unwilling to admit out loud that she was right. "You know how much I needed to see you. Just see you with my own eyes and know you were okay."

Brin shook her head, staring at her hands. "I couldn't let myself come here. Coming to Chicago would eventually lead to you and I couldn't trust myself around you. Even thinking about it made my palms sweat and…"

Marisol grinned at the suggestive way her words trailed off. She put her hand on Brin's thigh again, this time much higher, the hem of the short robe tickling the back of her hand. "Yes? What else happened beside your palms sweating, Governor Sloane?"

"Why don't you see for yourself?"

Brin pulled at the tie on her robe which had done a passable job of keeping the two sides together until now. The fabric flowed over her curves and off her body.

Marisol's mouth went dry at the sight. Brin had lost weight since Marisol had seen her last, but her visible hip bones did little to mar the pristine flesh. She was pale as marble but soft. Marisol traced the heavy curves with her eyes, followed by the lightest brush of her fingertips. They travelled from her smiling face, across the swell of her round breasts, pooled enticingly as she lay on her back, across the expanse of her stomach and the fleshy swell between her navel and the neatly trimmed patch of hair that brought moisture back into Marisol's mouth.

She leaned forward, prepared to take the journey yet again, with lips and tongue and perhaps just the barest hint of teeth the third time, when Brin caught her chin, drawing their eyes together. Marisol fell into those blue orbs, floating into their depths with ease. Brin touched a quavering hand to her cheek and then her jaw and then deep into her hair. Drawn by Brin's touch, Marisol slid her body up until they were face-to-face and she could look down into the limitless depths of those eyes.

Bringing Marisol's right hand to her mouth, Brin laid a full-lipped kiss on her palm. Then she turned Marisol's hand over, exposing her wrist. When Brin's lips touched the scars, Marisol hissed with mingled pleasure and pain. Brin stopped moving, holding her lips in place against Marisol's pounding pulse point.

Slowly, one pale, twisted inch at a time, Brin's lips made their way across the scar. The sensation of her kisses were overwhelming Marisol.

Her body quivered as Brin's lips circled her right hand. When she had finished her circuit, Brin placed another kiss in the center of Marisol's palm. Releasing her right hand, Brin took up Marisol's left and kissed the scars with the same reverence as the first. By the time she placed a final kiss on her palm, Marisol's body radiated need. Burned with the need to touch. To kiss. To taste. In her office they had been hungry and reckless. Here, with the yawning void of night stretched out deliciously before them, Marisol would force herself to move with all the delicacy Brin's body and heart deserved.

Instead of releasing her hand when she was done, Brin kept possession of it. She locked Marisol into her gaze and directed her hand down to her breast. The moment Marisol's calloused palm rested on soft flesh and hard nipple, Brin's eyes rolled back and she moaned with glorious abandon.

Marisol spent endless minutes reminding herself of Brin's body. In many ways, she was learning it for the first time. The first time they went to bed, a one-night stand that lasted all weekend all those years ago, Marisol had thought they'd never see each other again. She hadn't bothered to study a one-night stand's body.

When she knew neither of them could stand another moment of exquisite torture, Marisol dropped to her knees in front of the couch and wrapped Brin's thighs around her shoulders. She devoured her love, sampling every inch until Brin's moans became desperate and her body shivered. Then she focused her attention and tightened her grip on Brin's legs. Her lover exploded, screaming her release as her body shook into oblivion. Marisol held on through wave after wave, refusing to break free until every ounce of long-stored need had been released.

Her last cries had barely finished echoing from the dark windows when Brin reached down and yanked Marisol back into her arms. Their impatience was evenly matched and Marisol struggled out of jacket and boots as she was dragged back onto the couch. Brin only managed to get the skin-tight jeans down to Marisol's thighs, but that gave her all the access she needed and her impatience was unstoppable. She wrenched Marisol's shirt up with one hand and plunged between her legs with the other. The position was awkward, the half-removed clothes were uncomfortable and the cushions of the couch were narrow.

No moment had ever been more perfect for Marisol.

She hovered over Brin, holding herself up to keep from crushing her, but Brin pulled her down hard. Taking Marisol's nipple into her mouth, Brin plunged deep inside her and picked up a desperate rhythm. It was graceless and wanton and it had Marisol peaking in a few expert strokes. Brin didn't hesitate, only grinned around the ample flesh in her mouth as Marisol roared her name and continued until she roared again. And again.

Drenched in sweat, Marisol collapsed onto her body and begged for a break, which Brin granted with a pout and grumbled acceptance. The reward came when she wrapped arms and legs around Marisol's spent body and held her tight, smoothing her sweat-streaked hair and kissing her forehead until Marisol's breathing returned to normal.

They then made their way to Brin's bed, shedding Marisol's clothes along the way and leaving the robe crumpled on the couch. They made love slowly this time, under blankets and sheets and without the need for light or words. Brin cried as she peaked the final time, pulling Marisol close to her and sobbing into her neck. For the first time in her life, Marisol held a woman close and let herself cry as well. Let herself cry for the lonely nights and the women she couldn't save and the girl she had been for too few years. She let herself shed the last bits of The Queen of Humboldt. She let herself be Marisol Soltero, who needed this woman to be whole and needed to be needed in return.

"I missed you, Brin," Marisol said simply.

Brin turned to look at her, wiping the tears away with gentle fingertips and a sad, watery smile. "I missed you, too. I'm sorry I couldn't be here with you. It killed me every moment of every day and I know it killed you, too, but it was worth it because you're alive. I knew I could live with the pain then if only you would stay alive."

"And now?"

"And now I can't stay away. It's not perfect. He's still out there. But he's weaker now than ever. He lost his base in Colombia and last night's body count was high. Tyler secured a nice haul of cash and weapons. He's lost a crippling number of resources in a short time. We'll just have to risk it. If you'll take me back."

"Of course I will. You know we're stronger together, Brin."

Brin cupped her face and brought their lips together, featherlight. "Yes, we are. We always will be."

Marisol looked away and asked, "Why though? Why would you risk all that?"

"Because I love you, Marisol Soltero. And I love The Queen of Humboldt, too."

CHAPTER THIRTY-SEVEN

Marisol watched from the alleyway caddy-cornered from Brin's building as she crossed the sidewalk to the black town car. The two idiot men were already there, one in the passenger seat beside the driver and the other on the sidewalk beside the right rear tire, his eyes scanning the street, his face set. The obnoxious Tyler walked at Brin's side, her suit looking even cheaper than usual beside Brin's exquisitely tailored skirt suit.

There was a minor tussle between Tyler and the official bodyguard over who would open the door, but the agent won. Marisol allowed herself a quiet chuckle at the woman's swagger. If she didn't hate Special Agent Tyler Graham for the sin of being allowed to walk at Brin's side in the daylight, she might appreciate how she operated. Behind a pair of mirrored sunglasses Brin scanned the street. Marisol took a half-step forward, and the movement was enough to catch Brin's eye. One side of her mouth turned up and she puckered her lips almost imperceptivity, sending a quick kiss down Marisol's alley.

The cop hadn't noticed anything amiss, but Agent Graham had. Once Brin had ducked inside the car, Graham shot a hateful, angry glance at the alley and dropped into the car. The thought of that jackass sitting next to Brin for the three-hour drive back to Springfield made Marisol's blood boil, but she soothed her nerves with memories of the previous night.

With the car around the corner and out of sight, Marisol buckled her helmet, pulling down the tinted face shield to block prying eyes. Her Ducati waited behind a dumpster, its engine as anxious as Marisol to hit the road and let the wind tear at them. The drive to Humboldt was short, but it would give her enough time to buckle her armor back on. To hide Marisol behind the shield of The Queen of Humboldt.

She rode the fine line between neighborhoods, keeping to streets where police presence was less likely but she could open up her bike's engine. Instead of heading straight for Club Alhambra, she took a detour through the fringes of her domain. A few of her people saluted her as she whipped past. Others eyed her with something between wariness and awe. She dropped the kickstand and killed the engine in front of Justino's bodega.

Motorcycle helmet tucked under her arm, Marisol's eyes strayed across the street. A few slashes of green peeked out of the mud and straw in the medians. The bricks glowed red-brown in the afternoon sunlight. A team was hanging a sign over the front door of the community center, as a few staff members looked on. Marisol had paid for the sign but had ensured that information was well hidden. She had no interest in another confrontation.

"Humboldt Park Community Center and Shelter," Justino said, appearing at her shoulder. He held out a steaming paper cup and she accepted the coffee with an unsmiling nod. "It looks to be coming along nicely."

"No problems?"

"Not many," he said, chuckling as he entwined his fingers over his belly. "Some rowdy kids two days ago, but Gray took care of it."

"If there's anything else, you'll let me know." Not a question but somewhat short of a demand. She sipped her coffee before continuing, "Even if it's just kids being stupid. Understood?"

"Sí, mi reina. Sí."

One of the community-center staff members turned and spotted them. She wore a familiar sneer.

Marisol turned to go. She stopped once she could no longer see Justino's face. "I'm sorry about Analise."

"I knew she would not be coming home. She was gone too long."

Isabella hadn't been found either. No one was in the other room Mel had opened. Just a few broken beds and chains hanging from the wall. The SUVs hadn't come back and hadn't been located. Chances were good that the missing women were scattered to the wind at this point. The Bishop could have taken them anywhere to try rebuilding his shattered empire. They were probably beyond Marisol's ability to track them down, but she had Dominique making discreet inquiries. She owed that to Analise and Isabella. She would never give up on them.

"All Humboldt owes you a very great debt, mi reina. No one here had any doubt of that."

As she climbed onto her bike and roared away Marisol didn't look back at the woman across the street. She took the ride back to Club Alhambra much more slowly, noticing the cracks in the sidewalk and the trash. She noticed the eyes of the residents. There was a light in them that had been missing for the last few weeks. More people were out on the street. More women. More children. Humboldt was coming back to life.

Gray stood outside Alhambra's entrance. He glared down at her as she walked up the sidewalk. Before she reached the door, he slipped inside, moving with an alacrity that had Marisol's hackles raised. Normally Gray stormed around Humboldt like a barely contained grizzly bear. He thundered and roared so everyone knew where and who he was. It was in moments like these—moments when he moved like a cobra ready to strike— that Marisol knew her friend was enraged, beyond his usual.

Thinking of Gray like that—not as her most trusted underling, but like a friend—brought her to a stop in the center of the sidewalk. Gray was her friend. He always had been. There was no one, not even Dominique, that she trusted as she trusted Gray. Eventually—and that day was coming very quickly—she would have a conversation with him. She had always trusted him with her life, but she had never been willing to trust him with the lives of the women she rescued. Maybe it was time she did. Maybe he had earned that.

Shaking her head, Marisol wrenched open the front door and stepped into the warm, smoky shadows of Alhambra. Today wasn't that day. She entered just in time to see Gray climbing the stairs to her Throne Room.

"Hey, Boss."

Marisol turned to look at Mel. She was standing there, whole and solid, without bruises except under her eyes. Nothing about her had changed except her eyes. There was something new there. Something Marisol knew well and hated to see in any woman. Something that would never go away.

"So it turns out you were right," Mel said, trying gamely to smile and mean it. "That was a stupid plan."

"You can stay home for a while."

"Nah," Mel answered, scuffing her boot on the stained concrete floor. It squeaked at contact and she stopped. "H is driving me crazy. Keeps staring at me and crying. I told her nothing…bad happened. Doesn't help."

Marisol could understand how that tiny reassurance wouldn't help Helena. It didn't help alleviate Marisol's guilt.

"You're very lucky to have her," Marisol replied quietly, thinking of Brin.

"Hell, yes I am." Mel's eyes spoke of a ferocious protectiveness Marisol hadn't known was a part of their relationship.

It made her feel good to know how much those two women loved each other. That someone like Mel could be loved by someone like Helena. And that someone like Mel was capable of a love like that. That her life of petty violence and every despicable thing that came with running in Marisol's gang didn't keep her from happiness.

They fell silent, each lost in what Marisol assumed were very similar thoughts. Movement in the edge of her vision caught Marisol's eye. It was Gray, emerging from the shadows of the Throne Room to stand along the railing. He stared down at Marisol and the set of his jaw said that their awkward conversation was not as far off as Marisol had hoped. She avoided it by turning her attention back to Mel.

"How do you feel about some time away? Get out of the city." Marisol waited until Mel looked her in the eye and could see the meaning behind her words. "Like a vacation."

There was a glint in Mel's eye that told Marisol she knew it would not be a vacation. "Can H come, too?" She hesitated for a moment. "Neither of us are interested in being apart for a while."

"Definitely," Marisol said, clapping her hard on the shoulder and winning a smile. "You like hotels?"

Mel's eyebrows came together and she said, "Sure?"

"Come up to my office later," Marisol said as she headed toward her Throne Room. "I've got a job for you."

Gray stood at the top of the stairs like a monolith, stepping aside as she approached. It was good to know he wasn't so angry as to openly challenge her in public, but she shouldn't push it.

"How are you, Gray?"

"Confused," he replied, crossing his arms across his massive chest. "Concerned."

"Aw. I didn't know you cared."

He scowled down at her. "I don't wanna see you back in the lifer wing. Not for a skirt."

"Maybe not for one woman, but what about for a bunch of 'em?"

"What?"

"Later, Gray," she said, feeling the weight of her long night. "I'll explain later."

He was clearly annoyed, dropping his arms to make massive fists at his sides. It showed in the edge of his voice when he said, "Sure, Marisol. Sure."

He didn't follow when she headed for her office. He'd be pissed for a while. A long while, she guessed, but he'd get over it. He always did. There was a new door on her office thanks to that half-wit agent breaking down the last one. Gray and the gang had gone a little overboard, with a hollow metal exterior door rather than a straight replacement. The code was the same, though, and it pushed open easily when the lock clicked open.

Everything inside was the same, too, except for a new widescreen computer monitor. It wasn't just bigger than the one Brin had swept off the desk, but massive. At least forty inches. She could watch movies on the damn thing. Way more than she needed for her spreadsheets and email, but her people spoiled her. She smiled at Gray's efficiency.

Her smile had just finished growing when the desk chair moved. She should have noticed that the high leather back was facing the door. She never left it that way. She should have noticed that there was the warmth of a human presence in the room. She hadn't lived this double life this long by being sloppy. Fortunately, she was also fast.

Diving to her right, she went to the floor shoulder first. She tucked and rolled across the carpet, keeping her movements tight so she didn't roll out from behind the protective cover of the large desk. She wasn't wearing her vest. She hadn't sent anyone to search her office. She didn't have people stationed outside the door or even within earshot if her assailant had a silencer. Everything that had led her to this moment was monumentally stupid and now she was going to die the same day she got Brin back.

Landing in a ready crouch, she had her Colt balanced between her palms. She pushed her arms out in front of her as the chair finished its turn. Her finger was squeezing down on the trigger, ready to send The Bishop straight to hell.

She saw the bald head first, the skin entirely the wrong shade. Easing off on the trigger, she saw the thin beard with no mustache. Last was the eyes, gray like a thundercloud over the ocean. She hadn't looked into those eyes in years. Not since the best and worst day of her life. Marisol stood, gun still extended, and took a step toward the man who pulled her strings.

"Nice to see you again, Marisol," Anderson said in a voice that pulled at her nerves. "It's been a long time."

His words were bad enough, but it was his smile that really cracked open the vial of anger in her gut. "What the hell are you doing here?"

"Thought I'd come in person so I could ask after Governor Sloane. How is she? Did you both sleep well?"

"She's great, no thanks to you. Now tell me what this is about."

"I have an assignment for you, of course."

Bella Books, Inc.

Women. Books. Even Better Together.

P.O. Box 10543
Tallahassee, FL 32302

Phone: 800-729-4992
www.bellabooks.com